ALL THAT GLITTERS

Also by Jane Gorman

ALL THAT GLITTERS

*Book 3 in the Adam Kaminski
Mystery Series*

Jane Gorman

Blue Eagle Press

This is a work of fiction. Names, characters, places and incidents are the product of the author's imagination and used fictitiously. Any resemblance to actual events or persons, living or dead, is entirely coincidental.

To my friends and colleagues whose work supports
our national parks.

CHAPTER ONE

A GLIMMER OF LIGHT caught the polished wood, highlighting the stylized body of a man. A curve of mahogany captured a stern face, features set in determination and pride. A shield and axe appeared out of a sharp angle on one side. Turned wood at the top created the sense of motion, of power.

No more than a foot tall, the statue carried the weight of skill lovingly applied. It was a thing of strength and beauty. It blended into the night surrounding it, its deep brown balanced against the darkness of the dimly lit path.

The man holding the statue aloft bore no resemblance to the mythical figure carved into it.

He brought the wood down with all his strength. The unsuspecting man in front of him fell to the ground with only one strike.

The sound of the dull thud accompanied by a low grunt didn't carry far across the landscape, muffled as it was by the spray of water shooting up from the fountain in the middle of the square. A huddled figure on the ground next to a bench on the far side of the fountain shifted, then lay still. No one else appeared in the park, no other visitors at this time of night, no security patrol checking on the homeless.

The unconscious man fell sideways, landing at an awkward angle on a park bench.

The killer raised the wooden statue again. This time the glimmer of light caught the red wetness on the wood. He brought the wooden weapon down again. And again.

He held his breath, waiting. Still no one else appeared. Even the wind lay low, no telltale rustle from the branches overhead, no sprayed droplets of water falling on the ground around the limestone base of the fountain's pool.

Only the flicker of yellow light from the eternal flame showed signs of life. A flame dedicated to the legacy of those who had died for this country.

He tossed the statue into the boxwood behind the bench. It rolled as it landed, leaving a dark, wet patch in the dry dirt.

With one more glance around, he padded away from the still form. A stain of wetness spread from its head, creeping out over the wood underneath it and dripping down to darken the pavement below.

CHAPTER TWO

"ADAM, sorry I'm late."

Detective Adam Kaminski turned when he heard his partner calling and watched him cut across the grass toward the memorial. Pete Lawler had to bend double to duck beneath the yellow crime scene tape that stretched around the perimeter of the paved area, but he didn't let that slow him down. He hurried toward the crime scene, no more willing to waste his time while on duty than he was to waste police resources.

"No worries. Takes you longer to get here."

Adam lived only a few blocks away in an apartment in the Society Hill neighborhood of Philadelphia. Once he got the call, it had been a matter of minutes for him to get dressed and walk over to Washington Square. Not counting the minute he had stolen to watch Sylvia sleep, to wish he could crawl back into bed with her, wrap his arms around her under the warm blankets. Then again, Sylvia had never been much for cuddling. He'd taken another minute to set the coffeepot on a timer for her instead, the morning paper folded neatly beside it.

As if dreaming about his own warm bed, Pete shivered and rubbed his hands together. "What do you know so far?"

Adam glanced over at a group of National Park Service rangers standing on the far side of the pavement as he answered. "Body found about an hour ago —

about 5:30 — by a park ranger. Ranger Matt Thompson."

Pete turned to follow his gaze. "Is Ranger Thompson still here?"

"Yep. He called it in, then stayed with the body. That's his chief ranger with him, too, along with his colleagues."

"So this is federal land?"

Adam nodded. "Part of a national park. But we have concurrent jurisdiction."

Pete turned as if to approach the rangers, but Adam put a hand on his arm. "Let's take a look around before we talk to them. Get a sense of the scene."

Adam felt the rangers' eyes on him as he and Pete moved across the pavement around the fountain toward the corpse, covered in a plastic sheet as it lay on the bloodstained bench. Technicians with the PPD Crime Scene Unit were just setting up to analyze the scene, and Adam and Pete stopped at a safe distance.

Adam stood with his hands in the pockets of his chinos, his eyes scanning the area. Even the bustle of the techs and the crackle of law enforcement radios couldn't obscure the peacefulness of the square. Occasional drops of water splashed on the pavement from the grand fountain. The air was fresh with the scent of the last of the season's Russian sage, still struggling in the corner flower beds. The falling leaves added their own mustiness, along with colors that almost glowed in the bright fall light that followed the sunrise. If the square hadn't been cordoned off as a crime scene, he would already be seeing residents passing through, walking their dogs, enjoying an early morning jog. Instead, the only visitors this morning were law enforcement. And the dead.

"Likely that's the murder weapon." He pointed to a dark shape under one of the bushes behind the body. A battered piece of numbered yellow plastic stood next to it. A technician would soon be photographing and

4

bagging it to take back to the lab.

"Do we know anything about it yet?"

Adam shook his head and stepped to the side to get a better look. About a foot long, it looked like dark, carved wood. As he ran his eyes over the figure he could just make out the shape of a man. A memory flashed through his mind. It was gone as quickly, leaving only a flicker of recognition. A shadow of a doubt.

He glanced at Pete, who had lowered himself into a squat in order to get a better view of the weapon and the murder scene. Pete frowned as he stared at the statue, then moved his eyes over the ground around the scene. "No footprints, no signs of a scuffle."

"No." Adam shook his head. "The techs said he'd been hit on the back of the head. Multiple times. We'll know more once they finish their work."

Pete stood, straightening the legs of his khakis as he did so. "Okay. Let's talk to the park rangers."

The tallest of the rangers stepped toward them as they approached, his hand out. "Matt Thompson." His expression was eager, curious. Though his features were rough and irregular — his nose a little too long, his jaw a little too wide — there was something about the set of his eyes, the hint of his smile that looked comfortable, friendly. Like a pair of old jeans worn in just right.

Adam smiled to himself at the thought and shook his hand. "Detective Adam Kaminski, this is my partner Detective Pete Lawler. You found the body?"

"I did." Matt glanced back at his chief as he answered.

The chief stepped toward them, his back ramrod straight, the expression on his ebony face one of confident authority. "Chief Ranger Roger Burton," he introduced himself. "Are you taking the lead on this case?"

"I think we should, unless you have another idea."

Burton shook his head. "Nope, I think that's a great idea. We'll help in any way we can, but we don't have the resources or the capacity to manage a murder investigation."

Adam nodded and looked back as a team of technicians wrapped up the corpse to transport it for autopsy. He turned to Matt. "What can you tell us?"

"I did my patrol through the square at 5:30 this morning."

"Do you always come through at that time?" Pete interrupted.

"No, it's a big park so we cover more ground by varying our patrols." When Pete nodded, Matt continued, "I saw the body, thought it was another one of the homeless who live out here and went to do a wellness check."

"Wellness check?"

"It's how we try to manage the problem with homelessness in the park." Chief Burton answered this one. "We don't have any rules against homelessness, but we do prohibit camping in the park, including sleeping. If we know there are people sleeping here, we check on them periodically, wake them up, make sure they're okay. More often than not, once they're awake, they move on."

"So you move the problem to other streets, outside the park, is that it?" Pete raised an eyebrow as he asked the question.

Burton shrugged. "It's a citywide problem, friend, you know that as well as I do."

"Did you see anything else when you did the wellness check?" Adam directed his question back to Matt.

Matt raised his chin and pursed his lips, as if trying to recall every last detail of his discovery. Finally, he shook his head, his disappointment obvious. "Once I ascertained that he was dead, I called it in and checked the area. It was completely deserted, not even our usuals."

"So they may have seen something and got out, fast."

"We know who the regulars are, recognize them when we see them. We can do some digging, see if we can find any of them."

"Good," Adam agreed. "Not the most reliable witnesses, but someone may have seen something that could help."

"He spent a lot of time in the park." Matt's voice dropped a notch. "You know, walking through, maybe stopping to watch the kids play around the fountain." He looked around the square as he talked, as if seeing the scenes he was describing.

Adam glanced at Pete, then turned to Matt. "Who was he, what can you tell me?"

"Judge Oliver Ryan-Mills," Burton answered. Matt opened his mouth as if to jump in, but when Burton shook his head, he gave a subtle shrug and let Burton continue. "He lived in the complex behind you." He nodded toward the hulking modern apartment building across the street. A building where each unit went for over a million dollars. "A retired federal judge. We had a few cases before him, before he retired."

"How long had he been retired?" Pete pulled out a small notebook, his pen scratching on the paper.

Matt frowned, then looked toward his chief. "About two years?"

"Sounds about right." Burton stuffed his hands into the pockets of his cargo pants. "We've got a lot coming up, as you guys know. Between the convention itself and the protests that'll come with it, all of our resources are committed to prepping for that."

Adam and Pete both nodded their understanding. The Interfaith Peace Consortium was coming to Philadelphia next week, a convention that would bring religious leaders from around the world to look for ways the different faiths could work together to bridge gaps — sometimes chasms — between the religions and find ways to secure peace. It would also bring a host of protestors, and federal and local law enforcement were preparing for possible violence.

"Was Ryan-Mills connected to the convention?" Pete

asked.

Burton shook his head. "I don't think so, though of course I don't know for sure. He probably was connected to the event we're gonna have here this week."

"Event?"

"A tented gala thing," Matt said, distaste in his voice. "Some kind of support or fundraiser for convention delegates, something like that."

A white-robed technician approached them, a clear plastic bag in her hands. Adam could see the dark shape of the likely murder weapon in the bag and squinted as he stared at it.

"Blood on the statue, sir." The technician spoke to them all. "Thought you'd want to take a closer look before we take it back for processing."

Pete leaned toward the bag, his face reflecting nothing but interest in the statue. Adam glanced at it, then looked away as his flicker of recognition solidified into knowledge. He let his gaze move across the fountain to the memorial wall that stood behind the eternal flame.

"Something you want to share, partner?" Pete asked under his breath, indicating the statue with his chin.

Adam knew what he had seen. He recognized the statue. He'd seen it enough times before today.

He shook his head. "Nothing important." He gestured toward the memorial wall as he handed Burton and Thompson each one of his business cards and let them know he'd be in touch. "Freedom is a light for which many men have died in darkness?" He looked at Matt.

The ranger nodded. "George Washington. It's a great quote for a memorial to those who died fighting for our nation's freedom."

"It is," Adam agreed. "So who's going to help us shed some of that light on why Judge Ryan-Mills died in the darkness?"

CHAPTER THREE

LAW ENFORCEMENT RANGER Matt Thompson sat for a moment with the engine running. He closed his eyes and let his head fall back against the seat, keeping his breathing calm. He'd been involved with death before. Deadly falls, stranded hikers, even one manslaughter case. But not like this. Not when he knew the victim, at least superficially. He looked out at the park around him. Carpenters' Hall lay across the rolling expanse of grass. A place where many years ago great men had met to discuss the possibility of freedom. The pursuit of justice. Surely justice had been important to Oliver Ryan-Mills. He'd spent his career defending it. It was what he deserved now.

He took another breath, let it out slowly. Chief Burton hadn't let him down since he'd started in this park. There was no reason to doubt his judgment now. But he still wished he could be a part of this investigation.

Matt opened his eyes in time to catch a glimpse of Burton in the sideview mirror as he approached the vehicle from behind. He lowered the window even as the chief started to tap on it.

"You okay in there, Thompson?"

"Yeah, Chief, sorry. I'm coming in now."

Burton nodded as Matt turned off the car and stepped out. "That was quite a morning. You sure you're okay?"

Matt looked down at Burton, who stood about four inches shorter than him. The chief wasn't short; Matt was taller than almost everyone he knew. "I'm fine, really. I still want to work on this, you know. I could be our liaison with PPD."

Burton nodded with a wry frown, then looked away. Matt followed his eyes, taking in the eighteenth century building that housed their squad room, the brick and cobblestone path he had just followed through the landscaped grounds surrounding them. He was lucky to be working here. Lucky to have a chief ranger like Burton. He didn't want to push it.

Burton turned his eyes back up to Matt's. "We'll need a liaison, but you know John usually handles that. He's got the connections already established. Not that you wouldn't be good at it, Thompson. But I'm gonna need you along with everyone else to handle the protests that are coming. We've heard Anonymous will be out, along with a few neo-Nazi groups." Burton shook his head and grinned. "Anarchist hackers and anti-Semites. Maybe we can get them to turn on each other."

Matt grinned but didn't let the chief distract him. "I have some experience in this, too, Chief."

"Really? Didn't you just get back from FLETC?"

Matt nodded. He'd gotten back from the six-month training at the Federal Law Enforcement Training Center, referred to as "fletsee" by those in the program, only a couple of weeks ago. "Yeah. No, I mean at Shenandoah, when I was a seasonal."

"Tell me about it."

Matt paused as a jogger passed them on the narrow brick path. "A death, sir. Turned out to be manslaughter. We worked with the local PD on that, just like you want to do here. I assisted as liaison."

"Who'd you work with on that?"

"Our chief was Chris Duggan."

"Good guy, I know him." He glanced at Matt. "Let me think about this. I might give Duggan a call." He turned to walk through the wooden gate that led to the back entrance of their building.

Matt followed, taking off his uniform hat, the iconic Park Ranger campaign hat known informally as a flat hat. After a few steps, Burton turned his head and spoke to Matt over his shoulder.

"How well did you know the victim?"

"Only by sight, sir. To say hello to, that sort of thing. You know." Matt rubbed his fingers along the band of his flat hat. "He seemed like a good guy. Kept himself separate a little, didn't hang out and chat with the neighbors in the square."

"He was a judge. They play by a different rule book."

"He told me that once."

"Oh, yeah?"

"He just got involved in a community group. I ran into him leaving after a meeting, and I guess he was feeling chatty."

"You were patrolling in Washington Square?"

"He said it was the first time he was getting involved in anything in the community." Matt nodded as he answered. "He told me—" He laughed, cutting himself off. "I'm not making this up, Chief. He told me that a judge had to be isolated from the life of the multitudes. His words."

"Hmph." Burton laughed under his breath. "That sounds a little obnoxious."

"I don't think so." Matt recalled what the judge had said, struck only now by the loneliness it implied. "He said it happened naturally, by age, class, and training. But that it needed to happen, so he didn't get biased or subjective in his decisions. He kept himself apart because he thought it was the right thing to do."

"Did he have any family?"

"Yep. Two sons. His wife passed away a few years ago, pretty young. I think he was lonely, sir. He seemed unhappy. I always felt kind of bad for him."

Burton shrugged. "We all have to make choices,

Thompson. Your knowledge of the judge could be useful, but let me talk to John first and see how he wants to handle this. PPD has the lead, and we should have one point of contact. And that's not you." The chief patted him on the shoulder. "I know you're a good ranger, Thompson. After a couple years here, you'll be a strong candidate for that job you've got your eye on in Denali. I can trust you on this one, right?"

Matt nodded. "Absolutely, sir, of course." Even as he answered, he rubbed his fingers along the business card in his pocket with the phone number of Detective Adam Kaminski. One phone call wouldn't hurt anything, would it?

CHAPTER FOUR

"SYLVIA, YOU HOME?" Adam's voice filled their small apartment. He closed the door behind him as he pulled his phone out of his pocket and dropped his blazer on the futon that still served as their sofa despite their intention to invest in some real furniture. He had just decided she must have already left for work when she stepped through the bedroom door, closing it behind her.

"Adam, I didn't expect you back. Was it not a murder?"

He broke into a smile when he saw her. He couldn't help himself. "Yeah, I'm afraid it was." He planted a light kiss on her cheek, inhaling her lavender scent as he did so.

"Then why have you returned?"

He paused before answering, aware that what he was about to ask would threaten the wall he'd tried to build between his home life and his work. Everything about Sylvia was beautiful — her pale blue eyes, flawless skin, the elegant way she dressed and carried herself — even her Polish accent was sexy. He could so easily lose himself here, never return to the anger, hatred, and violence that made up his job.

"Adam, why are you here?" As always, Sylvia brought him back to reality.

"Sorry, I need to ask you for a favor."

He watched her as she crossed the room into the kitchen and put a kettle of water on to boil. After dropping two scoops of coffee into the French press, she turned back to him, leaning against the kitchen counter. "And how can I help you, darling?"

"You have a friend who's an expert in art and forgery, don't you?"

"Jim Murdsen, you mean?" Sylvia looked confused.

"That's him." Adam walked into the kitchen and stood facing her, leaning against the opposite counter. "I need his help with something. He consults for the FBI sometimes, right?"

"I'm sure he'd be happy to consult for the Philly PD as well, if that's what you're asking. But your department can contact him directly, you don't need to go through me."

Adam opened his mouth to respond, but the whistle of the kettle cut him off. Sylvia turned to pour the water.

He carried the mugs and cream over to the table, Sylvia following with the coffee.

"The thing is, I need to do this unofficially." He slid into a chair, setting his phone down next to his coffee mug. "I don't want to go through the department. At least not yet."

She pursed her lips as she looked at him. "You're not doing anything you shouldn't be, are you? That would hurt your career?"

He smiled. Of course she would ask about his career first. It was, after all, the most important thing to her. "I'm honestly trying to catch a killer. That'll be good for my career advancement, won't it?"

Sylvia pouted and shrugged, then reached to pour the coffee. "I suppose. But why do it so secretly?"

"I need to find out what I can about a statue. A wooden statue." He toyed with his cup before taking a sip, his eye dropping for a second to his phone, which remained dark. "I have a feeling about it. But it might turn out to be nothing, so I wanted to keep it quiet, look into it on my own first."

"That makes no sense. You follow leads all the time that turn out to be bad. Why would you do this thing unofficially?"

He paused, taking another drink. "It's just..." He looked across the table at Sylvia, reluctant to speak the words out loud. Uncertain she'd understand — or share his concern.

"It has to do with Julia," he said, finally shattering the wall. "I'm worried she might be involved somehow, and I want to keep that quiet."

"Ah." Sylvia sipped her coffee, then tapped her nails against the mug. "I understand that."

"You do?" His heart lifted at the words, at the knowledge that Sylvia would put family above his career.

"Of course I do, darling. Julia is your sister. If she needs your help, then you should help her. And I will help you. I will see Jim today and talk to him about it. What shall I do, invite him to dinner?"

"That would be perfect, thank you." Adam stood to kiss her again.

She smiled up at him. "Don't be so surprised I want to help you. But it's okay. I know your sister isn't really involved. Jim will look into this and clear things up, and no one in the department needs to know you were on this foolish errand."

Adam's smile faded. "So you are still trying to help my career."

Sylvia shook her head as she cleared away the coffee cups. "Of course I am, darling, I always do. And you should, too. You need to think about this as a career, not just a job."

He tried to hide his disappointment as he picked his blazer up from the sofa. The sound of horse hoofs carried up from the street below, and Adam realized how late it was. Tourists were already flooding the area. They'd be trying to get into Washington Square, too. Hopefully the rangers were keeping everyone out. "Do you know Washington Square?"

"The square up near Walnut Street with the fountain?"

"That's the one. Part of the national park."

Sylvia shivered as she turned to him. "Is that where it happened? The murder?"

"I'm sorry, I shouldn't have mentioned it." He stepped close to her, put his arms around her.

She rested her head against his shoulder. "That is a beautiful place. Peaceful. It is a cemetery, you know."

"Really?" Adam stepped back to look at her. "I didn't know that."

"Oh, yes, I took a tour not long after I moved here. That is why the memorial is there. Soldiers are buried there, some Americans, some British, from the Revolutionary War. And after that it was a burial ground for the free African community in Philadelphia. Many people don't know that as they walk over it, play games, picnic. It's a cemetery."

Adam nodded. "That's interesting. Makes sense. I wonder if the killer knew that."

"Or the victim."

Adam's phone chirped and he glanced down at it. He'd been expecting this call. And it wasn't going to be good news.

"PETE? WHAT'S UP?" Adam pulled the apartment door shut behind him as he jogged down the stairs, separating himself from Sylvia's curious stare.

"We ran the prints on the murder weapon. Based on your reaction earlier, I'm thinking you won't be surprised by what came back."

Adam bit down a retort. "Just tell me," he said through gritted teeth.

"They're Julia's prints. All over it."

He took a deep breath and nodded to himself. Julia's prints had been on file since the break-in at her loft over the summer. Pete was right, he had been expecting this. Hoping he was wrong, but knowing he was right.

"She's not involved in this, Pete, you know that, right?"

Pete didn't answer right away and Adam picked up his pace as he walked up toward Walnut Street. "Pete? You heard me?"

"I heard you, partner. But…"

"I don't want to hear it." Adam's voice dropped, the warning in his tone clear.

"Well, you gotta hear it. But not from me. Captain wants to meet with you."

"Can't you fill him in?"

He heard Pete's sharp inhale, as if he were laughing at him. "He's not looking for information, Kaminski, he's sharing it. You coming in?"

Adam glanced back down his street, toward the apartment where he knew Sylvia was in the process of helping him. Of reaching out to his first lead, taking the first step on what could be a long and winding investigation.

He knew what his captain wanted to say to him. Hell, it was the same thing he'd tell any other cop who had a personal connection to someone involved in a case. And he knew how important his career was to Sylvia. How much she had sacrificed to leave Warsaw and come with him to Philadelphia.

"I'm coming in. Be there in twenty."

It didn't really matter what his captain had to say. He had to protect Julia, no matter the cost. He only hoped it wouldn't cost him his job.

CHAPTER FIVE

CAPTAIN FARROW'S GLASSES lay on his desk, perched on top of uneven piles of paperwork. How he ever managed to put his hands on anything when he needed it, Adam couldn't figure out. An undulating sea of manila folders and white printed paper surrounded the brass pen set that took pride of place at the front of the cheap pressed-board desk. Adam kept his focus on the pens, trying to keep his anger under control.

"This can't be a surprise to you, Kaminski. You're a good cop. You know how this works."

"I know, sir, I do. But this is different." Adam searched for a way to convince Farrow to keep him on the case. To break just about every rule in the book. Even though he knew if he were in Farrow's position, he'd be doing exactly the same thing. He ignored the guilt growing in his gut, and the anger rising with it.

"Yeah, it is different. And we need to keep this investigation impartial."

"But I can do that, Captain. This situation… it's complicated."

"This is black and white, Kaminski, you know that as well as I do. I have no choice."

Adam knew just how black and white it was, but there was always a choice. His jaw worked overtime, biting back the words he really wanted to say. Propelled by his frustration, he stood, pushing himself off the captain's desk as if he could push the anger and guilt away with it. His fist hit the desk harder than he'd intended. The pen set shifted forward and toppled onto the ground, accompanied by a few stray papers.

"Damn it, Kaminski." Captain Farrow stood to retrieve his pens, shoving a pile of paper aside to replace it carefully center stage. "Your sister's involved. What the hell did you expect to happen?"

"She's not involved, sir. It's her statue, that's all. You said yourself she's not a suspect." They stood face to face, Adam far too aware that he risked appearing aggressive toward his boss but not willing to back down.

Captain Farrow glanced at Pete, sitting in the second chair facing Farrow's desk, his eyes moving between Adam and Farrow. "Not yet, is what I said, Kaminski. She's not a suspect yet. We're still gathering the facts, putting them together. Let's wait and see."

"That's crazy, sir. There's no way my sister's involved in this. No way."

Pete finally jumped in, standing and stepping between them, his back to the captain. "No way she's guilty. But she is involved, whether we like it or not."

Adam's anger shifted to fear for a moment, but he shook his head and let the anger back in. "You know her." His voice was quiet, talking only to Pete. "You know this isn't possible. I can help find the real killer. We're wasting time considering Julia."

"Not a chance." Farrow's voice was sharp and he held Adam's eyes without blinking. "You need to stay a mile away from this, Detective Kaminski. Or do I need to put you on administrative leave?"

"I can do this on my own, partner. You gotta trust me, you know I'll find the truth."

Adam took a deep breath, staring once more at the brass pen set. Losing his cool was only making the situation worse. One more breath, and he felt the heat draining from his face. "I trust you, Pete."

He looked over at Pete as he said it, his meaning clear

in his eyes. Trust wasn't the issue here.

Farrow grunted and nodded. "Okay then. Kaminski, you'll be working for Inspector Murphy on convention preparedness in the Tactical Field Support Division. They need all the help they can get 'til this damn convention is over. There's a briefing in the federal building on Sixth starting right about…" He glanced at his watch. "Now." He sat back in his chair, picking up his glasses on the way. Clearly, they were dismissed.

Adam followed Pete out of Farrow's office, his mind spinning. He trusted Pete, he did. But he couldn't walk away from this, walk away from Julia.

Pete turned to Adam as he pushed on the door to the stairwell. "It's a good assignment, partner. You know we need all the manpower we can get helping to make sure things don't get out of hand with these protests. If things get too bad, we'll be looking at more than one homicide."

"I know, you're right." He shut his mouth as a colleague passed them heading up, his shiny uniform shoes tapping on the concrete floor. Adam waited until he heard his footsteps on the next half-flight up. "But you know I gotta help Julia, right? Murphy's got most of the department helping him. And he's a good inspector, a good cop."

Pete raised an eyebrow. "And I'm not?"

"Come on, you know that's not what I meant."

They pushed out through the door to the small parking lot behind the district headquarters. A row of police vehicles stretched before them, lining the side of the building like sentries ready for battle. One or two still had the gleam of fresh paint and new tires, but most showed the wear and tear of a well-used car.

"I get it. But you need to leave this one alone. If you get involved, you'll put the case at risk. And that could jeopardize Julia even more."

He turned his back on Pete, took a step toward the closest vehicle. His face stared back at him in a grotesque mockery from the curved window. He knew Julia was completely innocent in this. Didn't he?

He shook his head and looked away. If she was innocent, Pete would clear her. But if she were somehow involved... he couldn't imagine what he would do then.

"Look, you heard the captain, she's not a suspect yet," Pete continued. "We just need to track the statue. See how it ended up in Washington Square."

"You know how it got there. It was taken during the robbery this summer. The one item that wasn't recovered."

"So that's it then. I find out who fenced it, track it 'til I find who ended up with it."

Adam nodded, thinking. "That's what I would do."

"But you won't, right? You're going to leave this to me?"

Adam grinned at his partner, wondering if Ranger Matt Thompson would be at the briefing. "You got it, partner. I'll leave it to you. Go check out this briefing I'm supposed to be at. But you'll let me know what you find, right? Keep me in the loop?"

Pete looked at Adam, his eyes narrowed, his mouth a grim line. He shook his head. "I can't do that. You gotta stay out of this. Right?"

Adam grinned again. "Sure, partner. Sure."

MATT THOMPSON STOPPED just before the entrance to the Liberty Bell Center. A teenage boy skulked in front of him, waiting his turn to go through security screening into the building. The boy kept his eyes down, hands in the pockets of his hoodie, picking at something on the ground with the toe of his sneakers. He didn't seem to care about the rally going on to his left. A middle-aged couple, presumably the boy's parents, stood directly behind him. They seemed to be trying to get the boy interested in what he was about to see, pointing to the park's brochure and saying things like "liberty" and "freedom." But every now and then one of them would glance toward the expanse of grass to their left that made up this part of Independence Mall, their attention only half on their child and his knowledge.

This protest was exactly the sort of thing covered in the briefing he'd just left. Federal and local law enforcement had met to talk about security plans for the interfaith convention scheduled for next week, and the rallies that were sure to accompany it.

Even while the line of people waiting to enter the Liberty Bell Center got longer, the crowd gathering on Independence Mall grew. They had no stage, but a podium had been set up on the paved area on the far side of the mall and the protestors gathered in front of this, waving placards and listening to speaker after speaker. With each speaker, the crowd seemed to grow, to surge not only in size but also in volume.

Another park ranger stepped next to Matt. "Looks like they're going to need our help after all."

She used her chin to gesture to the small group of park rangers gathered under the trees across the mall, setting up barricades to close off a section of the path in anticipation of what might happen.

"Maybe. It might still stay peaceful. I don't know how worked up people get about international food policy."

Barb laughed. "You never know what's gonna get folk worked up. And you saw Nancy's intel. We're expecting counter-protestors. That neo-Nazi group."

Matt wasn't entirely sure what the people in this rally were objecting to. Or fighting for. Or why they'd inspire a counter-protest. But the people gathering were clearly angry, as speaker after speaker talked about the need for more international support to feed the hungry around the world. About the need for religious organizations to coordinate their efforts. And about the problems the world faced whenever politics got in the way of access to healthy food.

As Matt and Barb watched from under the shelter of the Liberty Bell Center, a counter-protestor moved into the group. His head was shaved bald, his tall lanky form draped in a black leather jacket. Matt couldn't be sure about his age, somewhere between twenty-five and thirty-five. His shouted words slurred together, making them hard to understand, but the swastika painted onto the large cardboard sign he brandished made his position perfectly clear.

Bard shook her head. "Really? Are the neo-Nazis opposed to feeding the hungry?"

"I have no idea," Matt answered quietly, hearing the man's angry slurs against Muslims, against Jews, against homosexuals. Against everybody, it seemed.

"Should we stop him?" Barb took a step forward, but Matt put his hand on her arm.

"Not yet, not unless he starts interfering." Independence Mall was a public place, and that man had as much right to be there as the other protestors. Unless he took actions that interfered with their event, Matt and his colleagues wouldn't stop him. Regardless of what they thought about his shouted opinions.

As they watched, the neo-Nazi made his way through the crowd toward the podium. People who were in the rally turned away from him with looks of disgust. One looked over at the rangers and pointed at the man, mouthing something. But they all stayed out of his way. No one wanted to engage him. Which was good.

Finally, the neo-Nazi stepped in front of the podium. He lifted his sign into the air, blocking any view of the speaker. All the park rangers moved at once.

Matt and Barb stepped out of the shadows of the Liberty Bell Center and jogged toward the crowd. The rangers coming in from the other side got there first. The action was so smooth, so quiet, visitors waiting in line at the Liberty Bell Center might not even have noticed. With no scuffle or noise, the man was restrained, his sign was taken away from him, and he was brought over to the area the rangers had previously closed off.

Matt and Barb followed their colleagues to the secured area. "We better get used to this," Barb muttered. "There are gonna be a lot more like this once that convention starts next week."

Matt nodded his agreement, watching his colleagues take the man's name, run him through the system, then let him go with a warning.

Barb turned back to watch the ongoing rally. "Still got your eye on that job in Denali, Thompson? Aren't you going to miss this?" She kept her hands tight around her utility belt, but her eyes took in the green expanse of the mall, the brick-paved paths leading to Independence Hall, which stood proudly at the end of the block.

A fistfight broke out among the protestors. No counter-protestor involved this time, just a disagreement, apparently, within the ranks. Two rangers jogged out to break it up, bringing one of the more aggressive protestors back with them.

Matt grinned. "Don't get me wrong, I love this town. This history. Even a small group like this knows they're going to get more attention because they're standing in front of Independence Hall. Next to the Liberty Bell. Yeah, sure, I'll miss it."

As the man who had been picked out of the protest was led to a table to give his name, one of the two rangers with him broke away and approached them. His already stout form was exaggerated by the body armor he wore under his uniform, and his face glistened with sweat. He lifted his ball cap and ran a pudgy hand along his hairline, his blond hair stiff with sweat. "Did I hear you say there's a job opening at Denali? What job?"

"Thompson's got his eye on a supervisor position at Denali. Their chief of ops announced his retirement end of the year, so we figure once they fill that position there'll be an opening for a supervisor."

"What, and leave all this?" Even as he spoke, a shout

rose up. Two more counter-protestors had infiltrated the rally, the fighting this time between members of the rally and two new men carrying swastika-emblazoned signs.

"God, what idiots," Barb muttered under her breath as she jogged out to intervene.

"Where are these jackasses coming from?" The sweaty ranger, known as Moose, ran his hand over his hair one more time. "It's like they intentionally organized themselves to draw this out while costing them the least."

"You're right about that. They know we're not going to cite or fine them the first time, so if they come out one or two at a time, they each get off with a warning. Someone in their group must know the routine. And they clearly have funding."

"Nancy said they accept donations online. Can you believe that? There are people out there willing to give money to hate groups like this, and they solicit out in the open… online… in meetings. Crazy." Moose fanned his ball cap in front of his face again before putting it back on. The two rangers watched and waited.

Barb jogged back again, leaning against the wall next to Matt. "So you still want that Denali job?"

"Look, there's something appealing about protecting our great natural parks. Waking up every day to those sunrises, breathing in the fresh air, getting away from the noise and craziness of the city. Tell me you wouldn't love that, too."

"You wouldn't get to deal with scuttling the homeless," Barb pointed out.

"Or discovering murder victims," Moose added.

"Yeah." Matt looked down at his shoes. He had to remember to polish them; they were getting pretty scuffed up. "I guess."

"What's bugging you?" Barb nudged him, looking up at him.

"I want to help get that solved. The murder. I want to be a part of that investigation."

25

"So do." Moose leaned both elbows back against the low brick wall behind them, exposing the wet patches staining his uniform dark under his arms. "Talk to John."

"I will. We'll see. I spoke to the detective handling the case already."

"Without going through John? You're asking for trouble."

"Just checking in, that's all. We were both at the briefing, so I said hello. Let him know I'm free to help if he needs it."

"Yeah, but you're not." Moose stood up, pulled his sleeves down. "Look at that jackass. Will you get him or will I?"

"I'm on it." Matt jogged out onto the Mall.

CHAPTER SIX

"MOM?" ADAM'S call hung unanswered in the air, so he walked through the living room to the kitchen and out to the small square of yard behind the house.

His father looked up from the back of the yard, raising his head without straightening up. He nodded at Adam, then turned his attention back to the bits and pieces spread out on the wood in front of him. "Son. Good to see you."

"Whatcha fixing now, Dad?" It took only three steps for Adam to cross to the edge of the paved square where his father had created a makeshift worktable out of a plank of wood over two sawhorses. He patted his father's shoulder in an awkward greeting.

John Kaminski put a hand on the small of his back and straightened slowly. "Your mother's blender. Stopped working again… she wanted to buy a new one." He frowned. "Just need to clear out the gears, nothing wrong with this one."

Adam nodded, intimately familiar with the ongoing argument between his parents. "I'm looking for Julia. She said she'd be here."

"Yep." John rubbed a hand across his face, leaving a trail of dirt along his forehead, then bent down again to examine the parts in front of him. "She's with your mother. They ran out to the store, should be back soon."

Putting his hands in his pockets, Adam leaned against the low brick wall that ran along his parents' side of the wooden fence around the yard. The wall had been there before Adam was born. He didn't know if it predated the wooden fence the neighbor had installed or was added later, perhaps intended to be a decorative element. Now it served as a shelf for his father's well-worn tools and the occasional potted plant from his mother. John and Peggy Kaminski took pride in keeping their house and yard neat. Adam and Julia had been raised always to clean up after themselves and to treat their belongings with care.

But even so, the yard was spotted with stray flowerpots. A stain marred the woolen rug tossed haphazardly over the sofa in the living room he had just passed through. Signs of life that kept finding their way into the otherwise orderly space. Adam picked up a brass bucket his mother used as a planter. The bucket had lived in this backyard for as long as he could remember. He thought it might have belonged to his grandfather before his mother adopted it for her purposes.

"Dad?"

"Hmm?" His father kept his attention on the task in front of him.

Adam turned the bucket over in his hands, his brow furrowed. "I didn't get to know grandpa too well, you know? Before he died."

His father glanced over at him without straightening up. "What's brought this on? You're not dying, are you?"

"No." Adam chuckled. "I was just thinking, that's all. About family. How well we know each other."

His father straightened himself again. "We know each other plenty well enough, son. You're thinking about your trip to Warsaw last year, aren't you? Those things your cousin Łukasz told you about our family. Why're you thinking about that now? What's bothering you?"

"I need to see Julia, that's all. Ask her a few questions."

His father stayed where he was, the makeshift workbench between them, but he stared at Adam as if digging up an answer in his face. "You're angry."

Adam grinned. "I thought I was hiding it pretty well, considering."

John nodded, his hands still holding a greasy gear. "What's she done now?"

"Nothing, I hope. I think." Adam placed the bucket back on the wall.

"You need to stop thinking about those damn letters."

Adam nodded, still running his finger along the bucket. His cousin Łukasz Kaminski had given him the letters when Adam was in Warsaw a year earlier. Letters that told an admittedly one-sided story about his own grandfather and great-grandfather. Not a positive story.

He shrugged. "If it's true, if my great-grandfather abandoned the rest of his family to save himself, his wife, and his son…"

"Your great-grandfather was a hero. Don't you forget that." His father walked around the workbench toward him. "That's our legacy. He got his family out of Poland. It wasn't easy at the time, but he did what he needed to do to save his son." His father stopped directly in front of him. "It was the right thing to do, got it?"

Adam raised one side of his mouth in a lopsided smile. "I got it, Dad." Some things never changed. No matter how many years passed, when he was in his father's house he felt like he was a kid again. A kid who had to follow his father's rules.

His father waited a moment, then nodded and leaned back against the wall next to Adam. "So is this about your great-grandfather or about Julia?"

"Julia. I'm here to see Julia. It got me thinking, that's all."

"Well, they'll be home soon." He wiped his hands

down with an oil-stained cloth that looked like it would leave them dirtier than when he started. "But don't start something with her, whatever it is you got going on. She's having a bad day, apparently."

"Oh, yeah?" Adam turned to look at his father, trying to prise a meaning out of his lined brow and frowning mouth. "Why, what happened?"

"You're asking me?" John laughed. "Better ask your mother that one." He raised his chin as he jerked his head to his right. "There they are now."

Adam heard the sounds of women's voices in the house. He touched the bucket one more time, then stood to confront his sister.

JOHN HAMILTON clicked the end of his pen and folded the file closed. "I guess that's it, then." He looked across the desk at Matt. "Something else you want to add?"

Matt shrugged and frowned. "Nah, I guess that's all." He'd shared everything he could about the incident that morning, from the time to the temperature to the notable absence of the usual residents in the square.

"Uh-huh." John glanced at his watch. "You're on for a few more hours. I know for me it's gonna be a long night. Wanna get a cup of coffee? Then I'll set up camp in dispatch to stay in touch with PPD."

"Sure." Matt grabbed his gear as he stood, tapping his flat hat into place.

They stepped out of the eighteenth century row house that held John's office onto the Walnut Street sidewalk. Matt heard the click of the door locking behind him, but John's words, directed more toward the street than back at him, were drowned out by a passing bus. He just grinned and shook his head.

"I'll share everything you've told me with PPD," John repeated after the bus had passed. "I'm working with Detective Pete Lawler. You met him this morning."

Matt nodded distractedly. "Lawler, sure."

John glanced sideways at Matt, but whatever he read in Matt's expression he kept to himself. "Giving him all the basics, the full report."

He looked up and down 5th Street. The fastest thing moving toward them was a horse and carriage, clopping along at a leisurely pace as the driver passed on fanciful historical stories to the young couple sitting under the blanket behind him.

John crossed against the light. "He seems like a good cop, huh?"

When Matt didn't respond, John nudged him. "What's up?"

"Hmm?" Matt blinked and dragged his mind back to the present. "Nothing. Yeah, he seems great. I talked to his partner earlier today. Kaminski."

"You talked to Kaminski?" John raised his eyebrows and Matt steeled himself for a reprimand. "He's not working this case. Lawler's handling it alone. Something about a personal connection, Kaminski had to be pulled off it."

"You're kidding." Matt looked over at John in surprise and tripped over a loose brick in the path. "He didn't tell me that."

"Why would he?" John shrugged off the question, turning his steps toward the small coffee shop nestled between the hulking high-rise office buildings that lined the street across from Independence Hall, their glass and concrete facades looming ominously over the soft brick and wood of the historic square.

Why the hell hadn't Kaminski mentioned that when they spoke? Matt's first thought, that Kaminski was up to something, didn't last long. He had a good sense of the guy. Another cop trying to do the right thing. Sometimes fighting against the tide of the bureaucracy. Just like him.

The two rangers took their coffee to a table in the corner, a slice of Independence Hall visible through a small window across the room. Both men turned to look at the view, then scanned the room. Force of habit.

"You were at the briefing earlier, conference preparedness?"

Matt nodded as he took a sip of his coffee. It was weak and watery. "Yeah, where were you?"

"I had to help screen the setup for the event tomorrow night in Washington Square. What a mess, God." John grinned. He enjoyed every minute of his job, Matt knew, particularly when he got to work with the park's K-9 unit managing security screenings. "I can't believe the superintendent approved that circus."

"It's all politics, right? If the right people ask, you have to say yes."

"That's true." John glanced up as a man in a suit and tie passed their table on the way to the men's room. "And the folks in Washington Square, they have money."

"Money enough to make them good targets for murder." Matt pictured Washington Square as it had looked in those early hours of Wednesday morning, the deep brown stain pooling below the limp form draped across the bench. "Do we know who inherits Ryan-Mills' money?"

"Yeah, whatever, man, hold your horses. That's way too simplistic. Investigations are rarely that simple."

Matt opened his mouth to speak, but John put a hand up. "All right, you're right, they usually are that simple. But it's still none of our business." He shook his head and watched as the man in the suit passed again, heading in the opposite direction.

"I knew him, you know? Kind of."

John turned his eyes back to Matt. "The judge?"

Matt examined the surface of his coffee, cooling quickly in the paper cup in his hands and chose his words carefully. "He was a regular out in the square. I saw him when I did patrols. He liked to chat. Ask what was going on in the park. That sort of thing."

"Sorry, I guess I didn't think about that."

"I'm not complaining. I'm telling you because there are things about the man that might be helpful to know, you know? Earlier, when you were asking me about the case, you didn't ask about the man. Just the scene."

John let out a breath and closed his eyes, a light laugh escaping before he opened his eyes and said, "Yeah, that's all I asked about. That's all I need right now. From you, I mean."

"Why? I want to tell you everything I know. To tell PPD. Every little bit of information can be helpful. You know that."

"Yep, that's true." John folded his arms on the table, leaning forward towards Matt. "Look, I'm doing things by the book here, that's all. Right now, I'm not being asked for your opinion of the judge as a person. Just your knowledge of the facts. That's all I've been asked to provide, so it's all I'm giving them." He nodded once, as if closing the discussion. "By the book, get it?"

"But—"

"They haven't asked about his personal life. And don't think I don't care about this case. I do. Trust me, I've been doing this job for a lot of years. By the book is the only way to get things done."

Matt felt his face grow hot. He knew how to do his job. That's what he was trying to do. "They need to know about the victim as a person. Not just the facts at the scene."

John smiled. "No kidding, Sherlock. Of course they do. And they're gonna talk to his sons. To his neighbors. To his friends. To people who actually know him, not park rangers who run into him occasionally. What you know — what you think you know — how is that better than what PPD'll find by doing their job right, hmm?"

Matt toyed with his paper cup, considering what John had said. How well did he really know Ryan-Mills? And how much of what he thought he knew was just assumptions? He took a deep breath, looked up at John.

"I guess you're right."

"Damn straight I'm right. Is that what's been bothering you? That no one's asking your opinion? Because what you know, it's gossip, man, not facts."

"I know he was getting involved in a community dispute, related to one of his cases back before he retired. And he was getting a lot of people angry at him."

John took a sip of his coffee and grimaced. "He told you that?"

Matt nodded, waiting for John to ask for more details.

John shrugged as he stood. "If the judge was involved in something, PPD will know soon enough. They probably already know. Let them do their job, Matt. You focus on doing yours, you got it?"

John rapped his knuckles on the table as he walked away.

Matt waited a second before following, tossing his half empty cup into the trash can by the door. Maybe PPD would be looking in the right direction, but it didn't hurt for him to be in the loop, did it?

Another call to Kaminski wouldn't hurt, even though he wasn't on the case. Especially if he wasn't on the case. After all, neither of them were.

"ALL RIGHT, I'm listening. What's so secret you couldn't tell me in front of Mom?" Julia perched on the worn sofa, legs crossed. Their mother was busy banging the kitchen cupboard doors as she put away the groceries, the clatter expressing her displeasure at being left out of their conversation.

"Listen, I don't want you to worry…"

"Okay, if you don't want someone to worry, that's gotta be the worst way to start."

Adam grinned down at his little sister. She wore a loose black blouse over tight black jeans, her work garb for a gig she had that evening. But the somber clothes didn't dim the youthful blush in her cheeks or the shine of her strawberry blond hair as she pulled it over one shoulder. He took a seat on the chair opposite her.

"I know, sorry. I just need to tell you, we found that statue. The one that was stolen from your loft over the summer."

"That's great." Julia laughed and her shoulders lowered. Adam realized she'd been holding them tight. "So why all the mystery? I thought someone had died or something."

"That's the thing. Someone did die."

She shook her head. "What are you talking about? Who died?"

"A federal judge. Oliver Ryan-Mills." Julia opened her mouth to speak, but Adam kept going. "You don't know him, I know. The thing is, he was murdered."

Julia's hand flew up to cover her mouth. "Oh, that's terrible. Why are you telling me this?"

"It was your statue, Julia. It was the murder weapon."

"What? How could my statue kill someone? I mean… oh." Her eyes widened. "Oh, I see. Adam, that's horrible."

He was surprised to see a sheen of tears in her eyes, but chided himself for it. She'd always been empathetic, all their lives. "I'm so sorry, Jules. I know it is. I just… I wanted to be the one to tell you. And listen, you're not a suspect, okay? Everyone knows that statue was stolen."

Julia looked down at her hands, twisting in her lap. "But…" She looked up at him. "I don't…" She bit her lip.

"I know. It's okay. You had nothing to do with it. You didn't know the guy, you never met him. No one thinks you killed him. You got that, no one?"

Her sob came out as more of a gasp, and Adam leaned toward her, knowing there was more he needed to ask her but reluctant to draw this out any longer than he had to.

"What is going on in here?" Peggy Kaminski entered the room like an avenging angel. "What have you done to your sister?" She sat down and put her arm around Julia, who turned her face into her mother's shoulder and sobbed.

"Jules, honey, I'm sorry. I didn't think it would upset you this much."

"You didn't think, huh?" His mother chastised him with her eyes as much as her words. "Tell me, what's going on?"

"I can't, I'm sorry. Not right now. It's an open investigation. I can't talk about it."

"You could talk to your sister about it, clearly. Julia, are you okay, honey?" Her voice shifted from harsh to smooth within the same breath.

Julia sat up and ran a hand under her eyes. "I'm fine. I'm sorry, I overreacted."

"Did someone you know get hurt?"

"No, it's nothing personal," Adam answered. "I swear, otherwise I would tell you."

Peggy looked her son up and down, then turned back to her daughter. "Is that true?"

Julia nodded but kept her eyes turned down. "I'm sorry," she said again. "I'm fine, really."

"You don't need to worry, Julia. Really, you don't. I got your back, right? You'll be fine." Adam smiled at her. "Like I said, you didn't know the guy. I'm sure you've got an alibi—"

"An alibi?" His mother's shriek cut him off. "Why in God's name would Julia need an alibi?"

"Mom." Adam's impatience made his voice sound clipped, curt. "Please drop it. You're not helping." He should've had this conversation somewhere else. Anywhere else.

"Really, I'm fine. I just… I need to talk to Adam, okay?" Julia looked beseechingly at their mother.

"I know when I'm not wanted." Peggy stood, wiping her hands on her trouser legs. "But I'll be right here in the kitchen if you need me."

They watched her walk back into the kitchen, turning

once in the doorway to look back at them. Adam waved her on then turned back to his sister. "Julia, I'm sorry, I didn't expect it to upset you so much. I should have known better."

She sniffed and smiled. "No, it's not you. It's me. It's what you said, about an alibi. When was… when did it happen?"

"Sometime last night, I don't know exactly yet. But overnight, before 5 am."

Julia nodded and her face grew pale. "I can't give you an alibi, Adam." Her breathing got faster. "I mean, I don't—"

"It's okay." Adam laughed, trying to break the mood. "That doesn't matter. That's normal, in fact, most innocent people don't have alibis. Like I said, no one's looking at you for this murder."

"But…" Julia bit her lip, her eyes darting back and forth between Adam and a bookshelf behind him. "It's just, I did know…" She looked at him, her eyes pleading. For what, Adam couldn't tell.

He leaned forward, wanting to help but not knowing how. "Know what?"

She shut her eyes and shook her head. Adam waited, letting her get the words out in her own way.

"What the hell are you doing in here?" Their father's voice preceded him into the room. "Your mother says you're making your sister cry?"

"Calm down, Dad. We're fine, we simply need to talk." Julia's voice was strong, Adam was glad to hear.

"No, that's not okay. If there's something going on, I want to know."

Adam stood. He needed to end this now. He could talk to Julia again later. Somewhere more private. "It's nothing. I just told Julia we found her statue, the one that was stolen this summer that we didn't get back."

"Oh." John stood in the middle of the room. "Well, that's good, right?"

"Yes, that's good." Julia stood, too. "Adam, can I talk

to you later?"

"Sure. I need to get back to the precinct now. Talk to Pete, see what's going on."

"Sure, yeah, it can wait."

Adam leaned over and planted a kiss on her cheek. It was cold and its usual blush had faded. She had really taken this hard. He shook his head as he pulled the front door shut behind him. She was too good, cared too much about other people. It would get her hurt one day.

CHAPTER SEVEN

THE TINY BELL jingled as the door opened and closed. How elegant. How perfect. The customer smiled at the sound. Wood and brass statues cluttered the tabletops throughout the storefront, framed works of art and ornately detailed clocks covering all available wall space. He let his eyes roam the space, taking in the gleam of brass, the sheen of the wood. The musty smell, unfortunately, reminded him too much of old shoes, and he tried not to breathe too deeply.

His steps followed his eyes and he made a complete circuit of the small storefront before pausing in front of a statue. Its pale wood had been carved into a grotesque figure. A woman, he supposed, but like no woman you would meet on the street. Exaggerated breasts and bottom were highlighted further with added brass elements that wrapped around the form like a serpent.

His smile died as he spied the clerk hovering behind a high counter along the far wall. "May I help you, sir? Beautiful piece, that."

"I suppose." He looked up and around the room again, moving back from the table.

"Are you looking for anything in particular?" The clerk stepped out from behind the narrow shelf that served as a counter, its surface covered in receipts and forms. Her face was youthful, alert. Some might describe it as attractive, if you looked beyond the mousy hair and thick glasses. He couldn't.

"I'm looking for Sal. Is he around?"

The girl smiled thinly and nodded, then ducked through the small door in the back without saying another word.

"My friend." Sal's voice was silky smooth, his smile practiced.

The customer shook Sal's hand in greeting, noting that, as always, Sal's eyes held a smile that hinted at a secret, as if he were laughing at him, not with him. "How are you, Sal? Got anything new for me?"

Sal spread his hands wide. "My friend, it's only been a week. Nothing has come in recently, I'm sorry. But you know how it is." Sal put his hand out and stroked the statue that had caught the customer's eye. "We never know when a new delivery might be available."

The customer frowned. "Of course."

"But I have other products, you can see. These are all completely legitimate, I can prove the provenance of each of these."

The customer once again looked around the store. Every item displayed was on sale, some for prices that shocked even him. But none offered the thrill, the feeling of accomplishment and power the other items gave him. The black rhino horn, prized for its healing qualities and banned by the U.S. government. The ancient artifacts, dug up from old, abandoned tombs by bold grave robbers around the world. Weapons from the Civil War, with the thrill of history so close to hand.

The customer had started with legal items, years ago when he'd first started purchasing from Sal. But Sal must have seen something in his eyes, had recognized the need to own something special. Something unique.

He shook his head, disappointed. "Then for now, I'm looking for a statue. Something dark. Wood. Perhaps with gold." He raised an eyebrow as he spoke. "I liked the one you sold me last time, but I lost... that is, I had to give it away." He turned and let his eyes roam over the room as he spoke, hoping to look disinterested. "Quite distinctive. I really enjoyed having it."

Sal frowned now. "Yes, I remember. Dark wood, carved into the shape of a man, a Norse image, I think." He shook his head. "That was a piece of crap; I told you that when you bought it. I hope you sold it for a profit."

"I liked it." The customer gritted his teeth. "So what else do you have?"

Sal smiled again, lightening the mood. "We have a lot of options." He stepped around the customer and passed by him to the other side of the room, his smile constant. "We have a surprisingly complete collection of Konare's work. We picked these up at an estate sale." He turned back to him, waiting.

"I'm not interested in African art." He sniffed and looked around. "I want something elegant. Something unusual."

Sal laughed and the customer bristled. "These aren't African art; he's French. Though you should know Soalla is African and his pieces are quite distinctive. Unusual." He indicated the statue the customer had been admiring.

He felt his face burning at his mistake. Stupid. He clenched his fists, stuffing them into his jacket pockets.

"Of course." He forced a smile. "Let me see." He frowned again, looked around, then shook his head. "I don't see anything here I like. I don't know what you were thinking."

Sal grinned again. "The Soalla is a very precious piece. The piece that you were admiring earlier? It would speak volumes about the owner."

Was that a laugh? Was Sal laughing at him? He bristled, his chest visibly puffing out as he took a sharp breath in. "Do you have others by this artist?"

"No, my friend, that's the only one we have at the moment. But if you're interested..." He paused, his head on one side. "If you're interested in my special collections, I can certainly talk to some people, see what else is available. Check our networks, you know?"

This was better. "Yes. That sounds perfect. I am interested. And I'll take this one now."

"Very good." Sal snapped his fingers and the mousy assistant reappeared from the back room. She bustled about, lifting the heavy statue with both hands and placing it carefully on a pile of white paper. It made a satisfying thump as she placed it down, and he nodded with satisfaction. This would do very well indeed.

CHAPTER EIGHT

OVERHEAD FLUORESCENT LIGHTS cast a blue wash over the squad room. Windows that during the day looked out over city streets tonight showed Adam only his own reflection. A few other detectives hunkered down at the desks scattered around the room, but the place was quiet, everyone there trying to rush through the last paperwork of the day to get home to their families. Pete leaned forward over his desk, head hanging low. He looked like he was settled in for a long night.

"What's all that?" Adam dropped into the chair at the desk facing Pete's, the chair he should be occupying to help dig through all this paperwork. If he hadn't been pulled from the case.

Pete glanced up and smiled, but his eyes already looked tired, and both men knew his evening wasn't over yet. "I'm going through the judge's records, looking at cases that came before him over the past coupla years. It's what a murder investigation is all about, right?"

Adam nodded and made a sympathetic face. "Wish I could help, buddy, you know I do."

He meant it. It was dreary, sure, but reviewing Ryan-Mills' cases was the best way to find a connection to someone who might want him dead. As long as the motive was connected to his work. If the killer came from closer to home, then Pete's long night of research would turn out to be a waste of time. That's the way the job worked.

Adam reached across the desk and grabbed one of the files. Pete shook his head in warning, but didn't say anything as Adam flipped through it. Pete would be looking at everyone who appeared before the judge, from suspects to witnesses to lawyers. Anyone. Thank God the investigation was staying open, considering other leads. Not just Julia.

He tossed the file back onto Pete's desk. "Thanks, buddy." When Pete looked confused, he added, "For keeping on. For not giving up on Julia. I bet you'll find something in these files."

Adam looked hopefully at the piles covering Pete's desk. Each pile represented another set of cases the judge had heard. Another list of people who could have a grudge against the man or his family. Another possibility that might clear Julia's name.

"And if not, then tomorrow I go back to the family again. I don't really think this is going to produce any real leads." Pete shook his head at the paper he held in his hand. "But I gotta go through it, rule it out, anyway."

"You never know, a name might jump out at you. It's worth looking. So thanks." Adam stood and leaned over to pat Pete on the shoulder. "The investigation goes on, we're gonna find who did this, and you're stuck doing all the paperwork." He grinned. "The world is as it should be."

Pete's laugh came out more like a grunt, but he smiled.

"And Julia's still her same sweet self. Do you know she actually cried when I told her about Ryan-Mills' death?"

Pete gave Adam a look he couldn't interpret. "You shouldn't've done that. You shoulda let me talk to her first."

"What the hell, Pete, she's my sister, not a suspect. And I know her better than you do, trust me."

"Right, yeah… I know. Even so—" Pete dropped his eyes from Adam's face, turning his attention back to the papers in front of him. He cleared his throat. "Look, go do something useful. If you're not doing anything for Murphy, then at least go get me a cup of coffee or something."

"Sorry, buddy, no can do. I got dinner plans with Sylvia tonight." Adam gave Pete an exaggerated shrug, his palms open to the ceiling. "But I do appreciate you doing this. I know I owe you one, no kidding."

Pete looked up again, his eyes narrow. "Dinner plans? You know you need to stay far away from this investigation, right?"

"Damn, you're suspicious." Adam tried to deflect Pete's comment. It didn't work.

"'Cause I'm a good cop. So what are you planning?"

"Hey, I'm allowed to have dinner with my girlfriend. Meet her friends. No harm in that, is there?"

"That depends." Pete's voice was wary. "What friend?"

"Nobody special, someone who knows art, that's all."

Pete sighed and dropped the paper he'd been holding. "Adam, listen to me. Nothing you find, no information you learn, is gonna help me. I can't let you get involved. You know that."

"I know, we're just having dinner with a colleague, that's all. I promise, I won't repeat a word of what's said tonight. To anyone."

"Uh-huh." Pete narrowed his eyes as he looked at Adam, then shook his head and turned his attention back to the piles of papers in front of him.

With relief, Adam left him to his task of dredging through the hundreds of reports of Judge Ryan-Mills' cases. It was boring work, but Pete was right, he was a good cop. A rookie looking for excitement might see this type of research as a waste of time, but Pete's willingness to put in the long hours digging up every related piece of information revealed his dedication, his skills as a cop, his ability to scan through far too many facts to pull out the ones that were useful. Relevant. To find a needle in a haystack. Those files weren't just paperwork, they were hope.

Adam stuffed his hands in his pockets, whistling as he walked away. Now to see what Jim Murdsen had to say.

THE DIM LIGHTING inside the restaurant made the fake yellow gaslights outside seem bright in comparison. But light wasn't necessary. Adam was guided into the restaurant by waves of pungent spices: cumin, turmeric, cardamom, and others he couldn't begin to identify.

Sylvia and her friend were already seated at a table for four in the middle of the room. A low-hanging pendant lamp cast a romantic glow over the table that also created a sense of privacy built out of light and shadow. The warm sounds of an expertly played oud muted the voices of other diners. Swaths of fabric in golds, reds, and blacks draped over intricately carved wooden dividers throughout the restaurant enhanced the sense of intimacy. And excitement.

"Adam." Sylvia leaned forward to let him plant a light kiss on her cheek. She turned to her friend. "Jim, this is my... this is Adam."

Jim Murdsen stood as he shook Adam's hand. "A pleasure to meet you, Detective Kaminski. I've heard of you from Sylvia." He was shorter than Adam, his eyes wary under a deeply lined forehead. He didn't hold Adam's glance, simply nodded once, then looked back at Sylvia, then at the table. He retook his chair as Adam sat.

"All good, I hope." Adam smiled.

Murdsen's smile was thin. His fingers played with the cloth napkin spread across his lap, and he cleared his throat but didn't speak. His unease was obvious, though Adam couldn't imagine the cause.

Sylvia made small talk as they ordered their dinners of shish taouk and laham mishwe. Adam was relieved to see that, unlike Murdsen, she was relaxed, happy. Her usual beautiful self. The woman he'd fallen in love with. She laughed as she told a story from her day at work, resting her hand lovingly on Adam's as she spoke. She leaned in toward him, her hair brushing against his shoulder, and he inhaled, picking up a hint of her lavender perfume over the dominating scent of the spices.

Murdsen listened to Sylvia's story politely, occasionally smiling. But his smile didn't reach to his eyes, and when Sylvia's hand touched Adam's, he seemed to recoil. He stared at their intertwined fingers, then slid his eyes sideways to look at Sylvia. He gave a subtle shake of his head and looked away.

A waiter in severe black served their food, and Adam found himself distracted for a moment by the combination of scents that rose from their plates. He picked up his silverware, but spoke before taking his first bite. "So I'm curious to learn more about the black market in art here in Philly."

Murdsen nodded as he swallowed, took a sip of his wine. "Yes, Sylvia mentioned you had some interest in that. What can I tell you?"

"Well, for starters, how does someone go about getting their hands on a stolen piece of art?"

Murdsen frowned and shrugged, his wine glass following the movement. "That depends, of course, on how valuable the piece is. If we're talking about a Rodin, for example, or Renoir from the Museum of Art…"

"I was thinking of something a little less infamous. A piece by an unknown artist, for example, that was taken without permission."

Murdsen took a few more bites of his meal while considering the question. After a pause, he launched into an explanation of the illegal art trade, in Philadelphia and nationally. About how a piece could travel from a museum or personal collection to a dealer, from that dealer to a buyer. A buyer who wasn't too concerned about provenance. Or legality.

"So we're talking about crooked dealers?"

"Crooked, yes… but also legitimate."

"How do you mean?"

"Many dealers who trade in illegal art also run perfectly legitimate businesses. Buying and selling art, collectibles, antiques, all aboveboard."

"With a darker trade going on in a back room?"

"Exactly."

Adam reached into his jacket pocket and pulled out a photograph of Julia's statue. It wasn't the sort of picture that would appear in any catalogue. The image was clinical, the statue standing on a stainless-steel counter next to a black and yellow ruler that showed its exact size. It looked cold, if wood could be cold. Adam shivered.

"Dr. Murdsen, I'm trying to follow a very faint lead. The only breadcrumb I have is a piece of stolen art."

He tapped the picture that lay on the table next to his dinner plate. It seemed awkward, out of place in this elegant setting. Sinister.

"You know who owned it, from where it was stolen?"

"I do. I even know who stole it. He's behind bars. What I don't know, and need to know, is who he sold it to."

"It's very common to purchase through brokers. The person who purchased that may not be the person you are looking for, only the next breadcrumb on your trail."

"So the person who owned the piece last may not be involved in the black market at all?"

He paused, shrugged. "Maybe not. Of course, a true collector would be diligent in his purchases, ensuring appropriate provenance."

"Provenance?"

"Sure, it's not just for paintings. It applies to statues, photographs, even books."

Adam looked up from his meal at that, surprised. "There's a black market for books?"

"Of course." Murdsen's eyes widened, his expression excited.

"So the person who owns a stolen piece of art is either ignorant about what he or she owns, or simply doesn't care where it came from. Could they purchase it from a legitimate dealer, not realizing it could be stolen?"

Murdsen dabbed at his lips with the white napkin. "I suppose that's possible, though really it's unlikely. A dealer running an under-the-table side business will be very careful who he sells stolen pieces to. The FBI is known to run undercover operations. You wouldn't want to accidentally sell a stolen piece to an agent. May I ask why you are interested?"

"I'd rather not go into details. Let's say it's an unofficial investigation."

Sylvia had been eating quietly, simply observing the two men speak. At Adam's last comment, she inhaled sharply, choking on a piece of pita bread. Adam turned to her, but she waved a hand, nodding. "I'm fine, please."

She kept her smile pasted to her face as she turned to Adam, her voice low, so low Murdsen might not have been able to hear. "I understand you are helping Julia. I support you, that's why I set this up, but only if you are part of this investigation. Are you?"

Adam looked away. The photograph of the statue lay on the table, the wood twisted, the face of a man framed in guilt.

Murdsen had relaxed while Adam was quizzing him on the art trade, comfortable in a conversation he had had many times before, a subject he knew intimately. As soon as Sylvia mentioned Adam's job and her efforts to help him, Murdsen lowered his eyes, refusing to meet Adam's look. He coughed, dropped his napkin on the table, and excused himself.

Adam swallowed the rest of his wine, using his glass to indicate Murdsen's empty seat. "Do you know what's bugging him?"

"He's nervous because you are a cop, I am sure." Sylvia shook her head, her eyes shifting left toward the path Murdsen had followed to the restrooms. "That makes everyone feel uncomfortable, you know that. And you are asking him about illegal activities. Now, if you were a commissioner. Or even deputy commissioner. A nice political position, instead of digging up dirt on criminals."

She bit her tongue as Murdsen returned to the table. "I know a dealer you should speak with."

"Someone who might help me track this piece?"

"He might. I make no promises, mind you. He's just the best person I can think of. He works in the field, and he has some… unusual connections, I believe. I will ask him if he's willing to talk with you."

Adam handed his business card to Murdsen, who had remained standing, clearly eager to go. "Thank you, Jim, I appreciate it."

Murdsen nodded at them both, keeping his eyes down, and hurried out of the restaurant as the waiter approached the table with the bill.

As soon as he was out of earshot, Sylvia turned on Adam. "You're doing this against your captain's wishes, aren't you?"

"What if I am? What else can I do?" He knew he sounded resigned, not a trait Sylvia valued. He pulled out his wallet, handing his credit card to the waiter.

"I swear, for a smart man, you are blind when it comes to Julia. Maybe she did kill that judge and you just can't see the truth."

"So what, you want me to abandon her?"

"Do you know me so little? Do you think I would say such a thing?"

"Then what? What are you saying?"

"Things are not always so simple. Not always black and white, as you think. Support your sister. Support your family. But if it might cost you your job, then do it as a brother, not as a policeman. You can have both, you know, if you're smart. You should pursue this, but not at the cost of your career."

"I don't get you sometimes. I really don't." Adam tried to control his anger. It wouldn't do any good to turn her against him, but why the hell didn't she get it? "I *am* going to pursue this at any cost."

Her chair caught on the carpet as she jumped up. Her face was red, her eyes flashing. "I'll be home late. Don't wait up."

Adam stood to follow, but paused when he saw the waiter returning for his signature. When he finally got out of the restaurant, he could see only the back of Sylvia's retreating form as she hurried up Walnut Street, ignoring his calls.

"Detective Kaminski?"

Adam turned to see Matt Thompson walking toward him.

"Matt. What are you doing here?"

"Just heading home. You live around here?"

"Yeah, not far." Adam kept his eyes on Sylvia. Her pace didn't slow. She didn't turn around to see if he was following her. "Damn it."

Matt followed Adam's gaze to Sylvia, still visible the next block up. "I catch you at a bad time?"

"Yeah." Adam looked back at Matt, shaking his head. "Yeah, whatever, a fight with my girlfriend. About my sister."

Matt took a step back, his head to one side. "Is that the personal connection I heard about? Is it true, you were taken off the case?"

Adam bit back the anger that sprang immediately to his lips at the question. Instead, he tucked his hands into his pockets and turned away from the ranger. "You know what, it's been a long night. Good to see you, man. I'm heading home."

Matt stepped toward Adam, hands out in apology. "Hey, sorry, didn't mean to push your buttons. I get it, when family's involved it's hard to know the right thing to do, to see the truth. I just want to help."

Adam stopped walking, considering. He could certainly use the help of someone who was still officially involved in the case. Even tangentially. Matt picked up on his hesitation and kept talking. "I get wanting to help your sister, buddy. Whatever the situation is."

"Right." Adam shot one more glance toward Sylvia's retreating form, then turned back to Matt. "Maybe Sylvia's right. Maybe I can't see the truth when it comes to the women in my life. So yeah, I could use your help."

CHAPTER NINE

"RANGER THOMPSON, good morning." Ian Heyward turned in surprise, responding to Matt's call.

"Dr. Heyward." Matt cut across the grass to step into place beside Heyward as he followed the path that ran around the square. The regular inhabitants of the square had already returned. Matt had just woken two, and they were packing up their belongings, moving on for the day. Other than the homeless and Ian Heyward, the square was empty, too early still for commuters or yoga students. "What brings you out so early this morning?"

Heyward turned back to look at the Veriatus. "Just dropped by the office for a book I'd forgotten."

"Not working today?" Matt's glance followed Heyward's. The golden stone building seemed to stand alone, despite being closely bordered by red and gray brick buildings on either side.

Heyward saw Matt's look. "It's quite impressive, isn't it? Have you been inside? We have a world-renowned collection of written works. It's open to the public for viewing."

"No such luck." Matt shook his head.

Heyward glanced at his watch and stopped walking. "Shall I show you around?" His words were polite, but anxiety showed on his face. He lifted his glasses off his nose with the thumb and first finger of his left hand, as if to lift the weight of the lenses for a moment, then replaced them.

"Not this morning, thanks, I'm on duty. But I'd love to take you up on that another time."

Heyward smiled and nodded. Matt joined him as he resumed his march around the square. He walked with his shoulders hunched over, as if he'd spent too many years leaning over old books. He looked no older than forty, maybe forty-two, but Matt couldn't help but notice he carried a whiff of that mustiness unique to old places and old things. In contrast, his face was clear and unlined despite his age, a clear sign he hadn't led a particularly stressful life so far.

Matt matched his brisk pace. "What do you do in there?"

"Oh, this and that." Heyward patted his tan leather shoulder bag. "I'm the curator, you know. We have a significant collection of books. Quite impressive, really. But today, I'm refamiliarizing myself with Joseph Dennie. For my research, you see."

"I don't think I've heard of him."

"No? That's too bad. Fascinating person, wrote quite strident objections to certain forms of democracy during the early years of our country." Heyward's voice rose a level as he spoke about his research, clearly a subject that excited him, but Matt was glad when he left the description at that and said no more.

The two men walked on without speaking for a moment. Heyward broke the silence. "I heard about Judge Ryan-Mills." He glanced at Matt, then back at the path ahead of them. A lone jogger was out, running toward them. "I don't suppose you know anything about that investigation, do you?"

Matt waited until the young woman had passed, then responded. "No, not that I can discuss. What have you heard?"

Heyward shrugged. "Only that he was found dead here in Washington Square. And that he was murdered."

"That's about the gist of it. Not much more to tell,

really. Philly PD are investigating. It's tough with all the work going into preparing for the religious convention, you know?"

"Yes, and the fundraising event planned for right here in the square as well." Matt couldn't be sure, but he thought Heyward grinned when he added, "A murder can't be good for fundraising."

Matt's radio coughed out a noise. Matt listened to the call, responded with his usual check-in.

Heyward waited until Matt had completed his call, then added, "That's too bad, you know. About Oliver."

"You knew him well?"

Heyward frowned and moved his head from side to side. "I don't know if I would say well. We found ourselves working together recently on the casino issue."

"I've heard about that from a few of the other residents."

Heyward smiled up at Matt. "I've seen you chatting with the ladies. They do cozy up to you, don't they? Share a lot of gossip?"

Matt laughed. "I guess so. I'm just friendly, is all. But I didn't know you were involved in fighting the casinos, too."

"Sure. No one around here wants a casino built. Even if it's not in our neighborhood, the location they're planning is close enough, it will affect us. And not in a good way."

"So you and Judge Ryan-Mills were leading the civic association in its protest against the development?"

"Oliver provided some guidance, yes." Heyward's mouth clamped shut.

Matt noted the brevity of his response, but didn't push it. "Do you have any idea who might have killed him, Dr. Heyward?"

Heyward's mouth opened again in surprise. "Me? Of course I don't. How could I?"

Matt shrugged. "You might have seen him fighting with someone?"

"He was a judge, Ranger Thompson. Rich and powerful. No doubt he made many people very angry. That's the way of it. The reason he didn't usually want to be involved in the neighborhood. He always said he needed to keep himself separate. Objective. Safe."

Matt said nothing more, running through the conversation in his mind, preparing the summary he'd share with Adam as soon as he'd finished with Heyward.

Heyward looked over at him. "I'm glad you're asking these questions. You and the other rangers, you know this neighborhood. The people who live here. I'm glad to know you're helping on the investigation."

THE PHONE RANG again just as Adam disconnected from his conversation with Matt. He was grateful to Matt for doing the legwork and sharing what he'd found, though he wasn't sure how useful it was. He pulled his front door shut behind him and stepped onto the uneven brick sidewalk as he saw Julia's number pop up on the phone.

"Jules, you okay?"

"Finally. Where have you been?" Her anger crashed through the phone as though she were standing in front of him.

"What are you talking about?"

"I was trying to reach you all night, you didn't answer."

Adam grimaced. "Sorry, I didn't check my phone. Sylvia and I…"

"Oh, God, you're not fighting again, are you?"

Adam grinned. If Julia only knew what they'd been fighting about.

"Listen, Adam, I need to talk to you. It's important." The urgency in Julia's voice stopped him short. He stepped into the narrow alley that ran along his building, moving away from the noise of the traffic and leaning against one of the picturesque brick townhouses that lined the street.

"What's going on, what can I do?"

"That judge. Ryan-Mills."

"I know. I'm sorry I told you like that. But you were going to find out, and I figured it would be better if you heard it from me. Did Pete call you?"

Julia didn't answer, but Adam heard the rustle of fabric and knew she had tucked the phone between her shoulder and ear. "Yeah, he did. We talked about it. But I didn't tell him…"

"Tell him what?"

"I knew the judge. I was in his courtroom."

He stared at the numbers on the cornerstone of the house in front of him, trying to think rationally. 1762. That house had stood here for so many years. Before this country was a country. It had provided shelter and comfort to whatever family had lived here, a family that would've had to fight for their home, for their nation. Calmer, he focused his attention back on his sister.

"When? You've never been arrested."

"Not me, a friend of mine. He ran into problems in the park. It's a national park, so when he had a hearing, it was in federal court."

"What are you talking about? You're hanging out with criminals now?"

"Stop it. Just listen. He's not a criminal. He was smoking a little weed, that's all. It's legal in Philly now, you know? But he didn't realize he was in a national park. He got picked up and got a citation. He had to go to court."

"You knew the victim…" She had no alibi. The judge was killed with her statue. With her fingerprints all over it. And she had encountered the judge when he was alive.

"But you weren't on trial, you were there to support a friend, right? So your name won't show up in his records."

Julia's silence spoke volumes. Finally, she cleared her

throat. "I never testified, if that's what you mean."

"You were scheduled to testify?" Adam's body went cold. The sounds of the city around him stopped. He could hear his breath, in and out, in and out.

"His lawyer asked me to testify. I was on his list. But I never got a chance. The judge sentenced him without even hearing my testimony."

"Were you there with him? Were you smoking, too?"

"No, I wasn't. I wasn't there. I was just a character witness. He's a good guy, I swear. I've worked with him on a few projects. That's all I was going to say. But I didn't get the chance."

Adam nodded to himself. Not surprising the judge didn't want to hear her testimony. A case like this was open and shut. Not about the defendant's character, only about the facts.

"Shit."

"Adam, I'm sorry. I tried to tell you yesterday."

"Okay, I know. Did you tell Pete this?"

"I didn't... I couldn't."

Adam pictured the mound of files on Pete's desk and grew cold, files that yesterday gave him comfort, confidence in Pete's ability. Pete was skilled and he was fast. Those piles would shrink fast as Pete went through every case. Every name. Adam didn't have much time.

"Good. Don't tell anyone, let me handle this."

CHAPTER TEN

PETE LOOKED AS IF he hadn't moved. He still sat hunched over the pile of paper on his desk, still chewing the end of a pencil, tapping his fingers as he read. Only the color of his shirt gave away the fact that he'd made it home last night, at least to change his clothes. But he hadn't been gone for long. The pile was definitely smaller.

"What you find so far, partner?" Adam placed a paper cup of coffee on Pete's desk.

Pete leaned back and exhaled loudly, running both hands through his sandy hair until it stood on end. "Not much. Lots of names. Lots of motives. But nothing that connects. Not yet."

"You know the killer might not be in there. This murder might not be anything related to his cases."

Pete nodded as he took a sip of coffee. "I know, you're right. There is one case, though..." He reached across his desk to dig through a pile and Adam held his breath.

"Casinos."

Adam let his breath out. "Casinos?"

"Yeah. As a judge, Ryan-Mills struck down a proposed injunction by the governor's administration that would have stopped one of the Native American tribes from negotiating a new gambling compact with the U.S. Interior Department."

"Wait, Oliver Ryan-Mills struck down the injunction? You mean he helped the casino development move forward?"

Pete nodded at Adam, raising his eyebrows. "That surprises you? Because that part on its own didn't strike me as odd. Why wouldn't a rich judge support a casino being built in town?"

Adam thought of what Matt Thompson had learned, about Ian Heyward and the civic association. "Nothing, I guess. Sorry. Just not what I expected. Don't know why."

"Uh-huh. Because you think I can't tell when you're lying to me?" Pete smiled. "Never mind, I probably don't want to know. No, there are a couple things weird about it. For one, one of the defendants in the case, Roc Lubrano, has a known association with the mob."

"Known association? Known but not proven?"

Pete nodded. "That's about it. Someone who caught my attention, that's all." He dropped the file and looked up at Adam, who had perched on a neighboring desk. "Why're you asking, Kaminski? You're not on this case, remember?"

"I know, I know. I'm curious. It's my sister, Pete. You know I gotta care."

"I know." Pete looked down. He glanced around the squad room, but everyone else was minding their own business — on the phone, on the computer, talking to each other. The noise would have been overwhelming, but both men knew how to ignore it. How to use it to their advantage.

"Look, I'm not done yet. Still waiting for the tech's report. Still have this pile of papers to finish." He slapped his hand down on the pile remaining in front of him. "But what I know so far? We have a few people to look at."

"Like who?"

"The son. Harry Ryan-Mills. He lives in the area. And he'll inherit."

"Everything?"

"Well, he'll split it with his brother. But this is a substantial estate we're talking about. Half of twelve million is nothing to sneeze at. And the brother, Thomas, lives in Chicago with his wife and family and can prove he was there last night."

"Sounds promising." Adam nodded, indicating the other files with his chin. "What else?"

Pete looked down. "I'm still interested in this case on the casinos. First, as a judge, he blocks an injunction that would have stopped the casinos from being built. But interviews with his family and neighbors show he's been involved in a community movement against the casinos. A group led by a Dr. Ian Heyward."

"Yeah, I've heard of him."

"You have?" Pete looked up, surprised. "A curator of old books?"

Adam smiled. "I get around, all right?"

"Right. So, the developer involved, Roc Lubrano. Like I said, word is he's got connections. Always a red flag."

"And Julia?"

Pete shook his head. "She's still on our radar. She's probably fine, we just need to be thorough in crossing her off our list. She did own the murder weapon, after all, and they were her fingerprints."

He tapped his hand on the files in front of him. "Look, don't worry. More people may still be added to that list. I've got this whole pile of people to go through. Everyone who came before the judge over his last year on the bench, if you can believe that."

Adam took a breath and nodded, hoping his expression wasn't betraying him. He trusted Pete. He was a great cop. He could let Pete handle this. Find the truth.

But Pete worked for the captain, who worked for the deputy commissioner, and the list went on. It wasn't up to Pete. And it was just a matter of time before Pete found Julia's name on that list.

He needed to find the truth before that happened. Before his friends and colleagues got their hands on his little sister, bringing her in for questioning, linking her to this investigation.

CHAPTER ELEVEN

"FINALLY, THE LAST item on our agenda." The chairman sucked in his lips as he stared down at the notes in front of him on the podium. His already gaunt features tightened even more, and he ran a bony hand along the microphone in front of him. Nodding to himself, he raised his face to the audience in front of him. "I invite developer Roc Lubrano to present his plans for his latest casino, scheduled to be built on Market Street, outside our district's border. Mr. Lubrano."

A short, stocky man rose from a seat in the middle of the church hall. His barreling walk drove him to the front of the church with only a few powerful strides, and he scowled and pushed up the sleeves of his shirt as he moved, as if ready for a fight.

The audience moved with him, shifting in their seats. Adam sank down lower in his chair and checked out the room. It was a packed crowd. The civic association didn't usually hold their meetings in the church hall, but had arranged for the larger space given the higher than average turnout they expected for Roc's presentation. This was the reason Adam was there, why he'd waited through discussions of sidewalk cracks, parking problems, and leaf blowing. If Ryan-Mills had been involved in this, then Adam wanted to know if someone was angry enough about it to kill. And it didn't hurt that his attendance there passed the red-face test: if asked, he could always say he was working on community relations in advance of next week's protests.

Adam listened with half an ear as Roc described the height, materials, design, and setback of the casino and hotel he was building in Center City. He kept his attention mostly on the audience, though he refocused when Roc suggested that some undefined legal hurdles had recently been overcome, making it easier for him to move forward with development.

As Roc's presentation wound down, the chairman opened the floor to questions. Instead of the rush of questions Adam expected, everyone turned their heads to one man.

Ian Heyward coughed, lifted his glasses off his nose for a second with the thumb and first finger of his left hand, and stood.

"Mr. Lubrano. Thank you for deigning to offer us this presentation this afternoon. I'm sure you had other ways to spend your lunch hour."

Roc nodded, his face grim, but said nothing.

Ian continued, "I would like to make clear, so there is no misunderstanding. Nothing you have said today — nothing — has changed my mind about this casino." He turned as he spoke, addressing the other neighbors in attendance rather than the developer. "The way this is built, how it looks, what materials are used..." Ian waved his hand. "These are irrelevant."

A murmur ran through the audience, a few heads nodding in agreement.

"What matters... all that matters... is that we do not want a casino in, or near, our homes."

The murmur in the audience grew louder. Someone called out, "Hear, hear."

Roc's face grew a darker shade of red. He clenched his hands and took a step toward the audience. Adam sat forward on his seat, recognizing the anger in Roc's stance.

Ian either didn't notice it or didn't care. He walked out into the aisle as he spoke, the two men now facing off down the church aisle.

"You come here today with stories of blue granite and marble. As if any of those elements could hide the poverty... the crime... the alcohol that will surely follow your development to the borders of our residential neighborhood."

More calls from the audience proved that Roc was facing a hostile crowd, but he didn't look worried. He looked angry.

"Don't think we don't know what's going on." Ian was warming to his topic, his speech getting faster. "We know you're in league with the city, in league with the courts. You're flouting the law; you think you can do whatever you want. Well, we're on to you. You'll all get what you deserve."

Roc moved fast, a few long strides bringing him face to face with Ian. Ian adjusted his glasses again, coughed.

"Are you threatening me? Do you have any facts to back up your opinions? Your slander?" Roc's voice was low.

Adam stood up from his seat.

Now Ian's face was turning red to match Roc's. "Just look at Atlantic City. Look what casinos did to that town."

Roc shook his head. "You ignorant, biased, stupid little man. All you know is what you read in books. You don't know shit, you got that?"

Ian gasped, stepped back. Then stepped forward again. His hand flew forward, perhaps intending to slap Roc, perhaps simply intending to gesture wildly. Roc reacted. It took only a second, but his fist made contact with Ian's face. Ian landed flat on his back.

Everyone in the room was standing now, but Adam managed to push his way through, to step between the two men.

"That's enough. If you two want to fight this out, you

need to take it outside."

Two women had come up to help Ian, and Adam nodded to them as they helped him to a seat.

"You. Come with me." Adam pointed at Roc.

Roc sneered, pushing up the sleeves of his shirt. He glanced around the room one more time, then followed Adam out of the church.

Outside, children's voices carried from the school down the street. Yellow leaves littered the sidewalk. Adam took a few deep breaths of the crisp, cool air, letting Roc do the same. Once he'd given the man a minute to cool off, he introduced himself.

"Ha, a cop." Roc blew out the words on a laugh. "I should've known. What's your interest in this? Why're you here?"

"I'm looking into the murder of Judge Oliver Ryan-Mills." Adam looked Roc up and down. He looked relaxed, his feet apart, his arms hanging loosely by his side. But his fists were still clenched below the rolled-up sleeves of his black shirt. "Do you know anything about the murder?"

"Are you kidding?" Roc's expression was flat. "First of all, why would I know anything about a murder? What kind of person do you think I am?" Adam didn't answer that, so Roc continued, "Second of all, I didn't want him dead. Didn't you hear me in there? I'm grateful to the judge. He's the one who stopped the injunction to let us move forward with planning."

A stream of residents was now exiting the church, giving Roc, and Adam with him, dirty looks. Adam took a step back up the sidewalk and Roc followed his lead, moving away from the church entrance.

"I heard. But that was then. Since he retired, he changed tracks, taking steps to stop you, not help you. Seems to me you're in a better position now with Ryan-Mills dead."

Roc grunted as he readjusted his sleeves, this time taking care to roll them smoothly. "Yeah, you're right.

Ryan-Mills was implementing legal action to stop the casinos, close them down. Not to mention getting the rabble all worked up, along with Mr. Ian Heyward in there."

Adam caught a glimpse of dark green ink on the inside of Roc's arm, the edges of a spider web peeking out before Roc pulled the sleeve down. Adam recognized the familiar symbol of a man who'd spent time in prison. Something else he'd have to look into, but for now it was enough to know that Roc really was as rough a character as he was acting.

"So where were you when Ryan-Mills was killed?"

"Me?" Roc smiled and his whole face changed. He might have been a handsome man, if he hadn't let the scowl take up permanent residence over his eyes. "I was with someone on Wednesday night."

"He was killed Tuesday night, early hours of Wednesday morning."

"Yeah? I was with someone then, too. I'll give you her name, she'll vouch for me."

"For Tuesday night or Wednesday night?"

Roc grinned. "Whichever you want. Look" — he spread his hands open — "I'm an honest business man now. Yeah, I got a past. I don't deny it. I saw you looking at my ink. But I'm on the up-and-up now. I'm a legitimate businessman working on a legitimate deal. And I got the city's approval on this, too, don't forget."

Adam looked back up the street as the sound of children increased. A school was letting out, parents double-parking along the street, waiting to scoop up their precious cargo as soon as the school released them. Across the street, an elderly couple walked a miniature poodle, its black curls turned gray with age. Not a neighborhood where you'd expect to have a confrontation with a felon. He looked back at Roc.

"I understand exactly what you're saying to me, Roc. So who do you think I should be looking at?"

Roc shrugged. "You got the murder weapon? Look at

that. Isn't that what usually works for cops? Look for prints or something."

Adam stiffened. "You know something about the weapon you want to tell me?"

"Calm down, man." Roc put his hands up and took a step back. "It was just a suggestion. Hey, you asked. Look, I'm telling you, I wanted Ryan-Mills alive." Roc grinned again and winked before adding, "You have no idea how much. But life's too short, isn't it? For all of us."

He turned and headed up the street toward the school, patting a waiting boy on the head as he passed. Adam took a step to chase after him, but the boy's mother pulled up in a Volvo station wagon before Adam got there. The child was soon safely buckled into the back of the car and on his way.

There was something more Roc wasn't telling him. That much was clear. He'd as good as taunted him with it. Maybe Ian Heyward would know more.

Adam made his way back into the church hall, moving against the flow of residents leaving the building. But when he got back inside, the room was empty except for two elderly men folding up the chairs that had been set out. Adam watched them work for a moment, considering his options, then turned and left the church.

CHAPTER TWELVE

IT TOOK TWENTY minutes to walk from the civic association meeting north out of Society Hill, past the national park and through Old City toward Northern Liberties and the loft apartment that also served as Julia's studio. Whenever it was an option, Adam preferred to walk instead of cabbing it or taking the subway. Philly was an easy town to walk in. Everywhere in the city, but particularly here in the eastern, older sections, eighteenth and nineteenth century buildings lined the sidewalks, interspersed among the newer construction. The sidewalks were alive with residents, tourists, people from other parts of the city coming through to do their shopping or grab a bite to eat. You couldn't walk down these sidewalks without bumping into someone you knew.

He could see why Julia loved living in this part of town. She thrived on its nightlife, its artistic feel, its avant-garde culture. But Adam couldn't shake his fears for her, living alone in a building that hardly counted as secure. The break-in and robbery she'd been victim of last year had only confirmed his fears.

Adam passed the third church on his route, one where Benjamin Franklin himself had worshipped, and thought about the neighborhood. The number of old churches spoke volumes about the city and the people who'd lived here over the years. Philadelphia was the only city in the country, in the early years, where anyone of any faith could find a place to worship. It was no real surprise the Interfaith Peace Consortium had chosen to hold their convention here.

There was nothing wrong with this part of the city. It was still welcoming, still beautiful. It had character. Julia just needed to find a safer building. One with a doorman, maybe.

He was half a block away from her building when he saw an old man stepping out of the brick structure, pulling the front door closed firmly behind him. His shoulders were stooped, his hair almost completely gray. For only a second — half a second — something about the man looked familiar, but Adam couldn't place him.

"Shit." He spoke the word aloud as his brain clicked in and he realized the old man he was watching was his father. Did he look that old when Adam saw him yesterday? Or was it that seeing him unexpectedly like this, out of context, he saw him for how he really looked. Not how Adam expected him to look. The years were passing, and it showed. Adam picked up his pace to a jog.

"Dad!"

His father had already turned to walk the other direction, but stopped when he heard his voice. "Adam, what brings you up this way?"

"Looking for Julia. She in?"

John Kaminski shook his head. "No such luck. Not sure where she is." He held up a paper shopping bag. "Your mother wanted me to return this salad spinner to her. I thought I might just leave it outside her door, but then I remembered about that break-in last year..."

"Tell me the front door wasn't left open again?"

His father nodded, frowning. "She needs to move, Adam. Somewhere safer. I don't know where, but somewhere safer."

"I know, Dad, I keep telling her that." Adam walked beside his father up to the next street, where John would catch the bus that would take him back to Port Richmond. His father was saying something about the salad spinner, but Adam's mind kept going back to his conversation with Roc.

His alibi didn't prove anything, that much was obvious. What was he hiding? He'd spent time in prison. His nervousness could simply be a byproduct of dealing with law enforcement all his life. Perhaps he was always nervous around cops. But he was angry, too. He couldn't hide that. Was he just angry about the way this casino deal was shaping up? Or was it connected to the murder?

"You with me, Adam?"

"Hmm?"

"I said, what's on your mind, son?" John Kaminski laughed. "There's clearly something bothering you. And whatever it is, I'm guessing it's the same thing that upset Julia yesterday."

Adam acknowledged the truth of what his father was saying with a nod, but didn't answer the questions he knew his father had. "I'm trying to figure out what my best next move is, that's all."

"Next step in what?"

"It's nothing. Nothing I can talk about."

"Oh, but you want to talk to Julia about it? Since when do you two keep secrets from your old man?"

"Dad, you're not helping. I'm working on a case. Julia might have some information that would help."

"Now hold on there." John Kaminski stopped walking and turned to face his son. "You're not getting her mixed up in anything dangerous, are you?"

Adam's mind had already shifted back to his conversation with Roc, but the anger in his father's voice startled him back to the present. "Are you angry?" Adam felt his own heat rise. "I'm trying to do my job. You don't need to worry about Julia. I'm taking care of her, right? What do you think I'm doing?"

"I think you're not thinking, that's what I think.

Bringing your troubles to her."

"Yeah, well this time she brought her troubles to me."

"What are you talking about? What trouble?"

"Look, Dad." Adam took a breath. A fight with his dad was the last thing he needed. He bit down hard, biting back his anger and his stress, and tried to change the topic of conversation. "Don't worry about it, okay? I got it handled. Hey, I'm still planning to look more into those letters from Łukasz, you know? See what else I can find about Grandpa."

John Kaminski stayed silent for a moment more, assessing his son. He knew his dad could read him like a book. He was hoping he'd let this one go. No such luck.

"You do what you gotta do, son." John turned away from him as he spoke. "I know all I need to know about my father and his father before him. You know" — he turned back to Adam, his face red again — "I don't know what else you want to learn about your family. I may not have some great fortune to leave you. I'm sorry, my father didn't smuggle any gold or paintings out of Poland during the war. But we have a proud history. A proud legacy. Don't you forget that. You should be proud of it, not questioning it. And I'll tell you what else, you keep pushing me away like this, and I won't be there when you need me, got it?"

"Dad, I didn't mean…" But John Kaminski was striding up the sidewalk, ignoring his son's call.

CHAPTER THIRTEEN

A BEDRAGGLED CLUSTER of dark-clad individuals approached Independence Hall from Walnut Street, crossing Independence Square and heading toward the pointing brass finger of Commodore John Barry. Matt and Barb stood next to the Barry statue, focusing on the VIPs. At least, they'd been told the visitors were VIPs. Eyes glazed over, shoes scuffed and dirty, they limped toward the rangers looking more like a group of penitents seeking forgiveness from a religious leader. Or a group whose tour director had been driving them too hard to see too many things in too short a time.

"And why are they getting special attention?" Barb's skepticism matched his own.

He turned to her. "I have no idea. They know someone who knows someone."

"So they don't have to go through the normal visitor screening?"

"Maybe not. But we don't know them, so they still get screened, right? That's why we're here."

"Of course." Barb nodded once and tucked her hands around her utility belt, squaring her legs as the group approached. "Ladies and gentlemen." She raised her voice so they could hear. "Welcome to Independence Hall. Please hold your bags and coats open…"

Matt's attention shifted to a separate figure jogging across the square towards them. He could hear Barb

73

passing the visitors into the secure area one at a time, but kept his eyes on Ian Heyward.

"Ranger Thompson" — Heyward paused for breath, his hands on his knees — "I'm so glad I caught you." He stopped to take a few more deep breaths before standing upright.

"What can I do for you, Dr. Heyward?" Matt glanced back at Barb even as he asked the question. She gave him a quick nod, then turned her attention back to the group in front of them.

"It's that Roc Lubrano." Heyward had regained his breath, but not his composure. His voice wavered as he continued, "He's headlining at some big conference tomorrow. In Atlantic City. To talk about the casino!" Heyward's voice seemed to break on the last word and he choked on his own sharp inhale.

"Calm down." Matt took a step closer to him, gently shifting him away from the group of VIPs. "Why are you so upset about this?"

Heyward's eyes grew round behind his thick glasses. "Don't you get it? He's acting as if his casino is a done deal. He thinks…" Heyward turned to gaze around the square and Matt noticed a deep red mark under one eye. Almost as if he'd been in a fight, which didn't seem in character for him. Perhaps Matt had to learn a little bit more about Ian Heyward.

Heyward's gaze fastened once again on Matt. "He thinks we can't stop him. We have to do something. We must not let him continue like this."

"You gonna help at all, Matt?" Barb asked the question lightly, but he picked up on the impatience in her tone.

"Look, Dr. Heyward, I'm not sure why you're telling me this or what you want me to do. If you'd like to work with the park, you'll need to talk to the superintendent, not me."

"No, no, no." Heyward's eyebrows lowered as he shook his head. "You understand what I'm saying. You know the problem." He pointed a finger at Matt and nodded his head knowingly. "You know Roc Lubrano."

"And?" Matt took a step toward Barb as he asked the question.

"And I thought you should know about this. That's all." Heyward shrugged, his anger finally dissipating as his breathing returned to normal. "You should know what he's up to. So you can keep an eye on him." He looked down at the ground as he shook his head, shoving his hands into his pockets.

Matt glanced once more at Barb, who still had a few more people in the group to screen, then put a hand on Heyward's arm, intending to say a friendly goodbye.

Heyward took a step back. "Do you know he attacked me earlier today?" He raised a finger toward the mark on his face, then used the opportunity to adjust his glasses, as if trying to hide his injury.

That explained the bruise then. "He attacked you? For no reason?"

"For no good reason." Heyward's indignation returned and his voice rose. "I simply pointed out to him that we could see through his little scheme."

"We?"

"The community, Ranger Thompson. The neighbors. We will not let this continue."

"Will you be pressing charges?" Matt took another step toward Barb even as he asked the question, feeling her angry stare on his back.

Heyward's eyes dropped back to the ground and he took another step back. "I don't know... maybe." He wagged his head from side to side for a moment, then shook it like a dog shaking off water. "It's not just about me. The whole neighborhood was there, everyone saw the whole thing."

"Oh?" Matt stopped moving, wondering again what Heyward was hiding. Why wouldn't he file a police report?

"Oh, yes." Heyward nodded vigorously. "We all saw

Lubrano's true colors. And you need to, too. You need to know what type of man he is. Because I think he killed Judge Ryan-Mills."

"That's quite an accusation. What makes you so sure?"

"He punched me! He's a violent man."

"But that doesn't make him a killer."

"Oh, he's a killer all right. That's why I'm telling you this. You need to look closer at him. He's got to be your top suspect right now."

Matt felt his pulse quicken. Heyward was making sense. If Ryan-Mills had been helping lead the fight against the casinos, Lubrano could've wanted him dead. But something about Heyward's accusation was off. He shot one more glance at Barb, and this time couldn't ignore her stare. She was just letting the last visitor through the gate into the secure area.

"Look, Dr. Heyward, I need to get with this group. But thanks for letting me know about this, okay?"

"So you'll look into it? Find the proof that Roc Lubrano killed Oliver Ryan-Mills?"

Matt nodded noncommittally. "I'll see what I can do."

He jogged over to join Barb with the group as they followed an interpretive ranger into the shadows behind Independence Hall, wondering what the hell he should do next.

"DID MOOSE RESPOND to the call?" Matt directed his question to Barb as they headed toward the gate at 5th and Chestnut streets an hour later.

"Yep, he's on it. I let him know we'd get there as soon we finished up with this group."

Matt followed her out through the gate, turning to shut it behind them, blocking off the line of tourists eagerly hoping for a quicker way onto Independence Square. The call about the trip-and-fall had come in while they were still with the VIP group. Knowing

Moose was available, Matt had let Barb reply to dispatch with their location and status. Moose didn't really need their backup on a call like this one, but it didn't hurt to work their way over there and check things out.

Looking up 5th Street, he saw Adam Kaminski charging down the sidewalk towards them, his hands stuffed in his pockets, his face turned low to the ground. His failure to run right into the other pedestrians was due only to their maneuvering to get out of his way. He was a man on a mission. Or perhaps a man on the run.

"Thompson." Adam looked up just in time to stop in front of them. His eyes were dark, his face stern.

"We're on our way to a call, Kaminski. You okay?"

"Sure, sure." Adam looked away, his hands back in his pockets.

"How's the convention prep going?" Matt kept his voice light, Barb's presence next to him an impatient reminder that he wasn't supposed to be working on the murder case.

"You on that, too?" Barb jumped in, glancing at her watch as she did so. "We got a bit of that going on here. Gonna be crazy, it seems like, huh?"

Adam nodded but didn't answer.

After a moment of silence, Barb glanced up at Matt. "Look, we gotta run. Unless there's something you need from me?" Her voice trailed off as she looked back and forth between Matt and Adam.

Matt nodded but kept his eyes on Adam. "You go ahead, Barb, I'll be right behind you."

Barb's face darkened. "Sure, no problem. But Matt?" Barb gave him a look whose meaning was clear. "I'm only going to cover for you so many times, got it?"

"Got it." He watched Barb march up the street to meet up with Moose, then turned back to Adam. "Kaminski, what's going on?"

"Hmm?" Adam seemed startled by the question. "Nothing. It's nothing. Hey," some life came back into his eyes as he continued, "I stopped by the civic association meeting earlier, met Mr. Roc Lubrano."

"Yeah, I heard he made quite a scene there." Matt started walking up 5th Street and Adam kept pace.

"You heard? How?"

"Ian Heyward. Came by here sporting a shiny new bruise under his eye."

"Ah, that." Adam smiled. "Yeah, that was something else."

"It really set Heyward against Lubrano, I can tell you that. He's convinced Lubrano's the guy who killed Ryan-Mills."

"Oh, yeah? Does he have any reason for thinking that? I mean, beyond the fact that the man punched him?"

Matt laughed. "Nah, I think that's it. Except…"

"What?"

"He wanted me to go to some conference in Atlantic City. Lubrano's giving a presentation there, and Heyward seems to think that if I follow him around or something he'll trip up."

"Or get so nervous he confesses?"

"Yeah, something like that." Both men laughed, but Adam's smile faded before he'd let out his breath.

They paused when they got to the next corner. Matt knew he had to catch up with Barb, but didn't want to lose this chance. "I don't know what he's thinking, but no way I can head off to Atlantic City. I'm on shift all week. And the conference Heyward's talking about is tomorrow." He looked sideways at Adam. "Any chance you want to go?"

Adam shook his head. "Not likely, buddy. I can't just take off for AC. No way I can justify it. I heard Mr. Lubrano give his presentation to the civic association. He'll probably say all the same things again."

Matt nodded, frowning. "Yep, probably. I wish I knew why Heyward was so set on that conference and Roc Lubrano. There's something about Heyward…" Adam must have picked up on the doubt in Matt's voice, because he turned to look at him. Matt looked away from the scrutiny. "It's probably nothing, I'm probably looking too hard," he finished his sentence, knowing how lame it must sound.

"Maybe." Adam shrugged and stepped back from the curb as a bus careened a little too close. "If I were on the case, I'd be looking into Lubrano. See if there was anything more connecting Lubrano to the murder." He shook his head as he took a breath, his eyes looking ahead along the sidewalk. Finally, he turned back to Matt. "Heyward's right, we should be keeping an eye on Lubrano. I just don't see how I can."

"I know. Of everyone involved in this, he's certainly the most likely suspect. All right, I'll mention Heyward's comments to John Hamilton. By the book." He grinned at Adam. "Anything else you need from me? I gotta catch up with Barb."

Adam shook his head and Matt took a step to leave, then turned back with one more thought. "I'll tell you what, though. I'd really like to get to know a little more about Oliver Ryan-Mills, too. As a person."

"Yeah? How do you mean?"

"Just about him, as a man, not as a judge." Matt thought about his last conversation with John. "Tell me, how much is PPD really looking into Ryan-Mills personal life? As opposed to reading through his case files, I mean."

"Don't sweat it, Thompson. Pete Lawler's a good cop. He's looking at the cases now, but once he works through those he'll consider every angle."

Matt bit his lip and nodded. "Right."

"On the other hand" — Adam grinned at him — "you might be happy to know I've arranged to meet Harry Ryan-Mills as soon as I'm off duty."

Matt raised his chin. "I thought you weren't on this case."

"I'm not." Adam shrugged. "Just meeting a guy for a drink. Nothing wrong with that."

CHAPTER FOURTEEN

"THANKS FOR MEETING me, Mr. Ryan-Mills." Adam slid onto an empty bar stool.

Harry Ryan-Mills took a sip of his beer, eyeing Adam over his glass. A hard look came into his eye, the steel behind the man, then flitted away. He put the beer down and nodded. "Not at all. I'm surprised you were willing to conduct this interview here" — he waved a hand to indicate the Rittenhouse Square bar — "at this hour. And please, since we're in this setting, call me Harry."

Adam smiled and ordered a whiskey. Only after taking a sip did he turn back to Harry, who was by now growing impatient. "I should tell you, this is not an official interview."

"No." Harry twisted his mouth into a grin, looking at Adam's whiskey. "I suppose not."

Adam glanced around the room. Mostly business men, ties pulled loose or stuffed in pockets now that the work day was done. A few well-dressed young ladies. Out on the prowl, perhaps.

"I'm trying to get a sense of your father, Harry. Who he was. Who his friends were. Who his enemies were."

Harry snorted into his beer. "As if you could tell the difference."

Adam raised an interrogative eyebrow, so Harry continued, "Friends, enemies, who knew. His former colleagues... friends, right? Except that he didn't seem to stay in touch with them."

"No? Did he not have much of a social life after he retired?"

"Social life?" Harry spluttered again. "He had nothing but a social life. Constantly going out, traveling, womanizing even." He looked like he was as surprised as Adam at this description.

He waved over a waiter who had been hovering near the front door. "I'm going to need a table in about thirty minutes. I'm meeting someone, so something by the window if you have it."

The waiter nodded and moved off. Glancing around the restaurant, Adam figured the dinner Harry was about to eat would cost him a week's salary. As Sylvia surely would have reminded him.

Harry turned his attention back to Adam, staring for a moment, perhaps collecting his thoughts. Perhaps preparing a lie. "This has been hard on us, my brother and me."

"I understand."

"Do you?" Harry's expression suggested he didn't think so. "I'm concerned about Tom. We're both dealing with it, you know, but we're different, me and him. He's younger, you know?"

"I'm sorry if I'm reopening wounds you're trying to heal. I wanted to get a better sense of your father as a man. It could really help."

"Look, far be it from me to speak ill of the dead." Harry paused. In Adam's experience, a start like that meant the speaker was about to speak ill of the dead.

Harry continued, "It's just... my God. He was constantly going out, taking a jaunt to Paris or Rome. Fancy dinners, drinks. And the people he was associating with, well..."

Adam nodded and kept his mouth shut. Who was he to point out the obvious if Harry couldn't see it himself. Instead, he asked, "Was this unusual behavior for him?"

"Oh, yeah. God, when Mom was alive, things were

different, I'll tell you. She would never let him get away with throwing money around like this."

"When did your mother pass away?"

Harry stared down into his beer. He noticed it was empty and ordered another. "Two years ago, now. Doesn't seem that long, though."

A frown started at Harry's forehead. It worked its way down to crease the skin around his eyes, then form deep grooves around his mouth. He clamped his jaw together tight and blinked. He glanced up at Adam, managing a lopsided smile. "It's tough to think about, that's all."

Adam had no doubt this man was truly grieving. For his mother foremost, perhaps, but his father's death had clearly brought the pain all back again. He finished his whiskey, then waved the bartender away as he approached. "I'm sorry, I'm sure you miss her."

"Yeah." Harry's lips set into a firm line. "She kept a firm watch over him, I guess. And as soon as she died, what did he do? He laughed in the face of everything that was important to her. Being good citizens. Being frugal. Protecting her children."

Adam had to wonder if that last point was really the most important.

"What did you mean a minute ago, when you mentioned the kind of people he was associating with?"

"Oh, nothing… you know…"

"I really don't."

"There's this one… uh… activist type organization. With an agenda." Harry addressed his words to his beer, rather than to Adam. "A weird group that I didn't expect my father to support. Oh—" Harry perked up and finally looked Adam in the eye. "And that developer character. I mean, he can't be good news, can he?"

"What did your dad have to do with him?"

Harry shrugged. "Got me. But I overheard him talking to him on the phone. He hung up as soon as he saw me in the apartment. I don't know what they were talking about." He held up a hand to forestall Adam's question. "I just know it was him."

Adam accepted this for what it was worth. Harry pulled down the sleeves of his jacket, which had ridden up to expose a thick watch, the gold matching the gold ring on his finger.

"You'll be inheriting your father's estate now, right?"

Harry's head jerked up. "What's that supposed to mean? Yeah, Tom and I inherit. We split it. Assuming he didn't leave any more money to that stupid organization. But don't start reading into that, Detective. I don't need his money, I'm doing plenty well on my own."

"I see that."

"Right. You judge me based on what I'm wearing, don't you? Things like this?" He lifted his hand to show off the watch. "You don't have a clue. I work hard for my money, don't you forget that. I work hard for it and I'm careful how I spend it. Just ask— I mean, just ask me anything."

Adam tried to take a sip of his whiskey to cover up his smile, but realized too late his glass was still empty. He put the glass down again and coughed. "Who should I ask, Harry?"

"What?" Harry acted as if he didn't understand the question, then shook his head roughly. "Nobody. Nobody who'd interest you. A friend who has the same tastes I do. Look, Detective." He pointed a finger at Adam as he spoke, as if to underscore his seriousness. "I may like quality — this watch, art, houses. But that doesn't mean…" Harry took a breath and shook his head, his tongue working around his mouth as if trying to find the best word to use.

"I'm sorry if I upset you. That's how investigations work. We just keep digging until we find something. And sometimes that means leaving people feeling exposed. It's part of the process." Adam toyed with his empty glass, then changed tack. "So in this new life of your father's, anyone stand out?"

"Hah. They're all standing with their hands out, if you

know what I mean. But yeah, someone does stand out. Grace Evans." Harry grimaced as he said the name.

"A new woman in your father's life?"

"That's what she'd like to think. She seemed to believe they were getting married or something. But Dad wasn't about to settle down again, no way."

"You think she was after his money?"

"I don't see why, she had plenty of her own. She lived in the apartment next to his. She'd go on about how she was going to tear down the walls and give them one uber-huge condo. I only wish Dad would've married her. Then maybe he'd stop running around spending all of his own money."

Adam smiled.

Harry continued, "Look, I don't want to speak bad about her, either, but there's something off about her. Not to mention that creepy assistant of hers. I mean, Dad must have told her no at least a dozen times, but she just didn't get it."

A young woman entered the restaurant wearing a flimsy dress, far too much skin showing for this time of year. Harry stood, flagging down the waiter.

Adam wondered if this was the friend whose opinion of Harry he was supposed to trust. "Anything else you can add?"

Harry kept his eyes on the young woman and his answer was distracted. "He'd been spending time with that guy from the Veriatus. You know, the one all worked up about the casinos."

"Ian Heyward?"

"Yeah, that's the guy. But they were friends, not enemies. I'd look at that Grace Evans if I were you. Grace and her personal assistant, Marcus." Harry glanced at his watch. "She'll be at that fundraiser right about now, if you want to meet her."

"Fundraiser?"

"In Washington Square, you know? It's in a big tent on the square, you can't miss it."

CHAPTER FIFTEEN

ADAM WALKED ACROSS town, moving from the west side of Center City back to his neck of the woods. Past the subtle, inviting lights of the upscale boutiques that lined this end of Walnut Street. Past the five-star restaurants he could never afford to eat in.

As he walked, he thought about Harry Ryan-Mills. He had to be the prime suspect. He stood to inherit a good chunk of change, and despite his claims to the contrary, no one with tastes that expensive ever really had enough money.

On the other hand, Harry seemed relatively realistic about money. Oliver Ryan-Mills hadn't started out wealthy. Comfortable, sure, but not rich. He'd earned his money over Harry's lifetime. Harry's appreciation for the finer things might just mean that Harry had learned to value his money, to value the legacy his mother and father left him.

He turned down Broad Street and walked past the majestic beauty of the historic Academy of Music. Speaking of enjoying the finer things in life. The Academy's gaslights flickered gaily as men in dark coats and women in glittery high heels converged on its elegant steps. Cultured voices carried over the sound of clinking glasses that could be heard from the lobby inside. As he crossed the street, the bright blue and neon green signs to his right shouted out that this was the city's newly named Avenue of the Arts.

For the right type of artist. The right type of people. People like the Ryan-Millses.

Adam shook his head, readjusting his thoughts. Just because he was inheriting a fortune didn't mean Harry's grief wasn't real. Adam had seen the pain in Harry's eyes and believed it to be honest. It could be a holdover of his grief over his mother's death two years previously, but it was real.

Once across Broad Street, Adam entered into a completely different part of the city. One thing you could count on about Philadelphia, it changed neighborhood to neighborhood, block to block. He passed through blocks of rundown apartment buildings and cheap pizza joints. The city was upscaling from either end, and parts of the middle hadn't been touched yet. Windows remained boarded up, storefronts plastered with signs for cheap watches for sale and offers to buy gold. Perhaps the casino here wouldn't be such a bad thing, adding a well-managed, well-lit business to this part of town. No question, emotions were running high on that subject. That was his next step, then. He needed to look a little more into the decisions surrounding the casino and Mr. Roc Lubrano. After meeting Ms. Grace Evans.

As if passing through an invisible curtain, Adam suddenly found himself in the light again. Just a few blocks from Broad Street, pink, yellow, and orange banners defined the neighborhood as people in a crazy diversity of clothes — men, women and everything in-between — lined the sidewalks, talking, laughing, bargaining. He breathed out and enjoyed the lights, the excitement in the air as he picked up his pace, passing through Washington Square West and entering Washington Square from 7th Street.

The tent looked like a NASA eco-dome colonizing the land of Washington Square. Waiters in tuxedos moved in and out through the door flaps, bussing hors d'oeuvres and pouring wine. Small white lights seemed to be everywhere, as if floating in the air in and around the tent. For the second time this week, there were no homeless to be seen. They were getting a bum rap this month.

Adam saw an opportunity to sneak into the tent behind a harried waiter, grabbing a glass of champagne as he entered. Thank goodness for the classy wool coat and red cashmere scarf Sylvia had given him. At least he didn't stick out too much.

He paused to get a feel for the party, sipping his champagne as he relaxed, took a breath. Once he was sure no one had seen him come in, no one was on their way to politely ask him to leave, he turned to a passing waiter. "Excuse me, do you know which of the guests is Grace Evans?"

The waiter barely paused in his movement, simply pointing with a low finger toward a white-haired woman in a glimmering silver dress. Adam nodded his thanks and walked toward her.

MATT JOGGED UP the ancient stone steps into the vestibule. He felt lighter, as he always did when he wasn't weighed down by his uniform and belt. He raised a hand to remove his hat before he remembered he wasn't wearing one. Dipping the tips of his fingers into the holy water, he crossed himself quickly and passed into the church.

Anne Sentrick stood by the altar, a vase of flowers in one hand, the other resting on her pursed lips. She hadn't heard him enter.

He strode up the aisle toward her, his steps soft on the thick rug that covered the worn stone floor. As he took the few steps up to the altar, his heel brushed against uncovered stone. Anne turned. Saw him. Smiled.

He took a breath. "Evening. How's the arranging going?"

She shrugged, the vase in her hand wobbling a little with the motion. "Just trying to figure out where to put everything. I've got a little more than usual this time."

"Let me help." He took the vase from her and held it out to the side. "Where do you want this one?"

She turned back to the altar with her hands raised to her shoulders. "That's what I'm trying to figure out. Look, put it there, to the left, for now. Once we have everything inside, I'll get a better sense of where it all needs to go."

He placed it carefully where she'd instructed, then followed her back around the altar, through the heavy wooden door that opened onto the vestry and from there to the alley that ran by the side of the church. Anne's van blocked the alley, "Blooms and Blossoms" painted in scrawling letters across the side. She pulled the side door open with a jerk, and Matt saw what she meant.

"Wow, that's a lot of flowers."

She smiled up at him, laughter in her blue eyes. "I know. I should be upset my sales weren't as good this week, but hey, it's good for the church, right?"

"Sure is." Matt leaned in to look over the stock in the van, resting a hand on Anne's shoulders. She didn't step away, and he took that as a good sign. "I know I've told you before, but this is a nice thing you do, adding in your own donation to the flowers the church buys each week."

She shook her head and rolled her eyes at him. "Here, start with those." She indicated a pile of loose flowers wrapped in paper lying on the ground nearest the door.

"Yes, ma'am." He took an armload and made his way back into the church.

Ten trips back and forth later, the ground in front of the altar looked more like a forest than an eighteenth century church.

"Okay, now do you know where everything goes?" He wiped his hands down the legs of his pants and surveyed the space. If it were up to him, he'd just pile the blooms up wherever they fit. But Anne had an eye for this kind of thing. She always got it right.

One vase at a time, she directed him and he placed the flowers. As they worked, he let his mind wander over the events of the day. The murder. His chance to be involved and prove his worth. His connection with detectives Kaminski and Lawler.

"Matt, to the right, not left." Anne's voice expressed frustration, but she laughed as she said it. "That's the third time I said that. Where's your mind right now?"

"Oops, sorry." He set the offending vase in the correct place. "I was thinking about work. I got distracted."

"Is this because of the interfaith convention coming next week?" Her hands moved as she stared around the church, as if she were petting the flowers in front of her, even though they were out of her reach. Using her hands to visualize what each bloom would look like in various spaces. She really was an artist.

Matt inhaled the overpowering scent of the mounds of flowers, then coughed as pollen caught in his throat.

"Oh, are you okay?" She hurried over to him, and he waved her away.

"Fine, fine. No, it's not the convention. There was a death in the park yesterday."

Anne sat down on the top step toward the altar, one lone flower in her hand. "That's terrible."

"I know." Matt sat next to her, though not too close. "I'm working with the Philly PD to help solve the murder. A man was beaten to death with a wooden statue."

"Oh, that's horrible. I didn't think park rangers did that kind of thing. Investigating murders, I mean."

"We don't usually. But then there aren't usually murders in national parks."

"I see." She looked down at her flower, a pale peach tulip that bent away from her, leaning toward the ground. "I'm sorry you have to be involved in something like that. It can't be pleasant."

"You're right, it's not. So let's get back to work, huh?" He stood and offered her his hand to help her up.

As they turned back to the flowers, which were only half spread out around the church, Anne asked, "What are you doing to help, then?"

"I'm moving the flowers wherever you want them, aren't I?" He frowned and looked over at her.

She laughed, a beautiful, musical sound that lifted his spirits. "No, I mean with the investigation."

"Oh, I thought you didn't want to talk about that."

She shrugged and bent forward to lift a vase. She grunted with the effort and he jumped forward to take it from her.

"I'm supposed to be keeping an eye out for the homeless people who tend to sleep in Washington Square. See if they saw anything. Not very glamorous, I'm afraid."

"Back by the door, and the other one just like it." She pointed toward the front of the church and he followed her direction. "It sounds like it's something you can do, though. Like you're the best person for the job. That's good."

He thought about that as he placed the second display by the door. "That's true. The detectives on the case don't know our regulars like I do. Wouldn't recognize them if they saw them. So, yeah, I'm contributing something they can't do themselves."

"Good." She nodded and turned back to the few remaining bunches. "I think these each go under a window, and we're done here."

Matt started moving the displays, one at a time, as Anne followed, rearranging each after he set it on the sill under the window.

"It won't be easy though." He spoke the words aloud, but was thinking to himself as much as talking to her.

"What won't?" She didn't take her focus off the

flowers.

"Talking to the regulars from Washington Square. They're not all…" He winced, trying to find the right words.

"What?" She stopped her tinkering and stood before the altar, her face to the aisle in front of her, assessing the view.

He stood next to her, looking out over the beauty they had added to this already inspiring space.

"They're not all easy to talk to, that's all. Not entirely stable, in fact. I'll recognize them, sure, but I'm not sure how much I'll be able to get out of them."

Anne seemed to be thinking as she led the way back through the vestry, out into the narrow alley and her now empty van. "I suppose most things that are worth doing aren't easy, are they?"

"No, I guess not. And it's not like I'll find the clue that solves the case, either. I'd love it if I could find something about the killer."

"Like a witness?"

Matt laughed, then put a hand up as Anne looked offended. "I'm not laughing at you. Sorry. I'm laughing at myself. 'Cause, yeah, I was thinking about a witness. But no way that'll happen. These aren't people who are going to show up in court and testify."

"Then what do you think you might find?"

"Just a clue. Something that gives a hint about the killer. Who he is. Something about the person wielding that statue."

"QUITE A SUCCESSFUL event, wouldn't you say?"

Adam turned in surprise at Grace Evans' voice. He had been lingering near her, picking appetizers off a tray, looking for a way to approach her without raising her suspicions. Apparently hovering near her gorging on appetizers was the way to do it.

"Yes, it seems so." Adam glanced around the tent, big

enough to hold all of the Ringling Brothers' wild plans. "Were you part of the planning committee for this? If so, congratulations."

Grace covered her mouth with her hand and gave a girlish giggle that should have been coming from her great-granddaughter, not her. "Me, oh no. I simply benefit from others' hard work. Though I did lend them the use of my personal assistant for some of the planning. And Marcus is a genius when it comes to making things go as planned, believe me. But me? No, I am here to enjoy myself." She raised her champagne flute in a mock toast. "And of course to support the neighborhood."

Adam grinned and took a sip of champagne.

She joined suit, then fluttered her eyelashes at him over her glass. "You're being quite shameful, you know. You haven't introduced yourself."

"My apologies. Adam Kaminski, at your service."

"Kaminski?" Grace thought for a moment. "Related to…? No, I don't think I know any Kaminskis."

"No, we're based just north of here. So," Adam continued as Grace frowned at his vague description. "Did you hear about the murder that happened here? It all sounds very salacious."

"Did I hear?" Grace raised one side of her mouth and leaned toward Adam conspiratorially. "Not only did I hear, I knew the victim." Grace nodded as Adam looked surprised. "Quite well, I might add."

"Oh, I'm sorry, I didn't mean to upset you. I didn't realize it was someone you were close with."

Grace waved his concern away with her champagne flute. A passing waiter took the opportunity to replace it with a full one. "Don't worry yourself. Stingy bastard." She covered her mouth again in that girlish gesture that set Adam's hair on end. "Of course I shouldn't speak ill of the dead."

Adam's job was built on letting people speak ill of the dead. "You knew the judge well?"

Grace shrugged. "I lived next door to him, you know? We had a bit of a…" She shrugged one elegantly draped shoulder, and the sparkles on her dress caught the light. "I suppose you could say a fling."

She looked sideways at Adam, her eyelids fluttering again. "Even though he was a bit younger than me."

Adam shuddered and bit down with his jaw, keeping his mouth firmly shut.

"But as I said, he was cheap. He wouldn't give to the causes I was supporting, even when Marcus asked. And Marcus is usually so persuasive…" Grace's mind seemed to wander for a moment, then she shook her head and her voice grew stronger. "Said he had his own causes. But I never saw what they were. He wouldn't even pay to take a girl out to dinner; he expected us to go Dutch." Grace's expression made it clear that this was only one step shy of actually being murdered at the dinner table. "I have to get by on a quite a limited budget these days, you know, like everyone else. Fixed income." She nodded sagely, raising her glass once more. This time it was the ten karat diamond on her finger that caught the light.

He nodded and let her drone on about the challenges she faced, struggling to get by as a widow. His thoughts grew darker than he intended as he listened to her, knowing she had no real concept of what things cost. Of what life was like for seniors who really were on a fixed budget. She would never know, she would never have to learn. He bit back a retort, allowing her the luxury of thinking he agreed that times were tough for her, that she really had to struggle these days.

When she finally stopped complaining, she looked at him expectantly. He had nothing to add about the challenges of her life, so instead brought the subject back to where it had started. "It sounds like he was quite a hateful man. I'm sorry to hear that."

"Oh, I'll tell you, believe me."

"So perhaps he got what he deserved?"

"Well, I wouldn't go that far. I mean, after all, he was only human. Men do make mistakes, don't they? I'm sure he would have come around eventually."

"So you were still pursuing him?" Adam bit his lip as soon as the words were out, but couldn't bite back the words.

"Pursuing?" Her eyes widened and she moved her head to look him up and down. "Just who do you think you are, talking to me like that? What did you say your name was again?"

"Kaminski. Adam Kaminski."

"I see. You don't live in the neighborhood, you said. You're a guest of whom, exactly?" She pursed her lips as she asked the question, glancing around the room as if expecting Adam's host to step forward. Or security to do the same.

Adam saw no advantage in lying. "I'm not a guest, ma'am. I'm investigating the murder. I'm with the police."

"Well, I never. You dishonest, lying…"

"I never lied to you, ma'am."

"And stop calling me ma'am. You may not have lied, but you certainly misled. How dare you question me like this, without warning. Tomorrow morning I'm calling your commissioner. Oh, yes." She smiled at Adam's frown. "We're on a first-name basis. He played golf quite regularly with my second husband. You'll be hearing from your supervisor, young man. I'm going to make a formal complaint."

Adam watched her stalk towards one of the other guests, but ducked out of the tent before she could point him out. He'd accomplished all he could here. As he made his way home, he couldn't help but wonder if Grace's fury at his identity was because she thought he was beneath her — besmirching her reputation just by talking with her — or because she had something to hide from the police.

CHAPTER SIXTEEN

ADAM PAUSED IN the entranceway to admire the view. The hallway in front of him opened up into a cavernous library. Row upon row of books on polished wood shelves covered the walls, glimpses of gold wallpaper peeking out between the shelves. The low morning sun broke through small leaded glass windows, creating patterns that danced on the walls and bookshelves. The room glittered in the morning light, as if he'd walked into a bank vault instead of a library. Of course, these were all historical tomes, he reminded himself, worth a tidy sum in their own right.

He continued down the hall to the office door and knocked, entering on Heyward's call.

"I don't think this is the appropriate time or place, Detective." Heyward's response was curt when Adam introduced himself and explained the purpose of his visit. "This is my place of business."

"I understand that, sir. I knew this was where I would find you this morning."

Heyward nodded and stood from the small leather sofa on which he had been lounging. He placed the volume he'd been holding on his desk and guided Adam out of his office. He glanced up and down the hall as they walked. "Let's take this outside, hmm? It's a beautiful morning, just a little brisk. No reason for my colleagues to develop suspicions that I am being investigated by the police, eh?" He smiled, but Adam could see the nerves behind the smile.

"This is a wonderful place to work, I imagine?"

"Oh, yes, quite. The Veriatus is a library and museum that collects historical texts and displays them," Heyward continued to speak as they walked, as if offering a friendly tour to a neighbor. Adam didn't know if he truly was excited to share his work with Adam, or if he was covering in case someone saw them.

"Our organization relies on our members, you see," Heyward finished his tour. "Though my focus is really on the resource and how our members can interact with them. I am the curator, you see."

"And you live nearby, I understand?"

Heyward nodded, gesturing again toward the grand front entrance, encouraging Adam to follow him out to the square. "Yes, indeed. A five-minute walk to my home, through Washington Square. Quite a pleasant commute." He smiled thinly.

"I know that you knew Judge Ryan-Mills, Mr. Heyward."

"Dr. Heyward." He adjusted his glasses on his nose with the fingers of his left hand. Bruises from the day before still darkened his cheek.

"Yes, of course, sorry. Did you know the judge from graduate school?"

Heyward tipped his head to one side and narrowed his lips. "It's true, I went to Penn undergrad and grad, but I am younger than the judge, you know. I didn't know him then at all."

"Penn undergrad and grad? That's pretty impressive."

"Yes, Detective, I have been very fortunate. I grew up in a comfortable home, funded through grad school, fell into my job — to tell the truth, there's not a lot of competition in the field. Of course, I am one of the best." He lowered his eyes in modesty.

They crossed 6th Street and entered Washington Square, turning left to walk around the perimeter. "I understand from some of your neighbors that you're generally not outspoken except on one issue."

"You've been looking into me. Interesting. Yes, I'm not often outspoken, as you say. It's not that I'm shy, I'm quite confident in my abilities. I just don't see the need to be outspoken, to build networks, as they say. I have everything I need from my friends and family. I'm quite happy, you know."

He lifted his glasses off his nose for a second time with the thumb and first finger of his left hand.

"Do you have a large family?"

Heyward shook his head. "A son. From a blessedly short-lived marriage. That was a mistake, but it ended easily, without acrimony. And now I have a son, which is better than I ever imagined."

"That's great. I hope to have children myself one day." Adam smiled, then kept prodding. "So if you didn't know the judge from school, how did you get involved with him?"

Heyward gave an exaggerated sigh. "Oliver approached me after a civic association meeting with advice on launching a legal fight against the casinos. Well, at first I rebuffed him. After all, Oliver was the one who allowed them to move forward from the beginning. But over the past year I started to understand Oliver's position, his need to always do the right thing and the moral complexity that requires."

"So you became friends? You collaborated in your efforts?"

"To a degree, I suppose. I lead the committee against the casinos, and for that I relied on Oliver for support. But..."

"What?"

"Well, I will tell you that I didn't completely trust Oliver. His relationship with that developer." Heyward spit out the word.

"Roc Lubrano."

Heyward actually shuddered. "Yes. Oliver had a

relationship with him that… well… that didn't really make sense. Frankly, it made me suspicious of his motives."

"But you did work with Oliver, nevertheless?"

"Yes, it's true. I started working with him, taking his advice on what to read, who to talk to, what I needed to know. Oliver was only an advisor, nothing more, this was my fight to lead. To preserve our neighborhood, hold onto the legacy of the city's history and culture." He waved his arm to encapsulate the history before them.

A few people were out in the square this morning, some residents, some tourists taking pictures at the eternal flame. A team of workers was busy tearing down the fancy setup from the night before, a pile of black trash bags growing around one of the trees. A park ranger stood near the memorial, talking to a group of elderly women. As they walked closer, Adam recognized Matt Thompson.

"Now there's a man you should talk to, Detective." Heyward gestured toward a thin figure coming toward them from across the square. "Marcus Cory could probably tell you more than you ever wanted to know about everyone who lives in this neighborhood."

The young man coming toward them walked with a cool efficiency, as if using the least amount of energy necessary to propel himself across the square. He'd wrapped a gold scarf around his neck, over his impeccably fitted coat, a scarf with some sort of metallic thread running through it. In the morning light, he almost glittered while he walked.

His expression was calm, impenetrable, though as he passed the grounds crew working in the square his lips shifted into a shadow of a sneer. He saw Adam and Heyward watching him and slowed as he approached them.

"Marcus Cory, may I introduce Detective Adam Kaminski."

Adam shook Marcus' hand. The other man didn't remove his leather gloves.

"You must be the policeman who accosted Grace last night."

"I'll just leave you two to talk, shall I?" Without waiting for an answer, Heyward scuttled away across the square.

"So you work for Grace Evans, is that right?"

Marcus gave a slight nod but said nothing, waiting for Adam to continue, a small smile on his lips.

"I hear that Ms. Evans was close with Oliver Ryan-Mills. Can you tell me about that?"

"I can't speak about Grace's private life, Detective. You'd need to ask her about that." Marcus' voice was smooth as ice.

Adam nodded, considering. "What exactly do you do for Ms. Evans?"

"I serve as her personal assistant. I thought you knew that."

Adam bit his tongue. "Yes, but I don't know a lot of people who have personal assistants. What exactly does that entail?"

The other man frowned and shrugged, an elegant gesture, and slowly pulled his gloves off. "I support her in a number of ways. I have a background in business management. I oversee her finances and investments, I manage the household, I... well, I run errands as she needs them."

Adam thought about a life in which he had someone else to run his errands, do his shopping, pick up his dry cleaning. That would be nice. "So did you spend a lot of time with Oliver Ryan-Mills as well? Did you know him?"

"I knew him. But not well." A small electric truck passed them on the wide sidewalk, heading toward the grounds crew. Marcus sniffed and narrowed his eyes as the truck passed, driven by a large African American man who didn't seem like he would fit in the tiny vehicle. "He was a good man. Successful. Accomplished. He would come over for dinner occasionally."

"Do you cook as well?" Adam asked, surprised.

Marcus smiled, this time the smile actually reaching his eyes. "On special occasions. It's not really part of my job description, but I do enjoy whipping up a barigoule now and then. Or a crème brûlée."

Adam's phone trilled a light tune.

"Is that all, Detective? It seems you have a call."

"For now, thank you. If I have any more questions, I know where to find you." Adam smiled, baring his teeth.

Marcus' lips turned down into a thin line. He nodded once, turned on his heel, and continued toward whatever errand Grace Evans was sending him on this morning.

Adam tapped his phone to life. "Jim, I'm glad to hear from you."

"I'm afraid I don't have good news, Detective. I'm sorry."

"You weren't able to contact your friend?"

Jim Murdsen's voice, already tense, dropped even lower. "I'm not sure I can call him a friend. But he made it quite clear to me that he has no interest whatsoever in talking with the police."

"I see."

"Yes, perhaps." Murdsen correctly interpreted Adam's tone. "Though he assures me he has nothing he can share about the illegal art trade. He got quite upset that I'd asked, in fact. I had to apologize profusely for even thinking he could help."

"He protested a little too much?" Adam glanced over at Matt Thompson, still standing with the group of women, each of them looking up at him with adoration in their eyes.

"Perhaps, yes. But I won't be involved in exposing him. This is not my fight, you know." Murdsen paused long enough that Adam thought he'd said all he had to say, but a faint cough made it clear there was something else on his mind. "Detective, about Sylvia…"

"What's bothering you, Jim?"

"You have a good relationship, a strong relationship?"

Adam stopped walking, the hair on his arms tingling as he grew wary. "Why do you ask?"

"Just that there are rumors around the college—"

"I'm gonna stop you right there, Jim. If you're about to say something about Sylvia that you're gonna regret later, you should rethink that. I don't appreciate people spreading rumors about my girlfriend."

"Oh … of course, no, you're right. I do apologize. I'm putting my foot in it left and right these days, aren't I? Good luck with your case, Detective."

Adam stuffed his hands into the pockets of his cashmere coat and turned toward Ranger Thompson.

THE CUSTOMER scratched at an itch above his eye as he entered the lobby. No elegant tinkling bell greeted him here. Only the benign smile of the doorman from across the room. Why the hell did Sal want to meet here?

He glanced at his watch. Dammit, Sal was late, on top of everything. He tried to look casual, strolling across the shining marble floor toward the seating area. He chose a high-backed white chair with his back to the doorman and sat. He crossed his legs. Then slid his leg back so his ankle was on his knee. He didn't want to look feminine. Weak.

"My friend." Sal smiled widely as he slid into the chair next to him. "I'm glad I was able to get back to you so quickly."

"Sure, Sal, me too." He tried a smile, then felt his cheek vibrate and turned it into a frown. "Why'd you want to meet here, anyway? Anyone could recognize me." He glanced over his shoulder toward the doorman, who simply met his gaze.

Sal shrugged and laughed, a tinny sound. "You're an art collector. I'm an art dealer. So what if anyone recognizes you." He waved his hand dismissively, just the right amount of white cuff showing below his sleeve, a gold cufflink catching the light. "Anyway, I had to be in the neighborhood for some other business. This was convenient for me."

"Right. Uh-huh." He tried on another smile, then jumped as the elevator chimed. Out of the corner of his eye, he saw a man and a woman step out of the elevator, cross the thick white rug to the front doors. Heading out to work, perhaps. Or breakfast with clients. Through the glass front of the building, he saw the couple cross the street and walk into Washington Square.

A group of women standing in the square caught his eye, visible over the brick boundary wall. He couldn't identify them, but he did recognize the uniform of the man standing with them. A park ranger, standing head and shoulders taller than the women around him, his flat hat visible from far across the square. Dammit. He shouldn't have met Sal here.

"I have something to show you." Sal's eyes twinkled as he smiled again. How could he be so comfortable? So relaxed?

With a graceful gesture, Sal reached into his satchel and pulled out a small item wrapped in cloth. Slowly, carefully, Sal peeled back the layers of the cloth to expose the prize within.

He choked as he tried to swallow a gasp. It was beautiful. Black rhino horn. Carved into a small round cup that would fit in the palm of his hand, its center hollowed out and sanded until it shone. Intricate carvings danced around the lip of the cup, the light shades of the bone beneath the surface jumping out against the dark exterior.

It was a thing of beauty.

Sal had been watching him silently, letting him appreciate the work of art he held in his hand. Finally, he spoke. "These are said to have healing properties, you know that, right?"

He coughed, cleared his throat. "I do, yes. I've read up on them. They're highly valued."

Sam smiled. Nodded. He moved as if to cover the cup back up again. "Have you tried drinking from the other one you have?"

"Hardly." He gave Sal his strongest glare, but Sal didn't flinch. "I wouldn't dare dirty such a beautiful work of art."

Before Sal could finish wrapping it, he reached his hand out and picked it up. He cupped it in both hands, the fingers of his right hand running along the carvings. He closed his eyes for a moment and inhaled. He swore he could smell ancient Chinese herbs, even though this carved piece of bone had never made it to Asia as originally intended.

When he opened his eyes, Sal was grinning at him. "You understand that I'm doing you a favor, right? I can't sell you this sort of thing." Sal shrugged, his lips dancing around both a smile and a frown. "But since you are such a good customer, I'm willing to give this to you... as a gift. Depending on your next purchase, of course."

He cleared his throat again. "Of course, of course. And you know I'm interested. Anything you want to sell me, I'll buy."

He didn't care if he sounded desperate. This was what he deserved. It was his birthright. Who he was now. A member of the upper class, not just a working man, a rich man. A man with desires, a man who deserved to own beautiful things.

Sal had pulled out a ledger book. He made scratches in it with a tiny pen, his notes illegible to anyone but himself. After a few more notes, he nodded and glanced up. "I have a group of statues and some coins I can sell to you for fifty thousand."

He didn't need to think about it. "Perfect, wrap them up and ship them to me. I'll take this now?"

Sal looked into his eyes. As if he were unsure at first.

Then he leaned back and smiled. "Of course. I trust you — that is, I trust you not to do anything stupid, right? We understand each other?"

He barely nodded, just smiled and looked down at the cup in his hands. "We do."

He wasn't greedy, he knew that. He simply knew what he liked. And he was finally getting what he deserved.

THE THREE LATE middle-aged women clustered around Matt Thompson, their faces glowing as they smiled up at him, gathered in front of the memorial wall in Washington Square. Matt stood tall, his expression serious, though Adam was sure he could tell his audience was enamored of him.

"Matt, how are you?" Adam approached and nodded to the women.

"Adam. Ladies, may I introduce Detective Adam Kaminski. He's working on the investigation of the death of Judge Oliver Ryan-Mills."

The three women tut-tutted and shook their heads.

"Mary Godwin." The tallest stuck a hand out and Adam shook it. "And these are Joy French and Rachel Woodruff."

Adam nodded at all three. The women looked eerily similar to each other, as if cut from the same cloth. Fresh, clean faces, no heavy make-up attempting to cover the lines that cut across their foreheads and around their mouths. They were each dressed for exercise, well-fitting zip jerseys over sleek running pants. Neon stripes decorated the sides of their walking shoes. The expression on their faces looked honest. Fearless. Perhaps they simply had nothing to fear.

"I ran into these ladies as I was on my way back to headquarters. We were talking about Ryan-Mills," Matt explained.

"Such a good man, such a shame what happened to him." Mary Godwin nodded as she spoke. The other two nodded along, in clear agreement.

"Did you know him well?"

"Well? Only as one does, you know. A neighbor. He wasn't particularly involved in the community, though." Mary turned to look back at the building behind them. The building where Oliver Ryan-Mills had, until recently, lived.

"He kept himself apart," Joy added, her gaze following Mary's. "I believe he felt it was his duty. As a judge." Joy turned back to smile up at Matt as she spoke.

"Yeah, I heard that about him." Adam did his best to let his questions blend into their conversation, to keep the gossip going rather than turn this into an interview. "But I understand he'd been getting out more. Since his wife passed."

"Beautiful woman." The other two women murmured in agreement as Mary answered. "What a loss that was. She was so engaged in the community, you know. Very good woman."

Rachel chimed in, "We miss her, indeed. And I'm sure he did, too." The women seemed to turn toward each other as they spoke, as if they were sharing a chain of thoughts rather than having a discussion with Adam or Matt. Adam tried to follow as best he could, though he clearly didn't have the right expertise.

"He went out, but not locally. Despite Grace's best efforts." The others twittered in agreement.

"Oh?"

"Well, she did try, didn't she?"

"Try?"

"To catch the man, dear," Rachel explained.

"Husband number three he would have been," Joy added.

"Really?"

"Oh, yes. She seemed to work her way through them."

"Getting richer after each one, I might add."

"So her previous husbands died?" Adam tried to

jump in, but the women were moving forward even without his prompting.

"Yes, what was it…?"

"Heart attack, I think?"

"That would have been number two. The first, I don't remember the details…"

"Yes, there was something interesting about that one, wasn't there. But it was a few years ago, now. And so many of our friends have passed on since then."

"And that assistant"

"Marcus." Joy looked like she understood more than was being said. "Well, he's efficient."

"Oh yes, quite."

"But he has plans, doesn't he?"

"Plans?" Adam tried to keep up.

"You can see it in his eyes, he's looking for an opportunity."

"Exactly." Mary bobbed her head up and down. "To move on, to move up."

"So Grace was pursuing Ryan-Mills?" Matt brought the conversation back to the point.

"Oh, yes."

"And Grace is not one to take no for an answer."

"He told her no?" Adam asked.

"In that way that men have. He said no, but he was polite. He was kind. He was not firm."

"Hah, not firm enough for Grace, anyway."

"Yes, she would get what she wants. And she had decided she wanted him."

All three women laughed, then one laugh turned into a cough and Joy put a hand over her mouth.

Grace Evans strode toward them across the square, her mink coat — far too much for this balmy fall weather — flapping behind her as she walked. She wore running shoes that on anyone else would have looked ridiculous with the rest of her outfit, yet she managed to make them look elegant.

"You there," she raised her voice and waved at them.

"What's going on here?"

"That's my cue. Ladies." Adam turned back to the group. "Thank you, it's been a pleasure meeting you all." He patted Matt on the arm, then turned toward Grace.

He walked quickly toward her and for a second it almost seemed as if they would collide. But their routes stayed separate, Adam nodding at an angry Grace as he passed and kept walking the path that would lead him, eventually, back to his own home. He didn't need to check in at the precinct again for a couple more hours. He could still put a little more time into Pete's case before getting back into the work he was supposed to be doing.

CHAPTER SEVENTEEN

MATT SLID HIS ID over the card reader and pulled the heavy iron gate toward him. He passed through a brick-enclosed alley and up another flight of stairs. He swiped the internal card reader at the top of the stairs and the metal door clicked open.

One of the dispatchers on duty glanced in his direction. "Thompson, what's up?"

The other dispatcher kept his eyes on the bank of monitors in front of him, his attention on whoever he was speaking with through his headset.

"Nothing, Fred. Don't let me bother you, just need to get some work done." Matt pulled his hat off and tossed it on a table in the corner. It landed smoothly and slid until it hit a pile of folders on the table. The second dispatcher glanced over at that point, and Matt sheepishly grabbed his hat and settled it on the table, safely away from any paperwork.

"In here?" Fred shifted in his chair, his lanky frame twisting around to face him, a set of four monitors glowing behind him.

Matt recognized the question in Fred's eyes, but tried to ignore it. "Yeah, sorry. Look, I know it's not protocol, but I didn't want to be in the main offices, okay?"

Fred frowned but nodded. "I guess. But don't get in the way." A phone beeped and Fred returned to his work, grabbing the phone and turning his attention back to the monitors slowly cycling through all the cameras in the park.

Matt pulled a chair over to a free workstation. The computers here were already logged into IMARS, the Incident Management, Analysis and Reporting System used by Department of the Interior law enforcement units. The system connected him to all his law enforcement colleagues in the department as well as to the National Crime Information Center. He wasn't supposed to be working in here — the dispatchers had to keep their full attention on their job — but he'd have a lot more success working from these computers than his own workstation.

Plus he didn't want the chief to know what he was up to, and his desk in the squad room was way too open.

He typed in his search parameters and watched as the database compiled the relevant information. He scrolled through page after page of background. He wasn't surprised at how much was available on Roc Lubrano. He already knew the man had a record. He was surprised, however, at how much came up on Ian Heyward.

Matt already knew Heyward had no alibi for the time of the murder, but he also knew PPD wasn't taking him seriously as a suspect. His motive seemed weak, since he and the judge were, apparently, on the same side of the casino issue. Maybe this would change their attitude.

"Who you looking up?"

Matt jumped. He'd been lost in his work and hadn't noticed Sharea, another dispatcher on duty, return to the room.

"Whoa, didn't mean to scare you." She grinned. "Not sneaking around or anything, just got off my break. So what are you doing?"

"Oh, nothing. Sorry, am I in your way?" Matt turned sideways in an attempt to draw her attention away from the screen. It didn't work.

"Ian Heyward. You need data on him?" She leaned

over him as she read the screen. "I can help you with that, you know."

"No, that's okay. It's just…"

"He's doing something he doesn't want anyone to know about." Fred spoke up from his side of the room without turning to look at them. "It's either top secret or not by the book." The third dispatcher snickered at the standard joke, making fun of John Hamilton.

Matt shook his head and slumped down in his chair. Clearly, the life of a spy was not for him. "Look, guys. You're right. It's something I'm not supposed to be working on. But it is a legitimate case. Except that PPD has the lead. I'm supposed to be waiting until they ask for something."

Fred smiled. "And you don't want to wait around."

"You gonna tell the chief?"

Fred gestured toward a camera in the wall with his chin. "I don't need to tell him, friend, you know that. He could see that tape anytime he wants."

Matt nodded. "I'm hoping it won't be anytime soon."

He turned back to the sheet on his computer. The sheet detailing Ian Heyward's criminal record. The criminal record he had conveniently forgotten to mention and that PPD hadn't yet dug up.

MATT DIDN'T *have* to walk over to the precinct headquarters. John Hamilton was there now, but he'd said on the phone he'd be back in the park within the hour. Matt donned his flat hat and headed out toward Chinatown anyway.

He walked west on Cherry from 7th Street, bypassing the crowds that tended to gather at the Chinatown Gate on Arch Street. Of course, the streets were always packed in this neighborhood, no matter which way he walked. Chinese signs on everything from stores to banks to the local branch of the Free Library clearly defined the neighborhood. Crowds surged along the sidewalk, voices raised in a cacophony of languages, none of which Matt could understand. He kept his eyes forward, ignoring the looks from tourists intrigued by his park ranger uniform in this part of town.

One group of visitors managed to catch his eye. They waved him down, pointing energetically to their cameras. Matt smiled and took a breath as he posed with them for pictures. "The national park is just a few blocks east, people." He spoke under his breath. "There are plenty more rangers there."

It seemed like they would never stop, each person in the group wanting their own photo with him, each looking up at him, smiling, posing for the camera.

He finally broke away, holding his hands up and apologizing repeatedly as he backed away from the group. He crossed 10th Street, pausing to look south, to admire the gate. It was a remarkable structure. The unofficial entranceway to Philadelphia's Chinatown, it stood high above the street, green, blue, yellow, red, and orange paint glowing even from this distance. He didn't know when it had been built or why, but he knew it drew the tourists in, keeping the stores and restaurants along this stretch of the street packed at any time of year.

He turned to continue on to 11th Street, catching a whiff from a fishmonger setting up shop on the sidewalk. He stepped to the side to avoid a group of teenage girls moving fast and in the process managed to bump into someone else. "Sorry." He stopped to apologize and found himself face to face with Pete Lawler. "Pete, sorry. I was just heading to the precinct."

"Matt, hey." Pete looked confused for a moment. He put his hand out as if to stop the woman next to him. She looked over at Matt, her strawberry blond hair covering her shoulders, her smile warm in a lightly freckled face.

"Right, sorry." Pete regained control of whatever had thrown him. "Why're you going there?"

"I found some background on Ian Heyward, thought you might be interested."

"That's great, thanks." Pete glanced at the woman with him then looked up the street, as if checking to see if Matt was alone. "You should give that to John Hamilton, he'll share it with us."

"Right, I know." Matt drew his words out, looking back and forth between Pete and the woman. "I just found out John's at the district headquarters. That's why I'm going there."

"Oh, good. Fine. I'll see you later then." Pete turned as if to leave.

"Sorry." The woman smiled but there was a frown in her eyes even so. "Nice to meet you. Kind of." She shrugged as she stared at Pete, shaking her head, a question forming on her lips.

"We gotta go." Pete didn't hide the impatience in his voice. "Why don't you head back to the park, find John Hamilton." He finally had the grace to look apologetic as he finished his thought. "It's important that we work through one POC, you know that. To keep things clear, make sure everyone has the same information. Okay?"

"Right, got it." Matt bit back the embarrassment growing in his chest. "Sorry, like I said, I was looking for John Hamilton. By the book." He spit out the last few words.

"Julia Kaminski." The woman stuck out her hand, shooting a sideways glance at Pete, then turning a broad smile on Matt.

"Kaminski?" Matt shook her hand, surprised. "You're Adam's sister?"

"Right. Oh, I see." She kept her eyes away from Pete this time. "You know Adam."

"Julia, this is Matt Thompson, the park ranger working this case with me." Pete spoke slowly, enunciating as if speaking to a child.

"Got it." She gave a light wave and looked down at the ground as she turned away.

Pete nodded at him once more. "See you later then."

The two turned to head along Cherry Street, the convention center looming ahead of them in the distance. Matt watched them walk, moving quickly along the sidewalk. At one point, Julia peeked over her shoulder but looked away again quickly when she saw Matt watching them. What the hell had just happened?

Matt shoved his hands in his pocket and turned down 10th Street toward the Chinatown Gate. He ignored the crowds passing him on the sidewalk, barely avoided walking into the tables of vegetables set up along the storefronts.

Was Pete really that uninterested in what he'd found? Surely every little bit of information would help. Matt knew he was supposed to go through John Hamilton. Hell, that's what he'd been on his way to do. So why had Pete blown him off like that?

Whatever the reason, Matt wasn't going to make that mistake again.

CHAPTER EIGHTEEN

"I LOOKED FOR you at the precinct, but they said you hadn't gone in today. You not pulling your weight around there, son?" Adam hadn't been sure what to expect when he buzzed his father in from the street, but clearly John Kaminski was still upset.

"What, d'you come here to pick a fight?" Adam held his apartment door open as John entered. "I'm working on some stuff from home today, that's all."

John put a hand up in surrender. "No, I'm sorry, I didn't come here to fight. Just seems odd, you calling out sick today, that's all. You seemed perfectly fine yesterday."

"Then what brings you round, Dad? I'm busy." Adam moved back to the kitchen table, where he'd spread out what little information he had. Copies of the forensics reports he'd gotten before getting kicked off the case. His own notes of his interviews with Harry Ryan-Mills, Grace Evans, Roc Lubrano, and Ian Heyward. Photographs of the murder weapon.

John Kaminski's eye went right to the pictures of the wooden statue. "This about Julia?"

"Yeah." Adam nodded. "It is. And it's an open investigation. You know that means I can't talk to you about it."

He looked up, his hand on the back of one of the wooden chairs that stood around the table. His father had stopped at the other end of the table, hands in his pockets. The two men stood on either side of Adam's small kitchen, facing off like boxers sizing up the competition.

"If it's an open investigation, then why are you working on it from home?"

Adam shrugged but didn't lower his eyes. "I'm doing this on my own time. Pete has the lead on the case, officially."

"What's going on?" John's voice rose and he leaned over the table. "Julia won't talk to me. You're clearly up to something. And now it's keeping you from work — the work you're supposed to be doing. That's not like you."

Adam took a breath, looked down at the papers spread across his table. It was true this was an open investigation. But he wasn't supposed to be investigating it. If the captain found out he'd gotten this involved, he'd already be in deep shit. What difference would bringing his family into it make at this point?

He looked back up at his father. "Julia's a suspect in a case."

"A case? What kind of case?" John's expression stayed calm. If anything, he had actually relaxed at the news. "She didn't shoplift again, did she?" He laughed. "She hasn't done that since she was fourteen."

"It's more serious than that. It's murder."

Adam could hear John's intake of breath, saw the heat rise up his face. No question where Adam got his quick temper from. "What are you talking about?"

"A man was killed. Hit over the head with a statue. Julia's statue."

John's face sagged. He leaned heavily onto the table, then slid into a chair. His eyes moved around the room, occasionally landing on Adam but then moving on again, as if seeking something they couldn't find. "So Julia's a suspect." He nodded as he spoke, the red blotches on his face receding bit by bit as his color returned to

115

normal. "And you're working on clearing things up?"

"I'm working on it, trust me." He put a hand out, then pulled it back before he touched his father's shoulder. "The statue was stolen from her apartment this summer. You remember her break-in."

John nodded.

"It still had her prints on it. She has no alibi. And she knew the victim."

John nodded again, his fingers toying with a piece of torn notepaper lying on the table. "But you're not really on this case. Pete is?"

Adam nodded and took the seat next to his father. "Pete's looking into it, yeah. But I want to help."

"Your partner's a good cop. A good man. Julia could do a lot worse."

Adam blinked. "What? What does that mean?"

"Just that she's in good hands and you can trust him, that's all. I'm not telling you to back off, I'm telling to you to work with Pete. Don't try to do this on your own."

Adam watched his father slouching in the chair, his shoulders even more sloped than he remembered. The midday sun hit his hair, turning it silver in the light. "I know, Dad. I know when I need help." Adam looked down at the papers strewn across his table. He did need help. Sitting here by himself going back over ground he'd already covered wasn't getting him anywhere. Maybe Matt was having better luck.

John didn't look up as he asked, "Does Sylvia know?"

Adam nodded, looking back at his father.

"Good. You need her, too, you know. You're lucky to have found her. You don't want to have to be on your own."

"Is something else wrong?" Adam watched his father closely for some hint as to what else might be bugging him, but saw nothing beyond the signs of age that were so obvious to him now.

John shook his head. "No, no. It's just…" He reached

into his coat pocket and pulled out a folded envelope. "This is why I came by. To give you this."

Adam took the large manila envelope his father had carried rolled up in his jacket pocket. The paper was rubbed thin in places, torn on one corner. It looked like it had been through a wringer, though more likely just shoved onto a bookshelf somewhere and forgotten about for a few years. Adam had to hold the ends of the envelope to keep it from rolling back up again.

"I felt bad, last time I saw you. I guess I was angry. You were being cagey. Now I understand why, but at the time I thought you were unhappy about the legacy of my family. Your family."

"Our family is the most important thing to me. Always."

John nodded. "Good, at least I taught you something." He indicated the envelope. "I thought of these, after we spoke earlier."

"What is it?"

"You were asking about Grandpa. My dad, and his dad. I remembered that I had done some research, back when I was in high school. It was a family tree project. It took me some time to dig this up. There was no Internet then, you know."

"I know, back in the Dark Ages, right?" Adam grinned.

"Yeah, very funny." John smiled as he pushed himself up from his chair. "I found some old papers in the library. Newspaper stories from the time, about when my grandfather came to this country. I thought you might find them useful." John shrugged, as if it really didn't matter to him what Adam did with the clippings. "If you're interested."

"I am interested. Thank you. Hopefully once this is all cleared up, I can take a look. See what I can learn about our history."

"It's a proud legacy, son. You should be proud to be a Kaminski."

CHAPTER NINETEEN

ADAM AND MATT squeezed past the bikes leaning against the wall in the narrow hall and stepped into one of the squad rooms that lined this floor and the one above it.

"Interesting space," Adam observed.

"Yeah. Pros and cons of having our offices in an eighteenth century building." Matt smiled. "At least it looks like we have the room to ourselves this morning. Makes for a change. I'm glad you stopped by, Kaminski. I've got something I'd like to show you. I found some background on Heyward."

Matt pulled out a chair at a worn wooden table that stood in one corner and Adam sat opposite him. Matt flipped eagerly through the files he had printed on Ian Heyward.

"Destruction of private property… that's pretty serious, right?" Matt looked up at him, his expression expectant. Though Adam wasn't sure what he was expecting.

"It can be. Sure," Adam agreed. "Depends a lot on the situation, of course." He kept reading through the files as he asked, "Did you say you found something on Lubrano, too?"

"Lubrano? Yeah, it's in there. No surprises there. But aren't you a little surprised about Heyward?"

Adam kept reading.

"Kaminski?"

Adam looked up. "What?"

"Heyward?"

When Adam didn't answer right away, Matt stood and walked over to the window that looked out on the courtyard behind the house.

Adam glanced over and saw nothing but old flowerpots, a greenhouse with broken windows. Not very park-like. "What about him?"

"I figured he was hiding something. When he said he wasn't gonna file a complaint against Lubrano. Now we know he's got a record."

"It's just vandalism. He broke a window. I don't see the connection." Adam turned his attention back to the files on Lubrano. There was too much information. The background investigation on Lubrano had produced a string of police reports and arrests. And his real first name. Adam laughed out loud. "Thanks for pulling this all up, but it can't all be relevant, you know? We have to find the key."

"The key?"

"Sure. A way to sift through all these facts and find the relevant pieces. The pieces that fit into the puzzle we're trying to solve."

"Right, right. 'Cause of course I don't know how to do that." Matt turned his back to the window.

Adam knew he should find out what was bugging Matt, but a line from Lubrano's record jumped out at him. Grabbed his attention. He ignored Matt's sarcasm, saying, "Now that's interesting."

"What?" Matt leaned around to see what Adam was seeing.

"Here. Circumstantial evidence linking Lubrano to an illegal import-export business."

Even as Lubrano was building up his legitimate development company, he was funding it through potentially illegal activities. Activities also known as smuggling. It would have been easy enough for him. He was in the construction field, he saw where the money was and could have made friends with the right people. Adam looked up at Matt. "I've been looking for an art connection."

"Really? Why?"

Adam shook his head. "Just trying to follow the trail backward, to see how my sister's statue ended up in the murderer's hand."

"Okay, I get it." Matt nodded. "And you think this might be the connection you're looking for?"

"Could be. Who knows. Certainly worth looking into. Looks like he had connections, but was never charged. Not enough evidence, I assume."

"Anything more specific that could actually be helpful?"

Adam ignored Matt's tone. "A few associates are named, again no one who was charged, only people of interest the FBI is keeping an eye on." He ran his finger down the page as he scanned it. "Some art dealers here, Martin Cloche, Sal Rivieri, Terrance Brickworth... all still working in the Philly area, all still under suspicion."

"He says he's served his time and now he's an honest developer." Matt snorted, his tone expressing the same disbelief Adam was feeling.

Adam tapped the paper in front of him. "What else can you tell me about this casino development?"

"I know people are really worked up about it. The casino they're trying to build is one of the Salthill casinos."

"Those are owned by a Native American tribe, right?"

Matt nodded. "Yep. They're still working out the legalities, even though Lubrano's moving forward like it's a done deal. The tribe has until November 30 to secure a site and negotiate a compact with the state for the casino. If it fails to do so, the region opens up to a competitive bid."

"So they need to get this resolved, and fast, or they lose control over the area."

"And anyone else can start bidding on that license."

"Seems to me that that approach gives an unfair advantage to the tribe. They get first dibs, and if they can't work it out, then everyone else gets a crack at it."

"You're not the only one who thinks that. Couple of years ago, another developer filed suit saying just that. He got so far as to get an injunction in place against the Department of the Interior."

"I heard about that. Why is a federal agency involved if it's a Philly casino?"

"They're the ones who grant the licenses to the tribes." Matt shrugged. "It's how U.S. land is managed, buddy." He looked apologetic, even though he had no control over how Congress chose to manage federally owned land.

"Go on."

"So the developer got a preliminary injunction, but in U.S. District Court, a federal judge dismissed the lawsuit. And lifted the injunction."

"And that brings up back to our victim."

Matt nodded. "Judge Oliver Ryan-Mills."

The knock on the door startled them both. Adam pushed the papers he was looking at to the side as John Hamilton stuck his head through the doorway.

"Thompson, didn't know you were on today."

"Just putting in some overtime, sir. John, this is" — he caught Adam's warning glance and switched tracks — "Adam Kaminski, with PPD. We're talking about the religion convention. Kaminski's on the preparedness task force."

"Great, good." John looked Adam up and down. "Aren't you Pete Lawler's partner?"

Adam lifted one side of his mouth in a lopsided smile. "I am, but I'm here solely because of the convention."

John nodded again, then tapped the door once more on his way out, his words floating back into the room behind him. "As long as you're keeping it by the book."

Matt grinned, but Adam didn't get the joke. "Can I

take these? I gotta run, got a meeting with my captain at eleven, and I'll probably have some time to keep reading this while I'm waiting."

"Help yourself, those are copies. But Kaminski?"

"Yeah?"

"Just… thanks for keeping me in the loop."

CHAPTER TWENTY

"LET ME DO the talking, buddy." Mark Little, a man who lived up to his name, reached up to pat Adam on the shoulder as if to reassure him.

It didn't work. Adam nodded grimly. He'd always supported the union, but never thought he'd be the one who needed their help. Pete's presence offered more comfort, the knowledge that no matter what, Pete would have his back.

"Kaminski. Lawler." Farrow greeted them without smiling as they entered his office. "I see you brought your rep."

Adam opened his mouth to speak, but Mark got there first. "It's his right, Captain, you know that."

"I do know that, and I'm not complaining." Captain Farrow frowned and turned to Adam. "Look, I said you could bring a rep because the rules require me to… in this type of meeting."

"And what type of meeting is that?" Mark grinned as he took a seat in front of the captain's desk, looking completely comfortable.

Adam and Pete followed his lead, though Adam leaned forward on the edge of his chair, decidedly not comfortable. He couldn't get a clear read on Farrow's mood, a sense of what was about to happen, and that made him nervous.

The waves of folders on Farrow's desk didn't seem to

have moved. If anything, they'd grown. But the brass pen set still sat, pristine, front and center. Someday he was going to have to find out where they came from. What made them so special. He kept his focus on the pens, avoiding Farrow's eye.

Farrow looked at Mark, then back at Adam. "So I'm speaking to him, is that it?"

Adam looked down at his hands, the guilt growing in his gut. Mark started to respond, but Adam cut him off. "Just talk to me, Captain. You know me."

Mark raised an eyebrow and opened his mouth to speak, but closed it again and raised a hand as if to wave Adam on.

Farrow sighed and nodded. "I do, Kaminski, that's what makes this so hard. Why the hell couldn't you just follow orders?"

Adam started to answer, but the captain wasn't finished yet. "Yeah, I know. I do. Your little sister's involved. I do know you, remember?"

"I've been working the case, Captain." Pete jumped in. "I guess I may have talked a little too much. This doofus is my partner, you know." Pete kept his voice light, but his fingers tapped out a rhythm on his thighs, and his eyes moved quickly between Adam and Farrow, looking even more nervous than Adam felt.

"I had no choice." Adam kept his voice calm, quiet.

This time Mark cut him off physically, standing and digging his fingers into Adam's shoulder. "Don't say anything more, Kaminski. I'm here to advise you, and I'm telling you that is not a good move on your part."

Adam winced. Not from the pain, but from the knowledge that Mark was right. And that he didn't care.

Captain Farrow shook his head. "Look, it doesn't matter. I got a complaint." He lifted two pieces of paper off his desk, one in each hand. More lay below them. "Several, actually."

"Complaints?" Adam and Pete asked at the same time.

Pete finished his thought. "I've been following the rules on this one, Captain, by the book. No cause for complaints."

Adam grinned at the familiar turn of phrase, glad once more for Pete's presence in this meeting. He let out a breath, thinking this wasn't going as badly as he had feared. Judging by Mark's body language, he felt the same way. Pete and Farrow, on the other hand, seemed to be sitting in a different meeting.

Farrow caught his eye, then looked away. "Actually, some of them were meant to be helpful. But they still let me know that you were working the case. Against direct orders."

"Captain—" Pete started, but Farrow cut him off.

"This isn't only me saying this, Kaminski. You get involved, you could put our entire investigation at risk. Why the hell don't you see that?"

Adam shook his head. "I have no choice."

"Do you want to get fired, is that it?" Mark laughed to himself as he slid back into his chair. "'Cause you don't need me here for that, buddy." He looked around the room, as if waiting for an answer. "I'm here to help you, but there's only so much I can do, got it?"

"Sorry, no." Adam bit his lip. "I'm trying to be honest."

Mark sat, his arms folded across his chest. "Not always the best move, friend."

Farrow watched the interaction silently, and Adam noticed a slight tremor in his hands. As if noticing it himself, Farrow dropped the papers he still held. "Look, this is just a warning."

"Damn straight it is." Mark kept his voice low but his words were sharp.

The relief Adam felt at Farrow's words didn't shake his guilt for betraying the captain, for putting Pete in this position. He admired Captain Farrow, respected his work ethic. And he'd always followed the rules, taking pride in his work. How the hell did he get here, to this side of the desk? He glanced at Pete, but Pete hadn't relaxed at the news. If anything, his tension had grown.

"Captain, I appreciate the warning. I hear what you're saying. I will do a better job, I promise. And listen." He leaned forward even further. "This isn't anything to do with Pete, right? He didn't talk out of turn. I dug a little where I wasn't supposed to."

Farrow looked back down at his desk, frowning, and Adam knew he was missing something. "What else is going on here?" he asked.

"You may not've heard yet." Farrow glanced at Pete, who looked down at his hands.

"Heard what?" Adam looked back and forth between his captain and his partner, trying to read the meaning of their expressions. Pete wouldn't catch his eye.

"We brought your sister in earlier today for questioning."

Adam heard the words, but could make no sense of them. He felt the heat rising in his face, the sound of his own heartbeat pounding in his ears as he tried to understand what this meant.

He stood, his whole body shaking. "You what?"

"Turns out she knew the victim... the judge." Farrow wouldn't hold his eye. "She showed up in his case files. Pete found her name there. That's a connection we couldn't ignore."

Adam turned to his partner, who at least had the courage to meet his gaze. "Pete" — his voice broke with the effort to keep it calm — "How could you...?"

Pete stood, took a step closer to him, then stopped. "It was the only thing I could do, you know that."

Adam turned away, unable to look at his partner.

Pete continued, "Look, we both know she's innocent. The sooner we get this cleared up, the better, right?"

Adam tried to breathe, to regain control. He focused on Mark Little, who sat mutely, no longer relaxed. He gave Adam a look, sending him some kind of message, but Adam had no idea what. And didn't care.

"Where is she now?" He turned back to Farrow.

"She's already on her way home."

"I need to go." Adam turned to the door.

"Kaminski." Captain Farrow stood. "Take the rest of the day off."

"You can't suspend him like that, sir," Mark jumped in, though Adam couldn't care less if he was being suspended, fired, or worse.

Farrow waved his hands. "It's not a suspension, Mark, stand down. Call it administrative leave." He looked at Adam. "Just take the day. Hang out with your family. Talk to your sister. Get it out of your system. Tomorrow, when you're back on, you're on Murphy's team." He looked at Adam. "Full time, got it?"

"Yes, sir." Adam turned back to the door and kept walking, even as he heard Pete calling his name.

ADAM LET the front door slam shut behind him. He didn't want to be back at home again. He wanted to be out there. Helping the investigation. Helping Julia.

He took the two steps that brought him into the living room, where the late morning sun still cascaded through the sheer curtains, painting bright squares of light on the carpet and furniture. On the low counter that separated the living space from the kitchen. On the futon that sat there as a daily, constant reminder of the goals Adam had not yet managed to reach. God, he hated that futon and the volumes it spoke about the instability of his life, the uncertainty of his career so far.

"Adam?"

He turned when he heard Sylvia's voice from the doorway to the bedroom. She stood with one foot in front of the other, as if she had stopped suddenly and didn't know whether to continue forward or go back. She held a thin cashmere sweater in her hand. The dark ruby sweater he'd bought her on Valentine's Day. He loved that sweater, loved the way it looked on her, and even more, the way it slid off her.

"Sylvia." He smiled, feeling his tension release, at least a little, and walked over to her, wrapping his arms around her and pulling her close. "I love it when you wear that sweater. What's the occasion?"

"Darling, I'm just reorganizing my closet. I wasn't expecting you. Why are you home?"

Adam kissed her lightly on the forehead, then stepped away. "I got a day of admin leave. To spend with my family. Though I wasn't expecting you to be home, either."

"Really?" Sylvia's face lit up. "Some sort of time-off award?"

Adam bit his lip as he sank onto the futon. "Well... not exactly."

"Then what, exactly?"

He watched as she perched on the futon next to him, the ruby sweater draped over her arm. He knew how she'd react to the truth. And he was right.

"You stupid man." She snapped the sweater at him in her frustration after he'd explained the situation to her. "You need to trust Pete. Let him do his job."

He flinched, not from the hit but from the knowledge that Pete had betrayed him. Hadn't trusted him. "Yeah, that's what I thought, too. But he's not getting anywhere. I can't let him do this on his own. Or leave Julia on her own without helping."

She took a deep breath, refolding the sweater neatly in her lap, then looked back up at him. "You know, he probably knows more than he's saying to you."

"No kidding. But why would he keep details about the case from me? He's my partner. He understands the value of sharing information as much as I do."

She shrugged, her mouth a perfect pout. "You know he always follows the rules. He's careful. Correct. Besides, some of this information might not be about the case. But listen." She reached over and patted his arm as she stood and turned toward the bedroom before he had a chance to ask what she meant by that. "He will clear Julia. You know she's innocent."

"I can't just abandon her."

"And I don't want you to, darling." Her voice lowered as she sighed and walked back toward him, kneeling on the carpet in front of him. She grasped his hands in hers. "But don't jeopardize your career, for God's sake. Today it's administrative leave. What's next, suspension?"

Adam nodded, frowning. "Could be." He looked down at her, kneeling in front of him, her blond hair spread out about her shoulders, her eyes pleading with him. She wanted so much for him. For them. She was a strong, smart, successful woman, and he trusted her judgment. At least, he usually did.

"I want you to help Julia," she said. "Of course you need to support the people you love. But you need to trust Pete. Support Julia by talking to her. Spend time with her, be her big brother. Let Pete do his job."

When Adam didn't respond, she nodded and stood, once more turning toward the bedroom.

Adam felt a twinge of guilt as she walked out of view, and he followed her into the other room. Maybe it was unreasonable, but he didn't want to let her out of his sight. "Most of the city's resources are being focused on the religious convention next week. That's what I'll be doing when I'm back at work tomorrow."

Sylvia shrugged as she pulled open the door of her armoire. Adam had expected to see other sweaters or shirts piled on the bed, but they were all neatly folded. "Then do it well. So that Pete can stay on this case and get it solved. See?" She turned and smiled at him. "Then you will be helping."

Adam shook his head. "I feel like I'd be abandoning Julia. And I can't do that."

"Adam."

He heard the note of warning in her voice, saw the familiar glint in her eye. Knew her well enough to know it was the first sign of her anger. He ignored it, hoping his interest in the case would change her mind. "I think there's something going on with the developer, Roc Lubrano. Ian Heyward — he's another suspect — is convinced Lubrano's involved, and I can see the merit of his position." He bit his thumb as he paced back and forth next to their bed.

"Adam, why are you telling me this?" Sylvia hadn't moved from in front of her armoire. She still held her sweater in her hand.

"So you understand, honey. Heyward's no innocent, either, by the way. He's got an arrest record he was hoping we wouldn't dig up. Don't know what he was thinking."

"Adam."

He couldn't ignore the sharpness of Sylvia's tone this time. He stopped pacing to look at her. "What?"

Her eyes grew wide as her lips narrowed, her rage visible on her face. "You are not on this case. You should not be thinking about these things. Why are you torturing yourself like this? And, frankly, me?"

"What are you talking about? How am I hurting you by thinking about the case?"

She took a deep breath but it shuddered on its way out. If her goal had been to calm herself down, it hadn't worked. She pursed her lips, then asked, "Don't you care about me? About us, our future?"

"Of course I do, what does that have to do with anything?"

"Oh!" Sylvia threw the sweater down onto the bed. "If you don't understand how your actions affect me — affect us — then... then how can I live with you? How can I plan a future with you?"

She slammed the bedroom door behind her. A moment later, Adam heard the second slam of the front door. He knew what she was worried about. His career. But why didn't she understand that some things were more important than his career? Like family.

He stared at the sweater, lying in a mess on the bed.

Even tossed like that, it still made him think of romance. She hadn't been reorganizing her closet, that much was clear. But Adam had no idea why she was home at this time of day, getting changed. More to the point, he had no idea what she would do when she realized Adam wasn't giving up the case. He couldn't. As much as he loved Sylvia, he had an obligation to protect Julia the best way he knew how.

CHAPTER TWENTY-ONE

ADAM CATAPULTED HIS duffle bag into the back seat and squeezed into the rental car, cursing as his knee jammed into the steering wheel. He shifted the seat back with a grunt. Sylvia said she couldn't live with him. Captain Farrow told him to take time off to spend with his family. Julia was right, now seemed as good a time as any to head down to Atlantic City.

He steered the rental car over the Walt Whitman Bridge and headed for the Atlantic City Expressway. He'd known traffic would be heavy on a Friday afternoon, even at this time of year. Everyone was cutting out early to get a head start on the weekend. He swerved to avoid a tractor-trailer pulling into his lane and told himself again this was a good idea. Not a waste of time, as he'd claimed to Julia earlier.

He'd caught her at home this time, seeking her out after his fight with Sylvia.

"Adam, come up." Her words were welcoming but the tone was neutral as she buzzed him into her building. At least the door was locked. For once.

She stood in the middle of her loft, surrounded by easels displaying a variety of photographs. Garden scenes ranging from extreme closeups that made it impossible to identify the plant in the photograph to grand vistas that drew his eyes off into the sunrise. Urban scenes, beach scenes, portraits. Some in color, some black and white. Some a combination of styles and colors in a blend that only Julia could have come up with. He stopped to admire her work. He couldn't help it. He was impressed.

Julia did not look impressed. She stood in the midst of the easels, a frown etched across her forehead. She held a box cutter in her hand, and given her expression, Adam feared a little bit for what — or who — was to be the next victim of the knife.

"What can I do for you?" she asked without looking at him, her eyes focused intently on one of the images to her right.

"Just checking in, seeing how you're doing." He spoke casually as he slid sideways onto her sofa. She was obviously upset, and he did not want another woman yelling at him today. One was enough.

"Argh." She threw the knife onto the low table by the sofa and flung herself down next to Adam. "I can't do it."

"What exactly are you trying to do?" Adam tried to figure out from the spread of images around him, but could see no rhyme or reason to the display.

"Anything." She buried her face in her hands, her hair falling forward over her shoulders. "I'm just trying to do anything. To focus. To stop thinking about that judge. About my statue. About being a suspect."

Adam sank lower into the sofa, weighed down by the guilt of not being able to help his little sister. "Julia, I'm so sorry you had to go through that — that I couldn't stop it. I'm working the case, finding everything I can on the other suspects. I'm trying, I am."

"I know." She kept her face hidden and took a deep breath.

"Jules?"

She nodded.

He took a deep breath of his own. "Is there anything else you're not telling me, anything I'm missing?"

"How can I tell you that when I have no idea?" She

looked up at him finally, and the look in her eyes broke his heart.

He'd been expecting anger in response to his question. Defensiveness. Those he could handle. This... this was grief. He couldn't handle that.

He stood. "All right, then, I'm heading back out, see what I can find."

"What can I do to help?" She stood with him as she asked the question.

"Nothing. Just stay safe, stay out of trouble."

Finally, her anger flared. "How can I stay here? I can't work, I can't focus." She flung her arms around as if to demonstrate the futility of her efforts. "What are you going to do next? Tell me." She put her hands on her hips and stared at him.

He had no good answer to that. "I'm not sure," he thought out loud. "There are a couple of options. I can go back to the precinct, see what else I can dig up on some of the suspects in the case."

Julia shook her head. "I thought you weren't supposed to be working this case. You think you can sneak around right under your captain's nose?"

She had a point. He chewed on his lip as he stared at one of her photographs. One of the beach scenes, gentle waves lapping against a pale sandy beach. But in the distance, in the background of the shot, a larger wave was forming, breaking against a sandbar somewhere out in the water. Somewhere buried, unseen.

"I could always do what Heyward suggested and go to Atlantic City." He laughed as he said it.

"AC? Sounds good, I'm in."

He turned to look at her. "No way. First, I'm not really going. It's a long shot that will most likely go nowhere."

"And second of all?" She gave him an impatient look, one he'd seen far too many times over the course of their lives.

"Second of all, you're not getting any more involved

in this investigation. No way."

"Perfect, then." She grabbed her knife, mats, and images and started filing everything away into thin, wide drawers at the far end of the room.

"Perfect? What does that mean?"

She shook her head but didn't turn around from her work. "Look, you said yourself it's a long shot. A lead Pete probably wouldn't follow anyway, right?"

"Yeah…" Adam still didn't know where she was going with this.

"So, if you go to AC, you stay out of the way. You're still doing something useful, but you're not stepping on anyone's toes."

"Okay, but —"

"And if I go with you, I'm not in any danger, 'cause you said yourself this probably would turn out to be nothing. And I get a day off, away from this." She turned back to him, and he saw the worry forming in her eyes again. She turned to look around the room and shook her head one more time. "I need to get away."

ADAM GLANCED OVER at Julia in the passenger seat. She had her window rolled down, despite the chill in the air, and her hair billowed about her face. She stared into the fields as they passed them, though Adam wasn't sure how much she was seeing.

They were more than halfway to Atlantic City, driving past rows of blueberry bushes, bare now of their harvest. He saw signs for the New Jersey Wine Trail and thought how nice it would be if this really were a vacation. If Sylvia were sitting next to him, and they could stop at the wineries along the way, sipping whatever latest concoction the local wineries had come up with.

He must have made some sound, because Julia turned to him. "What else is bugging you? I don't think it's just about me."

He grinned. "Stop reading my mind. You know I hate

that." He waited for her to push, but she let it drop. After only a few more minutes, he caved anyway. "It's Sylvia."

"What's she done now?"

"Nothing. She's worried about me, that's all."

"Yeah, right." She rolled her eyes as she answered and turned back to the view of the blueberry fields.

"Why don't you like her, Jules?" His question was sincere. Ever since Sylvia had come back with him from Warsaw the previous year, Julia'd been difficult with her. He never could figure out why.

"I don't know, I can't put my finger on it. But there's something about her. She's not…"

"Not what, Kaminski material?"

"No." She shut her eyes before answering. "She's not honest, Adam."

"And you know this how?"

"Just a gut feeling."

Adam nodded, turning his eyes back to the road, and wondered what she wasn't telling him. Perhaps when it came to recognizing people with a secret, it was like the kids used to say. It took one to know one.

"So why can't you put that gut to work on this case. Think of anyone who might have ended up with your statue. Maybe someone's trying to frame you."

"What?" She sat up in her seat, lines of worry cutting across her face. "Why would anyone do that?"

"I don't know. I'm trying to think outside the box here."

"That's a terrible thought." She shook her head, her eyes back on the road. Traffic was slowing in front of them, the expressway lit up with red lights. And farther up the road, flashing red and blue lights.

"Great, traffic."

"Looks like an accident," Adam pointed out. Their drive came to a complete halt, then a slow jerk forward and another halt. This was not going to be a quick and easy drive after all.

"Okay." Julia sat up straighter, her face serious. "Let's use this time. Tell me, who are the suspects in the case?"

Adam laughed and shook his head. "I thought this was a day off for you — a chance to get away. Why would I tell you about the case?"

"Because we're stuck here." She gestured toward the back end of the car immediately in front of them. "We have to talk about something."

"Then I'll tell you about Dad's research."

Julia snorted. "Dad did research? I don't believe you."

"No, it's true." Adam's voice expressed his own surprise. "A few years back, when he was in high school."

Julia watched him, waiting for him to continue.

"He found some background info on our grandfather. And his father, too."

"You still bothered by the letters you found last summer, Adam? That's crazy. Why do you care if some relatives we never met said some bad things about our great-grandfather?"

Adam shrugged, pulling the car forward another twenty feet. It looked like they still had another mile like this ahead of them before they'd pass the accident. "I don't know, Jules. Aren't you curious? Don't you want to know more about our family history?"

"Me? Nah." Julia shook her head, slid down in her seat, and rested her feet on the dashboard. "I get enough family time as it is. I don't need to go back into the past to get more."

Adam grinned. Julia never had shared his interest in history. "There's a painting, apparently. Of our great-grandfather."

"Yeah?" Julia's question was polite, but her tone was light, her attention on the cluster of cars they were slowly approaching to their right.

"Yeah. Dad found it. In one of the branches of the Free Library."

"Really?" This seemed to have caught Julia's attention.

"Why would there be a painting of our great-grandfather in a Philly library?"

Adam shook his head, his eyes focusing on the bent mess of steel that used to be a car pulled over to the right side of the road. The ambulance was nowhere to be seen. Hopefully whoever had been in that car was well on his way to the nearest hospital. "I don't know, that's why I want to look into it. Maybe go see the painting, see what I can find out."

"Sure, sounds fun." Julia yawned and rested her head against the back of the chair.

Adam smiled and kept his mouth shut. A few hundred feet more, and he was past the accident, out of the mind-numbing traffic. Julia's head nodded to the side. He hit the accelerator and thought about why he was really going to Atlantic City.

Maybe because it had been Ian Heyward's suggestion, and he was curious about Dr. Heyward and his surprising past. Matt certainly wanted to keep the focus there. But Adam was still interested in Grace Evans, too. There was something about her. A woman who always got what she wanted. No matter the cost. And she wasn't above lashing out to hurt people who got in her way. Look at how fast she had lodged that complaint against him with his captain.

And then there was Roc Lubrano. A developer with ties to illegal smuggling, easy access to stolen artwork, and a clear motive. But not a motive to kill Oliver Ryan-Mills. To kill Ian Heyward, maybe. If he were Heyward, he'd be watching his back right about now. But Ryan-Mills? He'd helped the casino, blocking the injunction. Giving the tribe more time to move forward.

So why had Ryan-Mills partnered up with Heyward to fight the casino? Given his role in helping the casinos move forward, it didn't make any sense.

The scent of salt hung in the air as Adam hit the last toll on the expressway. Around one more bend, and the casinos and hotels of Atlantic City loomed before him, lights on and gaudy even at this time of day. Adam had to admit, he could understand why people were fighting to prevent something like this from being built in Center City Philadelphia.

But he wasn't here to judge the relative merits of casinos. He was here to form a judgment of Roc Lubrano, and gather whatever facts he could about the man, his connections, and his way of doing business.

CHAPTER TWENTY-TWO

MATT THOMPSON APPROACHED the still form. A gray bundle of rags, it looked like. But he knew beneath the filthy garments lay a man. "Hey, buddy, you okay?"

He spoke loudly, but the figure didn't move. He hated this part of the job. Usually, it was just a homeless person who found a comfortable place to sleep. Sometimes, though, kids or junkies slipped into this gated garden looking for privacy. Looking for a place to shoot up that, in a few dire cases, became their last resting place.

"Buddy, wake up." Matt reached a gloved hand out and shook the figure.

"Hmph." It stirred.

Matt let his breath out. Thank God. "Come on, get up. You can't stay here, you're not even supposed to be in here." Whoever had left that gate unlocked overnight was going to get grief from the chief, that was sure.

The man stirred and rolled over, now lying on his back on the bench. To his right, Matt could see the brick wall of the reconstructed house where Thomas Jefferson sat to draft the Declaration of Independence. To his left, the gray cement block wall of the local branch of Philly's Free Library, getting a constant stream of business, it looked like. Matt looked back down at the homeless man in front of him and saw a face he recognized.

"Hey, Frankie, what're you doing over here? This isn't

your usual turf."

Frankie grunted again and sat up, his legs still stretched out in front of him on the bench. The skin around his eyes and mouth looked gray, though Matt couldn't tell if it was from age or accumulated grime. His long hair hung in tattered bunches around his face, strings of black, white, and shades in-between. He rubbed a gloved hand over his face and turned his watery eyes toward Matt.

"Can't sleep in my square these days. Too much. Too many."

Matt interpreted his speech. He'd spoken with Frankie enough over the past year to have some sense of what the man was saying. "Too much going on there for you, huh? With that big party?"

Frankie mumbled something while he reached one hand out toward his legs, pushing them off the bench onto the ground. They landed with a thud and Frankie winced.

"You waking up? You ready to move?" Matt ran a practiced eye over Frankie, looking for any signs of injury. Any indication the man needed more help than Matt could give. He looked healthy enough, considering. He was moving his feet now, wiggling them up and down in preparation for standing on them.

Frankie shifted his weight and a crumpled piece of paper slipped out from beneath him, rolling onto the bench. Matt wouldn't have cared, but a logo just visible on one exposed edge caught his attention.

"You got a bank account now, Frankie?" Matt smiled as he asked the question, but he kept his eyes trained on Frankie's face, looking for his answer there.

"Wha? You got wha?" Frankie narrowed his eyes and shook his head.

Matt stepped to his right and leaned forward slowly, not wanting to make any moves that would startle Frankie. He wasn't looking for an altercation. He needn't have worried. Frankie was still groggy, still focusing on getting his feet to work so he could stand and walk out of the garden on his own. Matt slid his gloved hand around the crumpled paper.

"Where'd you get this, Frankie?"

"Tha's mine."

"Uh-huh." Matt looked at the bank statement he was holding. In the name of Oliver Ryan-Mills. "Where'd you get this, Frankie? You find it?"

Frankie shrugged. "He din't need it no more."

"Where'd you find it?"

"My place, man. Guy was sleeping hard. Some blood. No good." Frankie pushed himself off the bench, wobbled a bit, then stood. "I tol' you, din't need it."

"D'you know he was hurt? Did you see what happened to him?" Matt tried to keep Frankie's attention, but the man had turned and was picking his way across the garden toward the gate that led out to the sidewalk in front of the Free Library. His steps were short, shuffling. This would take awhile.

Matt walked next to him. "Did you see what happened to the man, before he was sleeping?"

Frankie slid his eyes sideways toward Matt. He saw the disbelief in the yellowed look, the small grin that cut across his face. "He weren't really sleeping, buddy, an' I tol' you, he din't need that no more."

"Tell me what you saw, Frankie."

Frankie shrugged. "Nothin'. I was there. I woke up an' he was there. He wan't gonna wake up, I tell you that. So I looked for what I needed."

"Did he have anything else on him?"

Frankie's eyes slid away. He shook his head sharply.

"Okay, he had some money on him and you took it. Anything else?"

Frankie grinned again, shook his head again.

Matt looked down at the bank statement. The man had a healthy bank account, that was for sure. But not surprising. What was surprising was why he'd been carrying his own bank statement when he went for an

142

early morning walk. Was that a rich person thing? Matt grinned as an image of a duck in a top hat rolling around in money flashed before his eyes.

Hell, if he had this much in his bank account, he'd probably carry the statement around with him, too.

Frankie turned to him, his face still gray. "Man, this in't good."

"What's not good, Frankie?" Matt waited for an answer, but he didn't have to wait long.

Frankie turned toward him as he leaned over and vomited.

"Crap!" Matt stepped to his left to avoid the rancid stream, but the paper in his right hand caught the edge of it. "Fuck." He dropped the sheet as it absorbed the liquid, turning yellow. "Frankie, you okay?"

"Better now… good." Frankie grinned, a few randomly placed teeth showing in his smile. "Off now."

"Shit." Matt bent down to retrieve the statement, holding it from one corner. He'd kind of screwed that up. No matter, it was just a statement, it wouldn't be a problem to get a copy from the bank if Adam or Pete needed it. Which they probably wouldn't, anyway.

He was disappointed. He'd really hoped that by seeking out and talking to the regular homeless who slept in Washington Square he'd find something useful. Something that would prove his worth as a law enforcement officer. Not something belonging to the victim, but a vital piece of evidence that would point toward the killer.

Matt turned to lock the garden gate behind them, dropping the sodden statement into a trash can, then watched Frankie amble away toward Market Street. Maybe next time.

CHAPTER TWENTY-THREE

THE MEETING ROOM stretched along the casino floor, from the west side of the building all the way to the boardwalk side on the east. Gold curtains draped over windows and walls, plush carpet covered the floor, and to the side, shining wooden tables held sweating pitchers of iced water, carafes of coffee, and pots of cream and sugar. A room half the size would have sufficed for the number of people gathered here. They clustered in the theater-style seating set up around the podium in the front of the room, leaning in to each other conspiratorially. A few men gathered in the back of the room, groups of two or three standing in close conversations.

Adam stood in the back as Roc finished his presentation. Some of the material Adam recognized from the presentation to the civic association earlier in the week. Some of it was data Roc had chosen not to share with the residents. Charts and graphs showed the huge profits he expected to raise from the Philly casino, compared to the losses experienced by the casinos in Atlantic City.

In the questions and answers following his presentation, the audience seemed to be in agreement that Atlantic City, as one central location for all state casinos, was a dying model. Participants considered locations from suburban strip malls to empty lots as locations for smaller establishments, with even bigger return on investment. The only challenging questions Roc faced surrounded the problems with the community. Participants wanted to know what he was going to do to bring the neighborhood around, to build support for the casino.

He got a laugh with his answer. "I'm going to keep meeting with them. Keep answering their questions. Convince them this will be good for their city. But at the end of the day, it really doesn't matter, does it? I don't need the residents' support, I just need the court's support. Once it's built, believe me, the gamblers will come. Including the gamblers who live in that neighborhood."

The audience mumbled its agreement as the next presenter stood from behind the long table at the front and walked toward the podium. Roc turned away, heading toward the back of the room instead of joining the other panelists at the front table. Two gorillas in blue suits followed him, arms out and at the ready in case Roc needed help.

Adam stayed where he was, leaning against a wall in the back, but he followed Roc with his eyes. Watching. Though he wasn't sure for what.

Roc made it to the back of the room, having been waylaid once or twice by audience members with questions. He headed toward a table laden with coffee, but two more men approached him. He didn't pick up the carafe, turning instead to the newcomers. The two men, one the size of a Volkswagen Beetle, the other short and skinny and wearing dark glasses, stepped a little too close to Roc.

Roc nodded his head toward his own bodyguards, a swift movement putting them off, then stepped out through an emergency exit that led toward the boardwalk. Adam waited to see if Roc's security team would follow him. When they turned away from the door, Adam slipped through it. Roc was outnumbered and that other guy was big. This could be trouble.

He needn't have worried. Roc had the situation well in hand. By the time Adam found them, in a dim alley that ran alongside the casino, the big guy was already down, crumpled into a heap at Roc's feet. Roc was wiping blood off his knuckles and rolling the sleeves of his shirt back up. The skinny guy stepped back, hands in the air.

"You think you can threaten me? Huh?" Roc stepped close to the skinny guy. "You think you can waltz in here with some muscle and suddenly I'm going to back down? How the hell do you think I got to the place I am? By being scared?"

"Sorry, Roc, I didn't mean—"

"Yeah, I know exactly what you meant. Now you listen to me. When I tell you to jump, you jump. Got it? I don't even wanna hear you ask how high."

By now he was standing close enough that the sweat from his brow dripped onto the skinny man's cheek. He didn't rub it away, and it worked its way down over his bony face and dripped off his chin. The guy didn't step back, just nodded.

"I got it, Roc. You got it."

Roc gave a sharp nod and Skinny Guy turned and ran. Roc looked up, saw Adam.

"What the hell are you doing here? You're a Philly cop. You got no jurisdiction here."

Adam pursed his lips and shook his head from side to side. "That's not entirely true, Roc. I do have jurisdiction when pursuing a felon across state lines." He stepped closer. "But that's not why I'm here. I just want to talk with you again."

"Talk? About what?"

"About Judge Oliver Ryan-Mills."

"Don't know the man personally, I already told you that."

Adam nodded. "Yeah, that's what you told me. But I know a little bit more now. Like that you and Ryan-Mills

146

had a closer connection than you're letting on. Like that you have a little experience in the 'import-export' business."

"So? That's old history, nothin' to do with today. And as for that judge, I didn't know him." Roc swiped an arm across his chin, wiping away the sweat that Adam could see budding there.

The sound of the emergency door opening caught their attention, and both men tensed. Roc stood facing the entrance to the alley and his eyes moved toward it. Adam stepped to the side, turning to an angle so he could see who was coming up behind him while still keeping an eye on Roc.

"You okay, Roc? I saw our friend go back inside and was wondering why you didn't come back yourself."

Roc grinned. "Sam. What perfect timing. Detective Kaminski, anything else you want to ask me, you gotta ask Sam first."

Adam eyed the man standing there. Tall, somewhat burly, but not tough looking, not mean. His suit was well cut and clean. He wasn't muscle.

"And why's that?"

"Because I'm his lawyer, Detective. Are you interviewing my client without legal representation present? Tsk, tsk."

Adam weighed his options, then nodded once and stepped back toward the end of the alley. As he passed him, Roc spoke up one more time.

"I didn't want him dead. You know that. Ryan-Mills was a lot more useful to me alive than dead. Think about that."

Adam gave Roc a small smile. "Thanks for talking, Ralph, I'll be in touch if I need more."

Roc made a sound that reminded Adam of a wounded animal at the use of his given name. Adam kept his eyes on the grimy pavement in front of him as he stepped around mounds of refuse mushrooming along the blackened brick walls, following the path back out to the boardwalk and the light. Leaving Roc standing in the filthy alley.

He found Julia waiting a few yards down the boardwalk, on a bench with a view of the casino entrance. A pedicab passed as he took the seat next to her, taking a deep breath of the clean salt air. Clearing his mind and his lungs.

"So how'd it go? Anything?" She seemed honestly interested, and Adam wasn't sure how to respond. The ringing of his phone saved him from either lying to her or telling her more than she needed to know.

"Sorry." He tensed as he saw who was calling. Not his favorite person right now. "Pete, what's up?"

"Nothing good, I'll tell you that. Just got a call from our friends in New Jersey."

"Oh?" Adam turned to look out at the waves behind him. "Why's that?"

"Body turned up. Might be related to my case."

Adam stood and took a few steps away from the bench, distancing himself from Julia. "A body? Whose?"

"You know I can't talk details with you, buddy. I just thought you'd like to know since this should put Julia out of the picture as a suspect. Unless she happens to be down at Brigantine right now."

Adam stared out across the sound, the clear white beaches of Brigantine easily visible, less than a mile away over the bridge across the bay.

When Adam said nothing, Pete added, "Adam, what's going on?"

"Nothing. It's... nothing." He disconnected, knowing he couldn't trust Pete with the truth. Not after he told the captain about Julia's connection to Ryan-Mills.

"Adam, what was that?" Julia asked as her phone started to ring.

"Don't answer that." Adam gave her a warning look. "I need to go to Brigantine."

CHAPTER TWENTY-FOUR

ADAM PULLED HIS car into the nearest cross street, parking on a yellow line and walking the rest of the way up the beach. It wasn't hard to find the scene. Emergency vehicles crowded the shoreline. A pop-up tent had already been set up over the spot where the body came ashore. The only thing missing was yellow crime scene tape fluttering in the heavy breeze, and Adam wondered if that was on its way.

He'd left Julia back in Atlantic City. Bad enough he'd brought her to the scene of another death, no point in linking her any more than she already was.

Despite the crowds of vehicles and people, sounds from the crime scene were barely audible from the back of the beach. As Adam approached, no voices carried over the pounding of the surf. Only the scent of salt water and seaweed filled the air. It could almost have been a family gathering if not for the flashing blue and red lights that cavorted along the waves of the sand as he walked toward them.

The team in place worked efficiently. Adam recognized the familiar motions as the body was lifted off the ground, all on-site evidence having already been collected. At least he was in time to see if he could identify the body. It would take a lot longer for the evidence, from the scene and from the body, to be collected and analyzed.

Out to sea, the water sparkled brilliantly, but behind him as he walked, gray clouds loomed. He looked over his shoulder and saw the bundle of clouds rolling across the sky, each bulging out as if being pushed from behind by an invisible breath, tumbling across each other in their race to get out to sea. The sky behind them was dark. Threatening.

The team working down the beach presumably saw the weather moving in and were working fast. An afternoon storm would obliterate anything that might be left to be found. Though Adam suspected there wasn't that much to begin with. A uniformed officer stopped him when he was still thirty feet away from the scene, but Adam produced his ID and the officer escorted him to the detective in charge on scene.

"What's Philly PD's interest in this?"

"Like they said when you called, the victim's involved in an ongoing homicide investigation."

The man nodded, eyeing Adam warily. "They didn't say they were sending anyone down."

"They didn't. I happened to be in AC. A day off."

"So are you back on the clock now?"

Adam shook his head. "Completely unofficial. I'm not even lead on the homicide." Only a slight bending of the truth. "My partner, Pete Lawler, called to let me know about this."

"Yeah, that's who I spoke to." The detective's shoulders lowered and the creases left his forehead. He gestured to the body, now wrapped in a thick black plastic bag, about to be loaded into the waiting ambulance.

"Wanna look?"

Adam nodded mutely.

The zipper was old, rusty from too much use in the salty air. It stuck a couple of times as one of the techs pulled it down from the top, the tech cursing with each delay. A grating sound accompanied the movement. Adam fleetingly wondered what it would be like to be on the inside of that bag, zipped in. He shook his head.

The sides of the bag were finally pulled apart and Adam leaned forward. The face was only partially bloated, its skin a Technicolor Rorschach test in pink and white and green. Adam knew enough about drowning to know the man couldn't have been in the water more than a day, probably less. He would have deteriorated a lot more after that. As it was, he was easily recognizable.

Matt Thompson would be disappointed. He'd lost his prime suspect. And now Adam had to figure out who had killed Ian Heyward. And why.

CHAPTER TWENTY-FIVE

ADAM FOUND JULIA at one of the casino's bars. She sat alone, staring down at the glass in front of her, apparently oblivious to the constant bells and whistles going off around her. She didn't notice Adam approach and only started out of her reverie when he took the stool next to hers.

"What's the news?" Her tone was light, but worry darkened her eyes and creased her forehead.

"Ian Heyward."

"Do I know him?"

"God, I hope not." Someone on the casino floor whooped and an even louder bell clanged. He leaned closer to Julia. "I'm sorry I brought you down here with me. Having you in the neighborhood when another murder happens is a really bad thing."

Julia shook her head. "This is insane. How could your department think I had anything to do with this? And make Pete seriously look into it?"

"He's just doing his job, you know that." Adam pulled his phone out of his pocket and placed it on the bar in front of him, in case Sylvia tried to reach out. "I'm only glad the captain kept him on this case. He could've pulled him off, too, since I'm his partner and you're my sister."

"He's good at what he does, I know." Julia played with the swizzle stick in her glass. "I'm glad he's on it, too. And I'm grateful to you, too, you know that, right?" She looked over at him.

Adam smiled, put his arm around her. "I know, but thanks for saying it."

"It's just, about Pete…"

"What about Pete?"

Julia's shoulder tensed under Adam's arm and he pulled away, turning to look directly at her. "What?"

"He may not be as objective about this case as the captain thinks, that's all." It was a statement but she said it like a question, her voice rising in tone but losing strength as she finished her thought.

Adam felt like she'd slapped him in the face. First Sylvia, now Julia. "You're questioning Pete's abilities? Why?"

"No, no. It's not that." Julia chewed on her lower lip, pink blushes growing on both cheeks. "I'm saying… Argh." She sat up straight on her stool, slapping the bar with her hand. "Pete asked me not to talk to you about this."

"I don't get you, Jules. First you say Pete can't handle the case. Now you don't want to talk to me about it because Pete asked you not to. If not him, and not me, who do you trust to figure this out?"

Julia smiled and shook her head, though the color in her cheeks remained. "I'm saying this all wrong, big brother. You're totally misunderstanding."

She grinned over at him and Adam couldn't help but smile back. He'd been taking care of her for as long as he could remember — for as long as she was around. Looking at her now, he still saw her in her sneakers and pigtails, chasing after him and his friends. Trying to prove she was strong enough to play with the big boys. She hadn't been, not really, but he'd let her play anyway. Basketball in the schoolyard. Kickball in the street. He'd watched out for her even then, making sure she always scored at least one point. He wasn't going to stop watching out for her now. No matter what Pete asked.

No matter what the captain ordered. No matter what Sylvia feared. Family always came first.

He put his arm back around her shoulder. "Look, this is a tough situation. I know what it's like to be accused of something you didn't do, believe me." Adam thought back to those few rough days in Warsaw last year. Julia needed his help right now, not his accusations. "I know it's horrible, but this murder could help get you off the suspect list. Ian Heyward was another suspect. He had some dealings with Ryan-Mills through their civic association."

"Rivals or something like that?"

"Actually, they were working together. Both trying to stop the casino from being built downtown."

Julia nodded. "So maybe the same person who killed Ryan-Mills also killed Heyward. Like this developer — Roc Lubrano. If they were trying to stop him, makes sense he would take them both out."

"Take them out?" Adam grinned. "You been watching too many cop shows on TV." He flagged down a waitress and ordered a whiskey. "Hey, it's after five somewhere," he responded to the look Julia gave him. "But I don't think you're right about that."

"What, am I too amateur?" She grinned.

Adam shook his head. "Roc wanted Ryan-Mills alive. He was the reason Roc's company had been able to move forward with the development with a noncompetitive bid."

"Because he was a judge?" Adam nodded so Julia continued, "But he was retired, wasn't he? So he wouldn't have still been involved in the case."

Adam shrugged, hit the button on his phone to check it was fully charged. "I know that on the force, when a cop retires, he still has a connection to the cases he worked. We still go back to them with questions or for advice. They're still the experts on the case. Maybe it's the same way with judges."

"Maybe." Julia looked skeptical. "But I thought you

said he was working in cahoots with Heyward, fighting the casinos?"

Adam nodded, frowning. "I know. He was definitely joining forces with Heyward. Well, publicly at least."

"What does that mean?"

Adam shrugged, dropped his phone back into his pocket. He couldn't sit around moping over Sylvia. He was here with Julia, they had a free evening together to enjoy the casinos, take some time off. Maybe down time was exactly what he needed to wrap his mind around this case. Sort out the wheat from the chaff.

He dropped a few bills on the bar as he downed his whiskey and stood. "Roc suspected that Ryan-Mills was actually working against Heyward. Hell, Heyward suspected the same thing."

"So what does that mean?" Julia slung her bag over her shoulder as she followed Adam out onto the casino floor.

"It proves nothing. But it makes me wonder... did Roc kill Heyward out of revenge for killing the judge? Or because with the judge gone, Heyward would have been a lot more successful?"

"THANKS FOR INCLUDING me in this." Matt shook Pete's hand outside the Washington Square building. A chill in the air kept pedestrians bundled into their coats, and the broad glass doors that welcomed guests to the building were both closed. He wondered why Pete had chosen to wait for him out here instead of inside the lobby.

Pete nodded a welcome. "John Hamilton said you'd be the best person for the job." He looked down at his feet before adding, "And I agree, you should be part of this case."

"No kidding? I kinda had the impression you wanted me to stay out of it." Matt let his surprise show on his face. He knew he was up to the job, he just hadn't thought Pete agreed. Or John Hamilton, for that matter.

"I know." Pete shrugged. "Look, sorry about earlier, okay? You caught me at a bad time, that's all. I called Hamilton to see if someone from your end could help me out on this, someone who knows Grace Evans. He suggested you."

Matt grinned. "And you need me since Kaminski's off the case?"

"Something like that. Look, it's nothing against Adam. He's too close to this, since his sister is a suspect." Pete frowned as he said it.

"For real?"

"Getting realer." Pete's jaw worked over time. "But not if I can help it."

"Oh, yeah? Am I picking up on something going on between you and Kaminski's sister?"

Pete shook his head once, an eyebrow raised. To Matt it seemed more of a warning than a denial, but he took the hint and changed the subject.

"So, Grace Evans, what d'you have on her?"

Pete nodded and gestured for Matt to follow as he pulled the glass door open. "Two husbands, both dead."

"Anything worth looking into there?" Matt tried to keep his question casual, not to be too obvious as he took in the lavish surroundings of the condo's lobby. Everything was gray or white marble, glass, or steel. Despite the cold colors it looked warm and inviting. Perhaps because of the five foot tall gold vases overflowing with out-of-season blooms. Or the thick white rug laid out before the elevators and around the modern seating area. Or the immaculately dressed doorman smiling at them from behind a high booth. He kept his mouth shut tight, worried his jaw was hanging open a bit.

Pete stopped just inside the door to answer, keeping his voice low. "Both deaths were aboveboard. First husband died in a hunting accident. Second had a heart attack."

"Hunting accident? That could be something."

Pete shook his head. "A friend of his pulled the trigger. Man stayed on the scene, called for help, admitted everything right off the bat. Really was an accident."

"Manslaughter, though."

Pete raised an eyebrow and nodded. "Yeah." He glanced at the doorman, who seemed to have nothing better to do than stand and watch them, waiting patiently for whatever assistance they would need from him.

"So you don't think she's a black widow?" Matt asked, thinking about the bank statement he'd found.

"No, I don't. But even if she were, that wouldn't make sense here. She wasn't married to the victim."

"She just wanted to be," Matt agreed.

"So I keep hearing." Pete let a small smile chase across his lips. "But that's not good enough. Not married means she doesn't benefit from his death."

Matt realized he was holding his breath and tried to let it out quietly. Definitely not worth mentioning the bank statement if Pete wasn't looking at the money angle. He didn't want to look like he wasn't able to sort out relevant clues from the useless piles of information that Adam had said inevitably accumulated during an investigation. Plus, he'd rather not have to admit he'd let someone puke all over the statement if it really was evidence.

"Look," Pete continued, "there's something else you need to know."

"Shoot."

Pete paused before answering, as if assessing him. Matt braced himself for whatever was coming. It clearly wasn't good.

"Ian Heyward was found dead this afternoon."

Blood rushed to Matt's head and he felt the world spin a little bit. He squared his feet and put his hands on his utility belt to stabilize himself. This was crazy. Two murders of people he knew?

Pete watched for a moment, then added, "He was found down in Brigantine, next to Atlantic City."

Matt nodded. He'd never been but knew the name.

"We're still waiting on the report on that. I don't have any more details yet," Pete continued. "I thought you should know."

"Yeah." Matt kept his voice calm. "Thanks. I appreciate that." He felt his adrenaline rise again and took a breath, then another. "He was a nice guy. I'm sorry to hear it."

Pete rested a hand on Matt's shoulder, left it there for a moment before stepping away. "Whatever Grace Evans' role was in the murder of Oliver Ryan-Mills, it would be a stretch to see her involved in the death of Ian Heyward."

Matt let out a light laugh. "Agreed. Her assistant on the other hand... I don't know about him."

"Maybe you'll have a better idea about him after we talk to him. He's upstairs with Ms. Evans now."

"Not surprising. It seems like he's always around. So what's your approach here?"

Pete turned as the elevator doors slid open. A young woman pushed a baby stroller out into the lobby, leaning forward and cooing over her child.

Pete watched as they crossed the lobby, then held the door for her. She nodded her thanks and kept moving. Pete turned back to Matt. "Just talk to both of them, get a sense of them."

"Not expecting to trick a confession out of her then?"

"Very funny. No, nothing that sneaky. I want to hear her tell her story in her own words, in her own voice. About her relationship with the deceased."

"About her plans for him, you mean?"

"Maybe. Let's see what she says."

Pete pulled out his badge and they approached the doorman.

CHAPTER TWENTY-SIX

"THEY GOT YOU working shifts now?" Pete asked the question lightly, but Adam recognized the sympathy in his eyes.

Adam shrugged and looked back over his shoulder at the marble building looming behind him. A little late for Pete to be concerned about him. "Yeah, it's just when the work needs to be done, you know?"

Even though it was Saturday, he'd spent the morning meeting with residents, businesses, churches, and synagogues throughout the neighborhood, letting them know what to expect over the coming week and listening to their ideas and suggestions for keeping the peace. It was amazing how effective a little community collaboration could be in law enforcement. Too bad Pete wasn't offering the same level of collaboration on this case.

"This related to the protest going through here next week?" Matt indicated the police "no parking" signs posted every ten feet.

Adam nodded. "Our friendly neo-Nazis, no less. Their march comes down here on Tuesday, so I'm meeting with the locals, making sure we're ready, getting familiar with exactly who's likely to be out in the neighborhood that day."

Pete looked up at the synagogue Adam had just left. "Not really something they can be ready for, is it?"

159

"No, maybe not." Adam shoved his hands in his jacket pockets as the breeze picked up. "But we'll make sure it stays peaceful at least. So, what have you two been up to?" He turned to walk west out of the historic neighborhood toward Center City and the other two followed.

"Still waiting on the medical examiner's report on Heyward." Pete sucked in his lips before adding, "Quite a coincidence you were there. With Julia."

Adam stopped walking and turned to face Pete. "You're mad at me? When you couldn't even bother telling me you were bringing my own sister in for questioning?"

"Hey, I'm not the one who dragged her off to another crime scene."

"She was in a casino in Atlantic City the whole time, buddy." Adam's hands tightened into fists as he spoke. "Nowhere near Brigantine. And not even near the shore when Heyward was likely killed."

"I sure as hell hope you're right."

The anger in Pete's voice only pissed him off more, and fighting with Pete wasn't going to help him. Or Julia. He closed his eyes and took a breath, then turned to Matt. "How did your talk with Grace Evans go? Better than mine, I hope."

"We talked, that's all. She's quite a character. And has a kinda strange relationship with her assistant."

"He's an odd one, for sure. But is he a killer? Or is she?" Adam asked.

The other men shook their heads at the same time. "She's angry," Matt answered.

"And vengeful," Adam added, remembering her complaint to his captain. "She knows how to get things done."

"But I don't see her as a killer." Matt shook his head. They had stopped at an intersection, waiting for the light to change, and Matt raised a hand to catch his flat hat as a gust of wind hit them. "She told us she spent the night with a friend."

"A man?"

"No," Pete answered, "a woman. Cousin."

"Out of town?"

"Nope. Rittenhouse Square."

"So it's still possible." Adam's doubt carried in his tone of voice.

Pete let out a light laugh, almost a sneer. "What, that she snuck out, ran across town, smacked Ryan-Mills over the head, and ran back to her friend's condo? All without being noticed?"

"I guess not," Adam agreed, still focusing on not letting his anger at Pete vent, not giving him the satisfaction. "Unless she paid someone else to do it for her."

"Now that's more likely." Pete nodded. "She has the money. Marcus Cory could be in it with her. He doesn't have an alibi. But I don't know. I mean, she's tough. Mean even. But I get the sense there's something else going on with her."

"Maybe Marcus took some initiative. On his own."

"Maybe," Adam pictured Marcus as he had looked on Washington Square, prim, proper, elegant. "But he strikes me more as the type who wouldn't want to get his hands dirty, either. Personally, I want to know more about Mr. Lubrano. He as much as told me he had some kind of arrangement with Ryan-Mills."

"Arrangement?" Matt asked. "Like what?"

"Got me. Something that made Ryan-Mills more valuable to him alive than dead. I dunno." Adam glanced to his left as they passed a well-used playground, its blacktop cracked and sprouting weeds, paint peeling off the jungle gym. A group of four children huddled in a corner, as far as possible from their minder, who leaned casually against a brick wall that lined one side of the playground, talking on the phone. "Unsavory characters, that's what Harry said."

Matt laughed out loud. "Unsavory characters? What

does that mean?"

"Just that Judge Ryan-Mills had been making some odd friendships over the past couple of years. People his son didn't want to talk about."

"Which could be connected to Roc Lubrano." Pete narrowed his eyes as he spoke. "That man has some connections that aren't legal, I'm pretty sure."

"So, what do we know?" Adam turned his back on Pete as they waited at another intersection. "A couple of years ago, Judge Ryan-Mills refused to uphold an injunction that would have stopped the Department of the Interior from negotiating a new gambling compact."

"And that allowed the tribe that hired Roc Lubrano to open a third casino in Philly." Matt finished the timeline.

"Right, but he's since retired," Pete pointed out.

"I've been speaking with one of the ADAs we work with at the park," Matt said. "As long as the judge is alive and still friends with everyone in the courthouse, his position will stand — no one's going to go against his stated will."

"But why wouldn't he have granted that injunction? He hated the casinos," Adam asked.

"Sure, but he hated the idea of going against his principles even more. Personally, he didn't want the casino. Legally, given the merits of this case as defined within the court of law, he did the right thing," Pete explained.

"Legally. Maybe not morally," Matt said. "That's a pretty weird gray area."

"So maybe he felt guilty about it?" Pete asked.

"I suppose he probably did, on some level. Which is why he was trying to help Heyward — guide him through the legal minefield of stopping the casino." Adam understood gray areas. He'd been in enough tough situations to know how hard it could be to do the right thing. To even know what the right thing was.

"But Heyward didn't appreciate his involvement," said Matt, interrupting his thoughts.

"And I bet his fellow judges worried that he was crossing the line," Pete jumped in. "Even as a retired judge, he needed to keep his distance from the multitudes."

"But that's exactly what Ryan-Mills was trying not to do — he was trying to get the chance to live his life like a normal person for the first time." Adam felt like he was finally getting to understand Ryan-Mills. A man with a complicated set of morals. Beliefs that forced him to act against his own self-interest.

"And someone killed him for it." Matt shook his head. "And then killed Ian Heyward."

"All right. So we look into the casino connection. I can dig into Roc Lubrano's background. Bank accounts, business interests, the whole shebang."

At Pete's mention of bank accounts, Matt's step faltered. He said nothing, though, and Adam didn't ask. He glanced at his watch. "Perfect. And I gotta get back to my new office. Yet one more report to write up about this morning's meetings."

"Just can't get away from the paperwork, can you, partner?"

Adam bit back his first response. "Don't worry about me, Pete. I'll get this report, request for resources, and budget estimate done in the next hour."

"You attending the funeral?"

Adam nodded. "So?"

"Stay of out sight, buddy, don't engage anyone. I'll be there. Officially, on duty. Let me do the talking. I don't want anyone there seeing you with me. Understand?"

"Sure, Pete. I get it."

CHAPTER TWENTY-SEVEN

THE BROWN EARTH lay exposed, chopped and turned on the surface, dark and cold below. The sun shone brightly and a light gust of wind encouraged the few red and yellow leaves that remained on the ground to dance across the thick carpet of grass.

Not the way it should be, Adam thought. It should be rain.

He stared at the dug earth, trying not to think. Trying not to remember.

It had been so long now. So much had happened. So much had changed. He didn't think about it as much now as he used to. The dead teenagers. The grieving mothers. His own inability to protect them from that racist cop years earlier.

But standing here, hands in his pockets, in a very different cemetery on a very different day, he couldn't ignore the memory. The pungent odor of the fresh dirt, the perfume of the lilies. There was no music here. This gravesite was depressingly silent. The group from the church had yet to arrive with the casket and only a handful of mourners gathered who hadn't made it to the service first.

Even though he stood alone, he felt the crowd surge around him as it did that day so long ago. Heard the low voices singing. He closed his eyes and it was as if he were there.

He felt the anger. The rage. The guilt.

He tightened the grip of his hands in his pockets, squeezing his fingers together. He opened his eyes in time to see a line of black cars approaching. The funeral train from the cemetery, the hearse in the lead.

The first black limo pulled up behind the hearse and Harry Ryan-Mills got out. A second man exited from the far side of the car, stopping to help a well-dressed woman who slid out behind him. Thomas Ryan-Mills and the daughter-in-law, presumably. It had to be Thomas. He was the spitting image of his brother, though a few years younger. The same sandy hair, worn short enough to be proper but long enough to be roguish, to look messy in the right kind of way. The same average height and build, with a lean, but not too lean, fitness. The kind that came from casual games on the squash or basketball court, not from hours in the gym.

Where they differed, however, was in their eyes. Thomas looked relaxed, almost happy, if that were really possible at a funeral. His father's funeral, no less. The woman with him kept her head down, her shoulders low. When she looked up to see where she was stepping, Adam saw the grief in her eyes. At least, it might have been grief. From this distance, her expression looked a little like fear.

Harry, on the other hand, showed no grief. No fear. He had an edge in his eye, a glint of steel that didn't quite fit with the grieving son persona he was trying to put forward. Adam watched him approach, considering him.

Other cars pulled up behind the limo. Other mourners crawled out of the vehicles, stepped their way cautiously across the grass of the cemetery to the exposed wound in the grass that awaited the coffin.

He took a deep breath and controlled his thoughts. He was there to observe. To see who showed up, how they behaved. The smallest clue, an unnoticeable tic, could be enough. The old myth was certainly true, the killer too often couldn't resist the thrill of attending the funeral.

Pete came towards the end of the movement of people. He had been at the funeral mass as well. He made eye contact with Adam as he approached, a slight nod, but then stepped to the far side of the grave, near the chairs set out for the immediate family.

Marcus Cory arrived in the same car as Grace Evans. Once at the grave, however, they headed in different directions. Marcus joined the group standing behind the chairs. He wore an inscrutable expression on his face, as if there were something not quite amusing about the situation. Not a smile, that would be too strong a word. Not a smirk, either. A hint, instead, that he knew something no one else there knew.

Grace Evans had the courtesy to stand away from the family. She settled on a location between two other elderly women draped in black quite close to where Adam stood. Perhaps she hadn't noticed him, perhaps she didn't care. She and the other women kept up a constant stream of gossip under their breath as they watched the other mourners approach, find a place to stand, shake hands, kiss cheeks.

"Hmm, he's just glad it isn't his own funeral." One of Grace's companions followed an elderly man with her eyes.

"Knows he won't get a crowd like this when it is." Grace nodded.

The other woman used her chin to point to a younger couple. "They're still together, I see. That's quite a surprise."

"George and Sarah didn't bring the children," Grace said as a middle-aged couple approached the family to offer condolences.

"And she must be pregnant." Another young woman fell under their critique. "That's not just weight gain. Wonder who the lucky fellow is." The ladies tittered in delight.

"Well, I never. He has some audacity." Grace didn't bother to keep her voice low as Roc Lubrano approached the grave. He skipped the traditional condolences for the family, instead walking directly to where Adam stood.

Grace and her friends followed him with their eyes. As he stationed himself near Adam, she sniffed and looked away, her eyes and posture clearly showing her distaste.

Adam nodded in recognition. "I'm surprised to see you here."

"Won't stay long." Roc spoke without looking at Adam, his eyes scanning the crowd. His hands were stuffed in his pockets, much like Adam's, but Adam could tell he was tense. Ready to respond if necessary. "Just paying my respects where respect is due."

Roc's gaze had settled on the two Ryan-Mills boys. Adam recognized the look; Roc was sizing them up. But for what?

He glanced at Pete and saw that Pete, too, was focused on Roc. Roc was evaluating Oliver Ryan-Mills' sons. And Adam needed to find out why.

By now Grace and her coterie had moved on to other unfortunate members of the community who fell under their critical gaze. They kept their voices even lower now, perhaps realizing that Adam was close enough to overhear. But Adam caught another name that struck a chord.

"He should be here now. It's not right."

"It's a terrible loss, a tragedy." One of the women wiped her eyes. "Two neighbors dead. Terrible."

Ian Heyward was remembered, even at this funeral for Oliver Ryan-Mills. An absence where a person should be.

HE KEPT ONE hand in his pocket, wrapped around

the gold coin he'd gotten from Sal. One of the items he'd purchased in order to acquire the rhino-horn cup. Not a bad purchase in itself, actually. He closed his eyes and let his shoulders relax as he ran a finger around the edge of the coin, feeling the etchings along the side. Not bad at all. He felt his lips turn up into a smile and opened his eyes.

He wiped the smile off his face as he saw other mourners looking at him. It was a funeral, after all. He looked down at the ground. At the brown earth that would soon swallow the coffin. Why wasn't he happier? He had everything he wanted now. He didn't need to worry anymore.

It was the setting, the cemetery, that must be it. They were always creepy. Made him tense. This wasn't his first funeral. God knew he'd been to enough when he was younger. His grandfather's, for one. He'd been what — five, maybe six at the time?

He could still picture his mother standing by that grave, bravely holding back the tears that had overwhelmed her all morning. His father did his best to support her back then, but he wasn't any good at it. He'd never been good at that.

"Buck up, Noodle." His father used the nickname that usually got his mother to smile, put an arm around her shoulders and pulled her tight.

She sniffed loudly, rested her head against his shoulder and closed her eyes.

"We'll get through this. Together," he whispered in her ear, loud enough that his boy could hear.

"I know, Cowboy, I know."

He was glad to hear her use her own nickname for Father. It was a good sign. He took a step back, tempted to wander off through the graveyard. A wicked glance from his father stopped his movement. He pulled his hands together in front of him and tried to look pious.

Other mourners approached his parents, offering their condolences. Mother just sniffled, occasionally nodding. Once even smiling. Father was stoic. As he always was.

Once the burial was over, Father left Mother sitting in a chair by the grave. Giving her space, he supposed, to be alone with her father one more time.

"You okay, Peanut?" God, he hated the nicknames. Why always a nickname? Did he not remember their real names?

"Just fine, Father. How are you?"

Father grinned and took his hand. "You wanted to walk around? Let's go."

Father set a quick pace. He had to trot to keep up, stepping over the obvious graves, trying not to think about the bodies buried below their feet.

A few quick strides ahead, around a copse of dark trees, leaves almost black in his memory, they came across another funeral. Much different from the one they'd left. They hung back, near the trees. He'd pulled a leaf off and slowly tore it into tiny little bits as he watched.

"Black bastards," Father muttered under his breath. "Stay away from them, Peanut. No good. They never are."

He nodded. He'd heard the same story before. He watched, wondering what made them so different from him. Not just their dark skin, but their attitude. Must be the wailing. They couldn't control themselves. Not like Father. Not even like Mother.

"Why are they even in this cemetery? I thought this was a better place to rest our dead." Father shook his head, one side of his mouth pulling up, his eyes lowered.

The unfamiliar mourners were louder than he expected. They hugged each other, they cried. A line waited to drop flowers into the still open grave. A voice jumped out from the crowd, floating high above the others. Some of the mourners stopped, turned to look in the direction of the woman singing.

It was a sad song. He didn't know it, couldn't repeat

it. Wouldn't want to. A low-life song, sung by a wicked woman mourning a wastrel who wouldn't be missed. He looked up at his father. That's what Father would say.

"Stupid." He dropped the last bit of the leaf and tried to grab Father's hand. Father shook him off.

"Cowboy?" Mother's voice startled them both. "What are you doing?"

"Oh, nothing, dear, we came across another funeral." He turned away, waved dismissively back at the group behind them.

"Oh, those poor people. We should show our respects."

She made as if to walk closer, but Father grabbed her. "Don't go there, Noodle." His voice held a note of warning, but Mother didn't seem scared. She seemed angry.

"What have you been saying? What have you been telling our son?" Her eyes were the driest he'd seen them all day. Maybe anger was good for her.

"Father was saying the cemetery never should have let this kind—"

He didn't get to finish his sentence. Mother grabbed his hand and pulled him around. He lost his footing and put his other hand out to catch himself. "Don't you repeat that nonsense. Don't you say things like that."

He chased after her as best he could, one hand still trapped in her vise of a grip. She didn't go far. She stopped. Took a deep breath. Another ragged breath. The tears were returning. Her anger must be fading. She turned back to Father.

"Cowboy?" Her voice was pleading now. No longer angry. Not even sad. "We've talked about this. You're better than this."

He'd approached her, took her free hand in his. "I know, Noodle, I'm so sorry. I didn't say much, I promise."

She glanced down at him, a smile flitting across her face, then disappearing into the creases around her eyes.

"You understand that that family has as much right to be here as we do, right, darling?"

He'd nodded. He'd only been trying to help. He shot an angry glance at Father, but Father only had eyes for Mother. They'd moved closer together, Father putting his arms around Mother's shoulders.

"Come on, Noodle. Peanut. It's a hard day today, we need to go home."

Father had always denied himself to Mother. Pretended to be something he wasn't.

Not him. He didn't need to hide. He had no hidden hatreds. No biases. He was better than that. Smarter than that. He'd taken charge of his life. Become a success.

Father would be proud. If he were alive.

CHAPTER TWENTY-EIGHT

A CROWD OF locals packed the South Philly diner, green and black hoodies, jackets, and jerseys filling the place and spilling out onto the sidewalk. It was a home game that weekend and fans were just warming up. Adam joined Matt and Pete waiting on the pavement outside, staring down the row house-lined street as they waited their turn for a seat inside.

A few doors down, two women sat out on a stoop, sipping beer and chatting with each other and with neighbors who passed by. They hadn't let the fall weather stop their usual entertainment, but had bundled up in layers of sweatshirts and blankets. Adam knew the residents of this neighborhood would be sitting out on their stoops as long as they could, well into winter, until heavy snowstorms forced them inside. The smell of burgers on a grill carried over the air, some fans barbecuing their own, even at this time of year, instead of waiting for a table in the diner.

Adam shifted his weight back and forth, his hands deep in his pockets. Standing out in a graveyard built up his appetite, apparently. And got his mind spinning. Pete used the time to tell Matt about the funeral. Adam kept his eyes on the street, his thoughts on Ian Heyward.

He felt a nudge as Pete stepped next to him. Matt had gone inside to see how much longer they had to wait.

"Pete."

Pete waited a three-count before speaking, collecting his thoughts perhaps. Or working up his anger again. "I'm sorry, okay?"

Not what Adam was expecting. He turned to look at his partner. Pete's head was bent forward, his gaze on the cracked sidewalk, but even from this angle Adam could see the worry lines across his forehead and around his eyes.

"Why didn't you call me, buddy? Why keep me out?"

Pete shrugged, looked back up the street, then in the diner. Anywhere but directly at Adam. "I knew I had to report what I found, you know that."

"And?"

Pete finally looked him in the eye. "Look, this was hard for me, too, okay? It came up at briefing. I reported out. Captain said we had to bring her in."

It wasn't good enough. It didn't explain. Adam shook his head but said nothing.

Pete continued, "Denardi brought her in. He went and picked her up. I couldn't go."

"You didn't even have the courage to do it yourself?" Adam felt his heat rising but didn't care. "What the hell happened to you, man? What were you thinking?"

"I don't know, all right? I just... I'm not thinking straight on this one." He turned back to Adam, his eyes pleading for understanding. "I needed to stay away, to keep out of it."

Adam kind of understood what Pete meant, but it wasn't enough. He knew that Pete had to follow the same rules he did. And that Pete was just as torn about it. Sometimes staying out of the way was the best thing to do. But not this time.

"Don't do that again, right?" Adam looked Pete squarely in the eye. "Right?"

Pete nodded, pursing his lips. "I need your help on this, Adam."

"Nah, you're a good cop, you know that." Adam said, trying to act calm. Despite his growing fear. If Pete couldn't handle this case, then Julia really was screwed.

"It's not that. I know. But we're a team for a reason, you know? We work better together."

"No kidding." Adam grinned. "Of course we work better as a team. That's what I've been trying to tell you, you jackass."

Pete let out a breath, not quite a laugh, but his shoulders relaxed a little. Adam glanced back as Matt came out of the diner door. "So we'll work on this together, then?"

"I think that's a very good idea, partner."

"What is?" Matt asked.

"Teamwork," Adam answered, then changed the topic. "Hey, so get this, I just learned about a portrait of my great-grandfather. I'm going to go take a look at it tomorrow."

"What, on display somewhere?" Pete asked the question but didn't seem particularly interested. His focus was still on the case, clearly.

"You're taking the day off?" Matt grinned. "I thought cops worked until a case was solved."

"I'm not on the case, remember? I'm on shift work now."

"You could use the time, though," Pete said. "Talk to the Ryan-Mills brothers again?"

Adam frowned as he nodded, considering the suggestion. "Yeah, I could drop in on them in the morning."

Pete punched Matt in the shoulder. "It's the guys on the lowest rung of the ladder who work through the night, buddy, and around here that's you, right?"

Matt laughed. "Tell me again about the funeral. What'd I miss?"

Adam was glad to see Matt take the dig well. Maybe there was hope for him yet. Adam stepped back as Pete and Matt launched back into another review of what little they knew so far.

BY THE TIME their table was ready, they'd finished rehashing what they already knew and were moving into the realm of prediction and guessing. Adam ordered a pastrami sandwich from the waitress who approached them, then settled into the booth.

"Was it the same killer?" Pete asked as he stacked the menus next to the napkin holder on the cracked Formica tabletop.

"I don't think so." Adam shook his head, his gaze on the house across the street, still visible despite the grime accumulated on the thick window. "It makes sense to me that Ian Heyward killed Ryan-Mills, then Roc Lubrano killed Heyward."

"Why?" Adam and Pete both turned to look at Matt, who went on, "I mean, why would Heyward kill Ryan-Mills? And why would Lubrano kill Heyward?"

"I can't answer the first part. Yet," Adam acknowledged. "But Lubrano's motives? God only knows. I think that man would kill just because someone looked at him wrong. Could be because he was mad that Heyward took the judge out of the equation. Could be that Heyward was more of a threat now that the judge was gone — now that his former colleagues may be more willing to revisit that injunction. Either makes a good motive."

Matt nodded as Adam spoke, but Pete shook his head. "Doesn't sit right for me."

"Which part?"

Adam looked up as their food was delivered, and they paused in conversation as the waitress handed out the dishes. Adam and Pete swapped plates as she turned to walk away, not noticing she'd gotten their orders mixed up.

"I don't believe Heyward killed Ryan-Mills," Pete explained as he added salt and pepper to his Italian hoagie. "Look, I met the man, I interviewed him. He's not a killer."

Adam couldn't disagree with Pete's assessment. "I

175

hear you, partner, I talked to him, too. I didn't take him for the type, either. But he's involved in the museum world, he'd have access to an art dealer, maybe a crooked one. And he does have a record."

Pete waved his hand, pieces of shredded lettuce descending onto the table from his hoagie like little green snowflakes. "Destruction of private property? No way, that's not even close to the same level. Uh-uh."

"Okay." Adam spoke as he chewed. "Other motives then. Money? Always a good option." He'd intended that to be the first of a list of possible motives, but stopped when Matt started choking on his cheesesteak. "You okay, buddy?"

Matt nodded as he took a sip of water. "You mentioned money. Ryan-Mills certainly had plenty of it. That could definitely be a motive. His sons inherit, right?"

"And Harry does seem to like the finer things in life, no doubt," Pete agreed.

"So we look at the financial angle. See if anyone else benefits from the death. Grace Evans' name keeps coming up in connection with Ryan-Mills' money." Adam grabbed a napkin and wiped a dribble of Russian dressing from his chin.

"And Marcus Cory is hiding something, that's for sure." Pete said. "I'll check out the financial angle."

"You can do that, right?" Matt asked, looking a little worried. "Pull the victim's bank statements, I mean?"

"Sure." Pete smiled, a questioning look in his eyes. "That's pretty routine in a case like this."

"Good, good." Matt looked like he was about to say more but a roar rose from a group on the far side of the diner, blocking out his words. One man in a black and green jacket stood, waving his hands above his head. The rest of the group cheered and laughed, eventually pulling him back down into his seat.

"All right, we'll look into Ryan-Mills' money, Harry's inheritance. But I still like Roc for Heyward's death."

Adam finished the last of his sandwich and pushed his plate away, wiping his fingers on his already greasy napkin.

"I get that. I do," Pete agreed. "We'll know more once we get the medical examiner's report on Heyward's death."

Adam nodded. "Good, hopefully there'll be something there to point to Roc."

"Or to whoever killed him, right?" Pete laughed. "We're not jumping to conclusions here, are we?"

Adam grinned at his partner. "I'm considering possibilities, that's all. Just talking, okay? Like maybe Roc thought Heyward killed the judge, Roc got it wrong and took out the wrong guy."

"Huh." Matt looked up. "There's an idea."

The waitress dropped the bill on the table, and the three men stood, pulling on their coats and making their way to the register near the door.

"So we've got some ideas?" Matt asked as Pete paid the bill, having lost the coin toss with Adam.

"Or we're back where we started." Adam nodded. "It was the same killer and he killed them both."

"Because of the casinos?"

"Or because of something we haven't figured out yet." Adam's tone was somber. It was helpful to toss around ideas like this, but of course Pete was right, he wasn't about to jump to any conclusions without evidence. Maybe his conversation with the Ryan-Mills brothers tomorrow would help shed more light on the motives at play.

Pete followed them out into the bright, chilly afternoon, the heavy glass door swinging shut behind them as another outcry erupted from the group in the back.

CHAPTER TWENTY-NINE

ADAM PASSED A rack of thick cotton shirts, a few leather and canvas bags stacked on a shelf, on his way to the counter to order a coffee. He couldn't tell if the place was a clothing store that sold coffee or a cafe that sold clothes and sundries. Either way, he knew from previous visits the espresso was good.

With the small cup in his hand, he turned to find Sylvia settled deep into a soft couch along one wall, bracketed on either side with shelves of soaps, candles, and jewelry. He lowered himself onto the sofa next to her, impressed, as always, by the ingenuity of Philly entrepreneurs. Anything to make a buck, and there was nothing wrong with that. Usually.

"Sorry I'm late, I got here as soon as I could."

She didn't look up from the magazine. "Jim just left, you missed him."

"I'm sorry." He meant it. He'd been looking forward to another opportunity to talk with Dr. Murdsen, to pick his brain about the illegal art trade in Philadelphia. Sylvia's call to let him know she was meeting with Murdsen again had been a pleasant surprise. He just hadn't had enough time to get up here from the diner in South Philly.

"Thank you for trying, anyway. I appreciate you coming around on this." He tried to catch her eye. "For agreeing to help."

178

"Do not misunderstand me, Adam." She snapped the magazine shut and looked over at him. Maybe it was better when her focus was elsewhere. "I don't want you involved in any investigation when you're not supposed to be, doing things in secret, ignoring the work you're supposed to be doing."

"Then why'd you meet with Jim?"

"Jim called me, asked me to meet. It wasn't my idea."

Adam took a sip of his espresso, sweet the way he liked it. "I wonder why he kept on it. He'd already told me his contact wasn't willing to talk."

Sylvia shrugged and tossed the magazine onto the worn table in front of them. "I suppose he feels bad that he wasn't much help before. He's still trying to find someone who will talk to you about the statue."

"Julia's statue."

Sylvia nodded, tightlipped, disapproval seeping through every movement.

"Pete asked for my help on this. Just now, when I met up with him."

"So are you back on the case then?"

The hope he saw in her expression hurt more than it helped. He couldn't lie to her. "No, not officially. But Pete agrees with me, we need to work on it together. Like we always do. As a team."

"I suppose that's something," she admitted with reluctance.

Adam seized the moment of goodwill. "So will you tell me what Jim Murdsen was so eager to share with you?"

"Do you promise you'll only share this with Pete? To help him, as he asked?"

"How can I promise that when I don't even know what you're going to tell me?"

"Just agree that you won't go chasing off after some new idea on your own."

Adam took a moment to finish his coffee, then looked around the shop. They had some nice shirts here.

He'd have to come back sometime.

"Adam?"

"I promise." He couldn't look her in the eye as he said it, knowing perfectly well that he wouldn't be bound by his words. He would do what he had to do. God, he hated lying to her.

"Thank you. I'm glad that Pete wants your help now. This way, you can talk with him, share information, and not get yourself in trouble. Right?"

"Sure. Whatever."

"And then we can think about the future. Isn't that what you want?"

The sudden turn in the conversation caught him by surprise. "What future?"

She took a sharp breath, leaned away from him. "What does that mean?"

"How can we sit here talking about our future when Julia's still a prime suspect in a murder investigation? What, you want to start house hunting or something?"

"You don't need to overreact." She turned away from him as she spoke, adjusting on the seat so her body faced the front of the store. "I just meant we could think about us. Our relationship. Where we're going."

He couldn't believe what he was hearing. Of course he thought about their future. All the time. But now was not the time to discuss it. "Look, let's focus on the present for now, okay? Let's get Julia's problems sorted out."

"And then we can talk about ours?" She asked the question dismissively, as if she already knew the answer. "Never mind, don't worry. Jim didn't really have all that much to say, anyway."

"Why'd he want to meet?"

"Just to let me know he was still working on it. He spoke with his friend again, the art dealer?"

"The one who won't talk with the cops."

Sylvia smiled. "He does make some strange friends in his business, I'm sure. He has worked with the FBI on a number of occasions."

She sipped her coffee, apparently already over whatever emotion had made her ask about their future. He really didn't understand the way she thought sometimes, how she moved from one topic to the next. She wasn't wrong, though, to think about it. He started picturing their future together. Imagined her holding his child. Their child. He smiled, shook his head, and brought his mind back to the present. Sylvia was talking again.

"Jim told me a little bit about the type of people who are involved in the black market for art."

"Like what?"

"Did you know that even if a piece is worth a million dollars, it can only be sold for five percent, maybe ten percent of that value on the black market?"

"Makes sense. Once it's hot, its value has got to drop." The dollar value on the street. Not the actual value, the historic or cultural value. These people were selling off masterpieces as if they were knock-offs.

"He told me about one man who was finally arrested, someone who'd purchased so many stolen works."

"Art?"

"Art, artifacts. Historical pieces from museums, cultural artifacts." Sylvia shook her head in awe. "Apparently they are all for sale."

"How'd they catch the guy?"

"He made a foolish mistake. He tried to buy something from an undercover agent."

"Seems stupid."

"Jim said the man was so rich and so bored he'd become careless. Perhaps he enjoyed the risk, the danger."

Adam knew the type. The spoiled rich boy whose life had become too secure, too easy. Someone who needed to find excitement somewhere, anywhere.

"Jim also said that sometimes these men and women, the people who purchase the stolen art, have them on display in their homes."

"Out in the open? They'd have to be careful who they invite over."

"Perhaps. But if no one knows what they are, or that they're stolen... I don't know." Sylvia shook her head. "Who would collect illegal art? Why go through all that?"

"They're greedy, pure and simple. They look for ways to make themselves feel better about themselves, even if it's in secret. It's not necessarily about letting other people know, more about knowing themselves."

"Art... money... all the things we work so hard for. To acquire." She shook her head again, and Adam could see the images she was conjuring in her mind. The collections of fine art, the displays of antiquities. Items that had great value, sure, but Adam knew they were still just things.

"It's not all it's cracked up to be, you know? It's like that saying, all that glitters isn't really gold. You think you know what you want, but it may not give you the satisfaction you were expecting."

Sylvia smiled. "Are you talking about me now? About my dreams for our future?"

He took her hand. "*Our* dreams for our future. Remember that. Hey, I have an idea. Will you come with me to the library tomorrow?"

She laughed. "The library? That's not a very romantic date."

"I know, but this should be interesting. I want to find a painting."

"Another stolen work of art?"

"Not this one, at least... well, to be honest, I have no idea. But it's a picture of my great-grandfather."

"Oh! That is exciting. And it's on display?"

"I don't know that either. I just know it was hanging in the library about forty years ago when my dad was in school."

"A mystery of your own to solve, is that it? That is

good. I will be happy to join you in this investigation."

CHAPTER THIRTY

A WIDE BANK of windows offered an expansive view of Washington Square below. From here, Adam could see not only the square, but also the tower of Independence Hall. Beyond that, the Customs House and a glint of sunlight on the river.

He turned back to the men standing staring at him.

"You weren't honest with me, Detective Kaminski. Or should I call you Mr. Kaminski?" Harry Ryan-Mills stood with his feet apart, his hands on his hips.

"I am a detective, Mr. Ryan-Mills. I didn't lie to you." Lying was wearying business, and Adam was sick of it. But he needed to fight on. He needed to find the truth. He turned to include the other man in his statement.

"My partner has the lead in the case, that's probably why they told you at the precinct that you needed to talk to him, not me."

"Hmph," Harry continued, not looking at his brother. "They told me you weren't on the case at all. Imagine my surprise."

"Look, I'm sorry. I'm not even supposed to be on duty today, it's Sunday." At least that part was true, he wasn't on duty. "Like I said, my partner, Pete Lawler, has the lead. In fact, I think you've both spoken to him."

"Yes, we have." Harry's voice still carried a note of suspicion, but he nevertheless turned to the other man. "I don't think you've met my brother yet, Detective.

184

Tom?"

Thomas gave his brother a nasty look and stuck out a hand. "Thomas Ryan-Mills, Detective. Pleasure to meet you."

Adam could pick out the hints of a Chicago accent as the man spoke. "You've lived out of this area for some time now?"

Thomas nodded. "Moved to Chicago for college and never came back. Met my wife, had children." He kept nodding as he talked.

Adam glanced around the apartment as he listened. The walls were dotted with oil paintings that, to Adam's untrained eye, looked expensive. Jim Murdsen might have a different opinion. A variety of statues covered different surfaces. In some ways, it reminded Adam of Julia's loft. A much more expensive, fashionable version, anyway.

"Are all of these items your father's?"

Harry frowned. "I have started bringing some of my own possessions in, actually."

"Oh? Are you moving in?"

Thomas frowned but didn't speak. Harry just nodded, adding, "Despite what Ms. Evans next door might want."

A photo across the room caught Adam's attention. There was something vaguely familiar and comforting about it. He crossed the room to take a look, Harry's and Thomas' eyes following him closely.

"My mother." Harry pulled the print out of Adam's hand, but not before he'd had a chance to get a better look. A blond, willowy, very thin woman smiled out from the silver frame, the wind blowing her hair. "She wasn't as frail as she looked, you know."

Adam turned to Harry, who placed the photograph back, exactly where it had been before. "No? Want to tell me about her?"

Harry nodded and slid into the large leather chair at the end of the room. Adam and Thomas took seats on the matching sofa and love seat, like an audience for Harry to address. Harry was already taking control of the apartment, it seemed.

"She was only sixty when she died. Far too young. My father didn't know what to do without her."

"They were married long?"

Thomas nodded but Harry answered. "To the great surprise of his family. She was from a different background, a lower middle-class background. She was working on campus when Oliver went to school — undergrad and law school at Penn, as you know. They met, fell in love, she stopped working. But she never lost that need to save, to prepare for retirement, to save something to leave for her sons. It was important to her that they leave an inheritance for their sons. For us."

"And after she died, your father's priorities changed?"

Thomas snorted but waited for Harry to respond.

Harry's mouth narrowed into a twisted frown. "You're not kidding."

"He was just living his life, you have to understand." Thomas spoke like he was trying to convince himself as well as Adam. "Looking for something to replace her, I'm sure. He didn't mean any harm by it. But he needed help, guidance."

Adam let their answer hang in the air for a moment before switching tack. "So were you staying here with your father before he died?" Adam addressed his question to Harry.

"No, I have my own place. And before you ask, I was home alone the night my father died. No one can corroborate that. In case you were wondering."

"Surely he was killed because of his involvement in the casino fight, wasn't he?" Thomas was really looking worried now.

"Might be. We're certainly looking into that."

"I think you should be looking a little closer to home, Detective." Harry wagged his head to indicate the apartment next door.

"You said Ms. Evans wanted to buy this condo, is that right?"

"Yep, she still does. Offered me a pretty penny for it." Harry looked around, tapping his hands lightly on the leather arms of his chair. "But I think I might stay here for a while."

Thomas frowned again. He looked away from Harry, took a deep breath, and turned back to him, but Harry cut him off.

"You don't mind, do you Tom?" Harry seemed to surprise himself by asking the question.

Thomas let out his breath. "No, no of course not."

Harry lifted his chin, folded his hands across his lap. "Yes, you need to focus your investigation on Ms. Evans. Look at her other dead husbands. Isn't that suspicious enough?"

"Your father wasn't her husband."

"And maybe that's why she killed him."

"She knew him better than we did, in a way." Thomas looked down at his hands as he spoke.

"How so?"

"She spent more time with him. I should have come back more often. I live so far away."

"Do you think your father confided in Ms. Evans?"

"No way." Harry was adamant.

Thomas was less certain. "Maybe. I don't know. He did talk about her occasionally."

"I am curious to learn more about Ms. Evans. She's not too eager to talk to me, though." Adam glanced at Harry. "I don't suppose you can help me with that?"

GRACE OPENED the door promptly after Harry's first knock. She wore a pale cashmere cardigan over loose silk trousers that flattered her gray complexion. She smiled when she saw Harry, who preyed on her expectations.

"Grace, good afternoon. I wanted to talk to you about

the apartment."

"Excellent, excellent. I'm glad to hear it. Please, come in."

She stepped back from the door to usher Harry in. As he stepped in, he added, "And I brought along a friend."

"What?" She turned back and her face closed as she saw Adam. "Oh, no." She reached for the door, but Adam had already stepped through.

"I'm sorry, Ms. Evans. I'm trying to find the truth about what happened to Oliver Ryan-Mills and I believe you can help."

She turned her back on him and walked to the far side of the room, picking up a wrap from the sofa as she walked and arranging it over her shoulders. The apartment was a mirror image of the one he had just left. Floor to ceiling windows looked out over Washington Square and the view beyond, though in this apartment thick filigree curtains draped around the windows while thinner sheer lace covered the glass, filtering both the light and the view. Everything about the apartment was plush, from the thick Oriental rug that cushioned his steps to the heavy mahogany furniture that filled every empty space to the rich tapestries that dotted the walls between oil paintings in ornately wrought frames. To the woman who stood with her back to him, her shoulders draped in a white fur wrap, an odd choice for something to wear around the house.

"Your colleagues were just here. Or perhaps not your colleagues, since they are actually on the case. And you're not." Grace looked back at Adam triumphantly.

"It's true." Adam nodded. "I'm not. But I am involved in this. It's personal."

She almost smiled at this, as if expecting it. "How so?"

"My sister is a suspect."

"Aha, I see." Grace turned back to the center of the long room and took a seat on the red silk sofa.

Harry did not react as smoothly, letting out a gasp he

tried to turn into a cough. "Your sister? But... how? I mean, what...?" He looked back and forth between Grace and Adam as if seeking an explanation, but Adam chose not to provide one, letting Harry splutter about for a moment longer.

Grace watched Harry with amusement, then turned back to Adam, her smile fading. She hadn't invited him or Harry to sit. "And why do you think I can help with your investigation?" Her expression looked as if asking those words brought the taste of bitter lemon to her tongue.

Adam stayed standing. "I think there are things about Oliver Ryan-Mills you're not telling me. And I don't know why."

She nodded once, then looked away, her gaze focusing on one of the red and gold wall hangings to her left. It looked Asian to Adam's eye, perhaps a memento of a long-ago trip. Shiny strands of gold threaded their way in and out of the dark weave, adding a hint of light and amusement to an image of a kimono-draped woman standing alone, looking out over a gray and wild sea.

"You knew him well, I think," Adam continued. "Tell me, did he often walk at that time of the morning?"

Her tight smile returned but she kept her gaze on the wall hanging. "Oddly, sometimes he did. He was a little strange that way. I think he didn't sleep well. He enjoyed the peace and quiet he encountered on his early morning walks."

Adam nodded. A regular habit; that was helpful, an opening. "Who else knew he was likely to do that?"

Harry stepped forward as he answered the question Adam had posed to Grace. "Nobody else knew that. Nobody beyond us, that is." His eyes narrowed as he looked down at Grace, his expression one of pure malice. Adam was taken aback by the strength of venom in his attitude to her. He hadn't been expecting that.

"That's true, nobody else." Grace nodded her agreement. "Unless, of course, someone else was in a similar habit and often ran into him."

"Bah." Harry dismissed the suggestion with a wave of his hand. "You wanted his money, Grace. His apartment. Admit it."

Grace's expression tightened, but she didn't rise to the insult, simply gripped her hands tighter on her lap and looked expectantly at Adam.

Adam moved on to his next question. "Did either of you recognize the statue?"

"What statue?" Grace asked, looking back and forth between the men standing in front of her.

"I'm sorry to have to show you this." Adam reached a hand into his inside coat pocket and retrieved the photograph he had shown to Jim Murdsen a few days earlier. "This is a photograph of the statue. This was used as the murder weapon, to kill Oliver Ryan-Mills."

Grace shuddered and shut her eyes, and Adam thought she might refuse to look at it. He set the photograph down on the polished table in front of her and took a step back. She took one deep breath and opened her eyes, looking first up at Adam, who nodded encouragingly, then down at the photo.

Adam saw the light of recognition in her eyes. "What do you see?"

"Well... I can't be sure." She looked away. At the windows. Then at Harry. Then back at the wall hanging that had drawn her attention earlier.

"What is it, Grace?"

She stood and moved back to the far side of the room, glancing once more at Harry, then away. "No, no, I could be wrong. I don't see as well as I used to." She leaned over and picked up a pair of pale gray reading glasses, the first that Adam had seen of them. Was she too vain to wear them in public, or did she really not need them?

When she turned back to Adam, her attitude had changed. The personality Adam had grown accustomed to had returned. The personality he had dared to hope he could break through.

"I've never seen that statue before, Detective. And I have no idea why you are in my apartment, deigning to interview me over something as disgusting as a murder. I had nothing to do with this, and I have nothing further to say to you." She raised her chin as she spoke, and a gleam in her eye showed her emotion. "Much good you've done on this case so far, anyway. Poor Ian."

"Yes, that was a tragedy, ma'am. But it may or may not be related to this case."

"Not related. Hah." She waved a hand, then grabbed at her fur wrap as it threatened to dislodge itself from around her shoulders. "You expect two murders of my neighbors in a few days not to be related? You must resolve this. Quickly."

"I will," Adam answered, amused that now she seemed to want him on the case.

"Good. But you will do so without my help. Now get out. Marcus!"

Marcus appeared silently through a doorway, as if he'd been standing there, waiting for his cue. He crossed the room and opened the door. "Detective."

Adam paused, hoping to come up with the question or the statement that would get through to her, crack her open and encourage her to reveal her true thoughts. To share what she really knew about Oliver Ryan-Mills. About the statue. About the killer.

But she remained silent and no brilliant question came to his mind. He thanked her for her time and followed Marcus into the hallway.

Harry was nowhere to be seen. Marcus glided along the hall ahead of him toward the elevator.

"You must know a lot about what goes on in this building, with the people who live around here?"

"How do you mean?" Marcus didn't turn around as he spoke, but his finger faltered before he pushed the button to call the elevator.

"I imagine you see a lot. Overhear a lot. Like my

conversation with Ms. Evans now. About the murder weapon."

Marcus slid his eyes toward Adam but didn't turn his head. "I may hear things, Detective, but I don't gossip about them."

Adam held out the photo of the statue, which he had folded back into his pocket. "Do you recognize this?"

Marcus didn't even blink. "I've never seen that before, no sir." He pushed the button for the elevator.

"If you know something about this investigation, you have to tell me."

"Do I? I understand you're not on the case. That, in fact, your sister is a potential suspect." Marcus' face didn't change, his voice and expression cool as ever, despite the admission that he'd overheard everything.

The elevator doors slid open.

"Good day, sir. Please call ahead next time you'd like to visit. I'll try to schedule you onto Grace's calendar."

CHAPTER THIRTY-ONE

ADAM TURNED AT the echo of footsteps approaching fast across the marble lobby. The doorman stood passively staring at something just out of sight through the building's glass sliding doors.

Thomas Ryan-Mills kept up his pace until he was shoulder to shoulder with Adam. He glanced at the doorman, who now appeared to be studying something on the tall podium behind which he stood. Thomas nodded at Adam. "Walk with me?"

Adam followed him out, buttoning up his cashmere coat as they walked, tucking his red scarf under the collar.

"How can I help you, Thomas?"

"I just... I haven't been here in a while, you know?"

Adam nodded. "Chicago."

"Chicago. Yes." He stared across the square as they walked, looking out toward the Veriatus, which loomed on a far corner. Once a sandstone giant, it was now dwarfed by the towering metal and glass apartment buildings that encircled the square.

"I should have come home more often. It's just... after Mom died..."

Adam nodded, thinking. Remembering the photo of Sarah Ryan-Mills in the apartment upstairs. A strong, independent woman with a frail appearance.

Neither man spoke as they continued their walk,

crossing behind the memorial wall and the eternal flame, the wall masking the spot where Oliver Ryan-Mills had died.

"I miss my mother, Detective. I mean, don't get me wrong, I miss my father, too. But he was... I don't know, it was like he was finding himself. After my mother died, I mean."

"How so?"

Thomas shook his head as he spoke, as if trying to put an emotion into words. Words he couldn't quite find. "He was doing so many new things. Travel. Dinner clubs. Wine clubs. Fishing clubs. He never had those hobbies before."

"It sounds to me like he didn't do a lot of things before." Adam thought about his own father, busier in retirement than he had been when he was working. It wasn't an unusual turn of events, a person finding new interests and new friends as his life changed direction. "Some people do pick up hobbies after they retire."

"That's true." Thomas sucked in his lips, his eyes on the path in front of them. "But I think this was more about my mother dying, not being there anymore to keep an eye on him."

"So Grace Evans...?"

"Hah. My father did like her, as I told you. They spent quite a lot of time together. But would he marry her? I don't know, maybe. I think he was looking for someone who would do these new, fun things with him. Someone not like my mother, you know?" He glanced sideways at Adam.

"So if he was seriously considering her, Grace had no reason to kill him."

Thomas shuddered. "What a horrible job you have, Detective. I may say things about people, judge them even. But not because I think they would actually murder someone, no."

"And Harry?"

Thomas smiled. "Harry. What about Harry?"

"He stayed in town, he didn't leave. Did he spend a lot of time with your father?"

Thomas shrugged. "He spent time telling him not to go out so much. Not to spend so much money. Which was pretty hypocritical, in my opinion."

"Oh?"

"He has very expensive tastes, my brother Harry."

"Such as?"

"Oh, trinkets he collects, artwork, photographs. He finds things in the oddest places. I assume it's all legal." Thomas laughed. When he saw Adam looking at him, he stopped laughing.

"I'm sure it is all legal, Detective. I'm not suggesting…"

"I understand, Thomas. But it is interesting to get your perspective on your brother."

"He's a character, that's for sure. He knows what he likes, knows what he wants, and is willing to do just about anything to get it." He cut himself off again, holding up one hand. "Within reason, Detective, within reason."

"Why did you want to talk with me, Thomas?"

Thomas stared out across the square, his eyes following a small black poodle as it chased a ball and brought it back to its owner, who scooped it up and threw it again. Around and around, back and forth. Adam waited a little longer, then repeated his question.

"Right, sorry." Thomas cleared his throat. "Harry told me what you said to Grace Evans. About your sister, I mean."

Adam bit his lip. He should never have let that slip. He wasn't used to working a case where he was so personally involved. His judgment was failing him. "And?"

"Families, huh?" Thomas gave a weak smile, more a crinkling of his lips and eyes than anything else. "We can't choose our families. Please remember that."

They had almost completed a full lap around the

square at this point, the memorial wall coming back into view to their left. Adam stopped walking and turned to Thomas, doing his best to keep his face a mask. He'd let enough slip already about his personal involvement in this. He had no intention of sharing anything more. But gaining information didn't always require sharing.

"You seem like there's something you want to tell me. Is that right? About your family?"

Thomas nodded and looked at the ground. Shuffled his feet a bit, then looked off over Adam's shoulder. "It's just… something about my father you might want to know."

Adam didn't wait as long this time before asking, "What is it, Thomas? Every little thing can help."

Thomas swallowed, clearly marshaling his emotions as well as his thoughts. "As I said, he was making new friends. Friends my mother wouldn't have liked."

"Such as?"

"I don't know for sure." Thomas straightened the buttons on his coat, pulled a pair of leather gloves out of his pocket and pulled them on as he spoke, as if creating a physical barrier between himself and his words. "My father had certain… well, biases, is the only way to say it."

"I don't understand."

"No?" Thomas looked at Adam with a sad, weak smile. "My father was actually quite a bigoted man, Detective. You may not know that. Before he met my mother, he'd been involved in some political movements. All legitimate, very conservative. Keep America pure, that sort of thing."

"Oh, I see…" Adam considered what Thomas was telling him. This added a new dimension to the case he hadn't anticipated.

"Do you?" Thomas smiled again. "I've spent my whole adult life trying not to be like my father. I'm involved in my local community. I support our church, our community center. My wife and I volunteer at a local soup kitchen every month. I try to give back… to help those who don't have as much as I do."

"That's admirable."

"Yes. And it's a trait I learned from my mother." He looked one more time directly at Adam. "From my mother, not my father."

He gave a light wave and walked briskly back the way they had come. Adam watched him cut across 7th Street and head east, toward the river, toward Society Hill. Walking as fast as he could away from the information he'd just shared about his father.

Whether or not this new information was relevant to the investigation still remained to be seen. For now, Adam filed it away mentally, adding it to the picture developing in his mind of Judge Oliver Ryan-Mills.

Glancing at his watch, he turned toward the Free Library branch on 7th Street. He planned to use the rest of his day off for his own purposes, to learn a little more about his great-grandfather and to spend time with Sylvia, hopefully resolving whatever was tearing into their relationship.

CHAPTER THIRTY-TWO

MATT SAW THE pale gold of Anne's hair as the light hit it, her head turning to greet a fellow parishioner. He took his leave of the elderly man he'd been talking to and worked his way through the crowd leaving the church to catch up to her.

"Anne," he called as got closer. "Afternoon."

"Matt, hi. I didn't think I'd see you today. Don't you usually go to the earlier mass?"

"I'm here today." He smiled. No reason for her to know he'd attended two other masses already that morning, waiting for her. "The flowers look great. You did another wonderful job laying them out."

"We did, you mean." She smiled and touched his hand. He felt the heat climbing up his face and hoped he wasn't blushing.

"Anne, gorgeous displays." A matronly woman pushed up against Anne as she spoke, her giant bosom pushing Anne even closer to Matt. He didn't mind.

"Thanks, Martha. I try."

"You do, dear, you do indeed."

Martha patted her on the arm, then pushed through to the next unsuspecting victim. Anne tried to hide her smile behind her hand, turning back to Matt. "So, how's the investigation going?"

"Ah, that." Matt looked down. This time he was sure he was blushing. He could feel the heat all the way from his face down through his collar.

"Uh-oh, that doesn't sound good." She started to ask a question, but another parishioner approached them, a man who was actively involved in the church himself.

"Anne, beautiful arrangements, thank you. You outdo yourself every week."

"Thank you, I appreciate the kind words." Anne shook his hand. "Matt helps, you know, I don't do it alone."

"Of course, of course. Matt, how are you?" He shook Matt's hand, waved, and took off through the front doors of the church.

Matt and Anne stopped where they were, in the vestibule, watching the rest of the congregation leaving the church.

"So, really, what's wrong?"

Matt took a deep breath, looked back into the church, where a few stray parishioners were still kneeling in the pews. The flowers he'd arranged with Anne earlier that week still bloomed proudly in front of the altar. "I screwed up."

"Oh." Anne looked like she was weighing her options, her head moving from side to side. "So? We all do that, sometimes. Can you fix it?"

He smiled down at her. "Maybe. I haven't really tried."

"Messing up I can understand. But if you know you made a mistake, you have to try to fix it. Don't you?"

"I guess." He looked down at his feet, his familiar uniform boots sticking out below his Sunday trousers. Damn, he still hadn't polished his shoes.

"Look." Anne turned to point to the flower arrangements on either side of the door. "See those vases?"

"Sure, I put them there on Thursday."

"Yes, you did. But they're different now."

"They are?" Matt looked more closely. He had to be honest, he didn't see the difference.

"No?" Anne laughed. "I pulled out the tulips. They used to have peach tulips in each vase. But they were wilting. I left them in because I thought they had enough life in them to make it through the weekend. But I came back on Friday to check, and I was wrong."

"About flowers?" Matt smiled. "I find that hard to believe."

"Everyone makes mistakes, Matt. You just need to fix things when you do, that's all. When I came back on Friday and saw they didn't look good, I pulled them all out. The arrangements are smaller now, but they look better."

Matt looked at the blooms. There was no indication that they weren't exactly as originally arranged. No empty slots where tulips should be. She'd caught her mistake and fixed it, and it looked perfect.

"I hate to admit to them that I made this mistake." He almost whispered the words, ashamed to have to say them out loud.

"Surely admitting it to yourself is the hardest part? Once you accept it, and take steps to fix it, telling other people should be the easy part."

"It's not just that I screwed up. I had a chance to tell them — to tell the detectives on the case what I found. But I didn't. In fact" — he bit his lip and looked down at his hands — "I kind of threw away the evidence." He thought about the ruined bank statement. Sure, Pete could get a copy of Ryan-Mills' statements easy enough, but he should know it was there, on the victim in the square when he was killed. Which was definitely weird.

Anne laughed loudly. That beautiful sound Matt loved to hear. He smiled at her. "Are you laughing at me now?"

"No. Well, sort of. You screwed up, I get it. You're embarrassed, I get it. It happens to all of us."

Matt looked back at the vases without tulips. "I wanted to do a good job on this. To prove that I'm good at this job. That I'm ready to move up."

"And what, now they'll know you're not perfect?"

Matt shrugged, smiled.

"Of course you're not perfect, Matt." Anne put a hand up to touch his face. "Of course you're not perfect. If you were perfect, I wouldn't like you as much as I do."

"Really?" He put his hand over hers.

"You have your whole life ahead of you to learn, to get better. As long as you're willing to learn from your mistakes. Are you?"

CHAPTER THIRTY-THREE

"I DON'T SEE IT." Adam looked around the entire wall space of the library branch. It didn't take long, it wasn't a big room. "The only walls we can't see are in the Asian Interest room, and I can't imagine it's in there."

"No." Sylvia nodded her agreement, herself turning to look at each of the four walls in view.

The Free Library branch in Chinatown had signs posted in English and Mandarin. The entire library seemed to be packed into one room. Each wall boasted signs atop the shelves indicating the books displayed below. African interest, history, geography. The lone reading room off to one side was dedicated to Asian interest. The few paintings that dotted the walls seemed to have been painted by children, maybe those studying at the high school next door.

"Perhaps it has been moved. It's some time since your father found it. He was in high school then, remember?"

"I know." Adam felt his spirits drop with his voice. "I guess I was being a little optimistic." Not just about finding the painting, either, if he was honest with himself. He was hoping this little diversion with Sylvia would help resolve whatever was growing between them.

"Excuse me." Sylvia reached out to grab the arm of a passing librarian. She was moving fast, a pile of books clutched in her arms, and didn't seem too pleased to be stopped. "We're looking for a painting. Can you help us?"

The librarian gave them a quizzical look. "This is a library."

"Yes, we know." Sylvia smiled graciously, demonstrating all her diplomatic skills. "It is rather important, though. Police business, you see. Adam, show her your badge."

Adam felt his face grow red. Sylvia always blurred the boundaries of ethical behavior. He shouldn't be surprised. "Well, it's not really police business." He saw the anger in Sylvia's eyes. "I mean, not officially. Very unofficial…" He let his voice trail off as he pulled out his badge and held it low, so no one else but the librarian could see. "It's really more personal."

"We have reason to believe," Sylvia continued, shooting an aggressive look at Adam, "that a painting is hanging somewhere here in this library."

The librarian balanced her load of books on a nearby table. "Tell me about the painting. What is it? Who's the artist? Our collection isn't large; if it's here, I'll know."

"Thank you." Adam smiled, pocketing his badge. "It's a portrait. From Poland. I know the subject, but not the artist. His name is Kaminski."

"Ah, yes." Her face lit up. "The Polish soldier. Of course. Follow me." She collected her stash of books, which she dumped unceremoniously at the checkout desk before turning to her right. Sylvia and Adam followed her along the wall toward a set of double doors and from there through a doorway marked Staff Only.

A barren flight of stairs led to a hallway on the second floor lined with closed doors, each with a narrow window. Adam tried to peek through the windows as they passed along the hallway, but couldn't make anything out. The librarian pushed open the double doors at the far end.

"Is this it?" She turned triumphantly to Adam and

Sylvia.

They stood in a square conference room, almost filled with a round table. Random, mismatched chairs pushed haphazardly up against the table, with more tucked into each corner of the room. Adam's attention was caught by the painting hanging on the far side of the table.

A gray, almost blue background enticed the eye to focus on the pale face staring back at them. A drawn, narrow face, prominent cheekbones under tired eyes. Sunken cheeks suggested the subject hadn't been eating well, an impression strengthened by the look in his eyes. A haunted, fearful look, his focus on something in his view. Adam had to resist the urge to turn and look over his own shoulder.

"This must be it," Sylvia whispered, pushing some chairs out of her way to pass closer to the picture. "This is your great-grandfather, Adam."

The librarian raised an eyebrow but didn't speak.

Adam coughed to clear his throat. "Sorry, like I said, very unofficial. But thank you for showing us this. I've been looking for it for a while."

He followed Sylvia, peering at the portrait from within a foot or two. Further examination revealed that the man was wearing a soldier's uniform, but no insignia showed on his jacket. The colors of the painting were muted. Grays, browns, blacks, and blues. The pale blue of the man's eyes jumped out of the picture, the only sign of brightness in an otherwise bleak image.

"Do you know anything about this painting?" he asked the librarian without taking his eyes from it.

"No, not really." She had stayed on the far side of the room. "We believe it was painted during World War II. The signature of the artist is there, you see? In the bottom corner?"

Adam and Sylvia both leaned in together, Adam placing his hand on Sylvia's back as they moved. "I see it," she whispered again.

Adam coughed, turned it into a laugh. Why were they

whispering?

"I can't read that." He forced himself to turn away from those bright eyes, to look back at the librarian. "Who's the artist?"

"He's well known. Well, no Picasso or anything. But he has produced some work that received moderate recognition. He was imprisoned during the war, held by the Germans. But only for a little while, a surprisingly short period of time in fact."

"So this painting is probably worth something then, given its provenance?" Sylvia asked.

The librarian smiled sadly. "Oh, we wish it were. We believe the person who donated it to the library thought so. Perhaps he thought it was a generous donation."

"But it's not?" Adam asked, confused.

"It's really not, despite its age."

"Why is that?"

"It's the artist's history, you see. Somewhat dubious." She coughed into her hand, then looked back at them.

"Dubious? As in, you're not really sure if he painted it, if it's a fake?"

"Oh, no, that's clear. Those are his initials, it's clearly his style." She backed toward the door, and Adam and Sylvia reluctantly followed her, Adam taking one more look back at the painting before she pulled the doors shut.

"So what's dubious?" he pressed as they headed back down the stairs.

"It's the artist himself. There are rumors — unsubstantiated, mind you — that he was somehow affiliated with the Nazi party in Germany at the time."

"I thought you said he was imprisoned?" Sylvia asked.

"He was, yes." She nodded thoughtfully. "But so briefly, that alone raises suspicions."

"Is he still alive?" Adam asked.

"I couldn't tell you that, I'm afraid. They looked into the painting when it was donated, to see what it was worth. That's all I know. I haven't followed anything about the painting or the artist since then. At that time, he had settled in Ireland, somewhere near Galway."

It was crazy to think that the political actions of the artist could so negatively affect the value of his painting, but Adam had learned many new things about the fine arts market over the past few days, both the legal and illicit. It seemed like anyone who created something needed to worry about his or her legacy.

They had made it back to the main room of the library, and the librarian was clearly eager to return to her duties, but Adam put a hand out to ask one more question.

"Can you at least tell me who donated it?"

"I'm afraid I can't."

"Surely that can't be confidential information." Sylvia frowned.

"No, of course not, it would be quite public. But it was anonymous, you see. The donation. The donor didn't give his name."

THE WAIL OF the sirens hit Adam as soon as they stepped onto 7th Street. He tensed and reached for his radio, forgetting he was off duty. It didn't matter. His phone rang.

"Sorry to bug you on your day off, Kaminski." Adam recognized the voice of their lead dispatcher. "Murphy's called an all-hands briefing."

"What happened?"

"A beating. Convention delegate was attacked down near South Street."

"Damn."

Sylvia looked over when Adam swore, a question forming in her eyes.

Adam shook his head at her and kept his attention on the phone. "I'll be there. Where and when?"

"Twenty minutes, here at the 6th District."

Adam tucked his phone back in his pocket. "Sorry,

honey, I gotta go back to work."

"Is this about Julia?"

"No, this is the job I'm supposed to be doing. The one I'm actually assigned to."

"Oh, but that's good, right?"

"Not good for the man who just got attacked."

He kissed her and headed up the street without looking back. Their discussion about the future would have to wait. Again.

It took only a few minutes to walk to the precinct headquarters, but it looked like most of the team had already gathered in the squad room when he arrived. Planning for this event had brought together staff from a variety of units and divisions, including Adam. He recognized other homicide detectives, detectives from other divisions, and some familiar faces from his detail to dignitary protection. It was an unlikely gathering, but Inspector Murphy was working closely with Chief Inspector O'Brien of the Investigations Bureau. They would use whatever manpower they could to control the violence that threatened to bring the interfaith convention down.

The windowless conference room wasn't designed for a group this size, and officers stood leaning against the wall, some crouched on the floor, waiting for the briefing to begin. The air smelled of sweat and leather, with a hint of anger seething just below the surface. Things weren't going as planned.

Inspector Tim Murphy, lead for the Tactical Field Support Division, was answering questions from the law enforcement officers gathered there and Adam picked up enough to get a good sense of what had likely happened.

"Witnesses are saying it was a group of drunks. Might even have been kids." Murphy's tone made it clear he didn't believe that for a minute. "Rabbi Newmann is still unconscious, he can't tell us anything."

"Why not? It happens. Could've been drunks,

couldn't it?" a young officer asked.

Detective Hank Burrough, an accomplished veteran on the force, answered him. "To a rabbi? A community leader? Doesn't really fit, does it? You'd expect that if he was the type to hang out in the South Street bars. But this? Nah."

"We're still talking to witnesses." Murphy held up a hand. "We're not taking anything at face value. We'll get at the truth."

"He'll be okay, though, right?" Burroughs asked.

Murphy nodded, looking around the room to see who else he was still waiting for.

"He's a local character," another officer pointed out. "Very outspoken. And actively engaged in planning this interfaith convention, right? So that's gotta have something to do with it."

Murphy nodded. He saw Adam and waved him in. "Kaminski, glad you could join us."

Adam leaned against the wall in the back of the room. As he listened to the questions and heard the information these officers already shared, he was hit with the realization of just how bad it was. And how much he was to blame. He hadn't been spending enough time on this. Pete had warned him this could happen, but he'd ignored the warning.

"So you think his political views weren't a coincidence?" Adam didn't see who had asked this question.

"I find it hard to believe in coincidences right now." Murphy shook his head. "He had strong opinions on U.S.-Israel relations. And we've got a group of neo-Nazis in town, protesting, causing problems. You think that's a coincidence?"

Adam looked around the room. He saw a group of exhausted men and women who'd been working around the clock. Making plans, working with federal agencies. Attending meetings, writing extra reports. They were already stretched thin as it was, and this convention was bringing even more whackos to town and bringing more law enforcement agencies into the mix. Now they were working overtime, policing the crowds growing in the city, and still trying to stay in the loop with external agencies.

Murphy checked the clock on the wall. "Okay, let's get started. Jeremy, you're running this one."

Murphy took a seat while his deputy stood and started walking the group through the events of that afternoon. Where and when the attack had taken place. What they all thought about the real motives behind the crime. He laid out the plans for the investigation of the attack, assigning duties, reminding them that the detectives assigned to the south division of the bureau would be taking the lead on the investigation. The detectives gathered there needed to focus more on prevention. On making sure this didn't happen again.

Adam couldn't help but think about how it could have been prevented. Maybe if they'd had one more cop out on the street, keeping an eye on the neighborhood, instead of spending time on someone else's case.

These were good people. Good cops. Adam was letting them down, chasing after an investigation that Pete could handle. Even if he didn't realize it.

He needed to focus on what was important. Help Pete, connect Pete to Jim Murdsen, like Sylvia said. But he needed to help Murphy and his team as best he could. Before anyone else got hurt.

CHAPTER THIRTY-FOUR

MONDAY MORNINGS were rarely good. This week proved to be no exception. Adam started his day at the precinct headquarters with the intention of focusing on the community maps he was developing for the convention prep. His plans, however, were cut short by a call from Captain Farrow's assistant.

He went to Captain Farrow's office as soon as he was summoned. He didn't invite Mark Little this time. He didn't doubt what the topic would be, and if he was going to convince Farrow he was following orders now, he needed to do it himself, not through his union rep.

"Why are you doing this, Kaminski?" Farrow looked like his Monday was starting out as badly as Adam's, though his expression held more sadness than anger as he leaned forward over the desk, his arms crossed in front of him.

He didn't bother with any pleasantries and didn't even bother explaining what Adam had done wrong. It could only be one thing. Word of Adam's involvement in the investigation must have come through. Again. Last time he'd gotten a warning; no way he'd get off so easy this time.

Adam wasn't sure what he could offer in his defense, other than the truth. "I'm trying to help Pete, Captain. That's all. To help solve this."

"And you think Lawler needs your help? That's pretty

arrogant."

"It's not that he needs my help. That's not what I'm saying." Adam searched for the words that would express how his experience could be an asset. How his unique perspective could open new ideas and new possibilities. To explain his physical need to be part of the investigation. He couldn't find those words. "I've been digging, that's all. Just helping out. But I'm working full-time for Murphy now, you gotta believe me."

"A little late for that, Kaminski. And all for what — to clear your sister's good name, is that it?"

Adam saw the understanding in the captain's eyes, but saw the anger growing there as well, displacing whatever friendlier emotions the captain had been trying to hold onto. Anger he was trying very hard to control.

"Isn't that enough? Look, I've got a good rapport with the neighbors, with the sons, with the park ranger who's helping on the case. I know the area, I know the people, and I can help."

"I told you to stay away, Kaminski. For a good reason. Your involvement compromises the investigation. Anything Pete finds that you were involved with is immediately suspect. Why don't you get that? You're making it worse, not better."

He ignored the wisdom in Captain Farrow's words, ignored the fact that he understood everything the captain was saying. "I'm getting a good picture of the victim. I think I understand the motive here."

"Yeah, and what's that?"

Adam almost winced as he said what was in his mind, knowing how it would sound. "I think it's his legacy."

Farrow stared at him for half a minute, shaking his head. "What does that even mean?"

"This guy, this judge. He made a lot of decisions when he was on the bench, some of them he didn't want to live with anymore. Some he was trying to change. Like the casinos."

"So you think his fight against the casinos is the key

here."

"Not just that. It's not only his legacy from his time on the bench. But also who he was as a man. What he left behind for his sons."

"So, money then? You think this is about the inheritance?"

Adam felt his leg bouncing up and down as he sought for the right words. "He'd become someone else over the course of his life, because of his wife. Because of his relationship with his sons. He was falling back into the person he used to be, before all that. Maybe he saw it as returning to his true self, I don't know."

"So you think that this... this change in his personality is what got him killed?"

"I do."

Farrow shook his head, reached a hand out to straighten his brass pen set. "Getting a good feel for the victim is the right way to approach this. Something you've always been good at." He looked up at Adam, and Adam was disappointed to see no understanding smile, no acceptance of Adam's position. "That's why you're a good cop, but it's not enough. You haven't narrowed down the suspects. You haven't even eliminated your sister." Farrow shook his head. "You're not helping. I don't know what else I can do to convince you of that. You need to go home."

Adam looked at his captain. He knew what was coming next. He'd known from the minute he'd walked into the office and seen Farrow's expression. He'd hoped to avoid it, hoped to talk his way out of it, to be able to count on Farrow's knowledge of him as a person and a cop. He'd hoped wrong.

"This isn't a suggestion. And it's not administrative leave this time. I'm sorry." He held up a hand as Adam started to protest. "This isn't coming from me, this is straight from the Deputy Commissioner — who has some connection to Grace Evans."

Adam took a deep breath and let it out with an

audible "ahh."

"Yeah. Ahh." Captain Farrow drew the word out, just as Adam had done. "You're on suspension. Indefinite, pending a full investigation of your activities over the past week."

CHAPTER THIRTY-FIVE

THEIR APARTMENT seemed quiet when Adam entered. He resisted the urge to slam the door behind him, embracing the quiet solitude instead. He tossed his coat on the sofa and had just crossed to the kitchen to put some coffee on when a noise from the bedroom caught his attention.

He paused in his tracks, his hand on the kettle. He replaced the kettle on the stove as quietly as he could, then turned toward the bedroom, grabbing a rolling pin as he moved.

Another noise, but this one stopped him for a different reason. It was a giggle. He'd recognize Sylvia's laugh anywhere. He let his breath out. She must have come home early from work. Maybe not feeling well, lying in bed watching TV. Or maybe reading, since he didn't hear the TV. Still holding onto the rolling pin, he stepped down the short hallway to their bedroom, pushing the door open.

Sylvia was home early, but she wasn't alone. Her shirt was draped across the dresser. One of her shoes lay on its side near the bed. Next to a man's shoe.

Adam raised his eyes slowly, afraid to look at the bed. Afraid of what he would see there. He heard Sylvia gasp. Heard a man's voice.

He couldn't look. He closed his eyes, turned, and walked back to the living room.

"Adam!" Sylvia called. He heard the sounds of her gathering her clothes, pulling things together. He heard another person moving in the bedroom. The heavy steps of a man.

He walked forward until his leg bumped into the edge of the futon in the living room, then stopped, unsure what to do next. He felt his rage rise as he bounced the rolling pin against his left hand.

He tried to stay calm, to wrap his mind around what was happening. But all he saw was Sylvia's shoe, tucked up against another man's shoe. As he stared at the futon, his vision clouded, red points of light inching into his view from the edges. He no longer heard the sounds from the bedroom, only a roaring sound that filled his head, filled his mind.

He had come home seeking solace. He needed help, comfort. Instead he'd found betrayal.

He raised the rolling pin and stormed back into the bedroom.

CHAPTER THIRTY-SIX

PETE AND MATT looked up with surprise as Adam banged the squad room door shut behind him. The eighteenth century doorframe didn't provide the satisfying slam Adam had been hoping for.

"What's up, partner? You okay?"

"I just got suspended."

Pete shook his head, pursing his lips. "I'm sorry, man, I really am. You knew you were pushing it, though, pursuing this against orders."

"What, you're blaming me for this?" The words came out through gritted teeth, and Pete leaned back in his chair away from Adam.

"Calm down, Kaminski. I know you're upset, but don't take it out on me."

Adam glared at Pete, then turned to pace across the far side of the room. He stared once again at the tiny patio behind the old row house, littered with broken windows, old gardening equipment, plants in trays waiting to be planted. It seemed empty. Vacant. Depressed. Why weren't there more rangers here whenever he came by?

He turned back to the only two men who'd been willing to help him. Matt sat back in his chair, watching him through narrowed eyes, probably waiting for the dynamic to play out. Pete had turned his attention to the table in front of him, pulling out a few case files, reviewing the information.

As he felt his anger subsiding, Adam stopped pacing and leaned against one of the chairs.

"Want to tell me what's really bugging you?" Pete looked up at him.

Adam glanced at Matt before answering. "I went home early. Since I was suspended and all." He gave Pete a wry smile.

Pete nodded, eyebrows raised. "And?"

"Sylvia was there. She wasn't alone."

Matt's mouth formed a silent "oh."

Pete lowered his brow and pulled his hands back from the table until they were tight up against his body, but he didn't move. "What did you do." It wasn't expressed as a question, more of a statement. Of fear. Of doubt.

Adam gave a dry, hacking laugh. "What could I do? I scared the shit out of him and I left. I came here."

Pete looked back down at the table and shook his head, slowly letting his breath out. God knows how Pete had expected him to react.

"I'm sorry, man, I really am." Pete glanced at Matt, then turned back to Adam. He opened his mouth as if to say something else, then shut it again.

Adam resumed his pacing. Matt watched him for a while, then turned to Pete. "What now?"

"Let him be." Pete watched Adam for a moment longer, then turned back to Matt. "These payments from Ryan-Mills have gotta be significant."

Adam stopped pacing. "What payments?"

Pete tapped a printout in front of him. "Multiple large withdrawals from Ryan-Mills' accounts. Some of them are cash. Plus he wrote several very large checks to someone; it doesn't say here who."

"Someone? Or an organization?" Adam leaned over the table to look at the bank statements. "That's worth looking into, seeing who he was giving his money to. Thomas told me he was concerned about who his father

217

was associating with. Bigoted, that's how he described him. Maybe Thomas was really upset because his father wasn't just theorizing, he was supporting the group financially."

"But why?" Matt asked.

"And even more important, who else knew?" Adam looked down at the statements. "What made you think to look for these?"

Pete shrugged, cast a quick eye over to Matt. "Just something Matt — uh — thought of. And it was a good idea, a good lead."

"Okay." Adam looked back and forth between the two of them, but it seemed they had nothing to add to that explanation.

"Tell me again about Harry and Thomas Ryan-Mills."

"Thomas is active in a number of church and community groups," Adam answered Matt, leaning heavily on a chair as he spoke. "What d'you think, driven by guilt because he thinks his father is a bad man? Trying to make up for his father's sins?"

Pete nodded as he shrugged. "Could be. He told you his father had some strange connections."

"That's right, they both did, Harry and Thomas, in their own ways."

"Sounds to me like his sons knew a lot about their father, who he was, who he was paying," Pete said.

"So what?" Matt asked. "Was Thomas so angry about some club membership he snapped and killed his dad? That doesn't make sense."

"You know that would depend on what club we're talking about. But he wasn't in town when it happened, anyway," Adam pointed out.

"So Harry did it, for the same reason?" Matt sounded less convinced.

"That doesn't sound like Harry, does it?" Pete shook his head.

"Why, what's your impression of Harry Ryan-Mills?" Adam asked his partner. "What else have you found on him?"

"Just that he's been suspected of playing outside the rules. You know the stuff: hiding the value of his assets for tax purposes, possible insider trading, that kind of thing. Nothing that's ever been proven though."

Adam felt his rage rise, thinking about the inequities exposed in this investigation. The rules that only applied to some people, but not others. Why was he always on the losing side of that divide? He focused on channeling his anger into the investigation. "We have to go back to the beginning. Track that statue. If we can place that statue in somebody's hands, then we have the murderer."

"Didn't you have someone looking into it?"

"Yeah, a friend of—" Adam cut himself off.

"Right." Pete nodded. "That's okay, we have other resources. I can track the statue. I'm hoping to get the medical examiner's report later today with more details on Heyward's death, too. That should help."

"Maybe."

"What, you don't think they're connected?" Matt asked in surprise.

"They gotta be connected, I know. But connected doesn't mean the same killer."

"So now we have two killers roaming around our neighborhood?"

Adam grinned. "Sorry to break it to you, Matt, but in a city this size you probably got more than two."

"So what are you thinking?" Pete asked.

"Check out the medical examiner's report on Heyward. We'll see if Roc killed him. He probably did, it's got his fingerprints all over it. But then we need to track the statue and see if Roc killed the judge, too, or if that was a little closer to home."

CHAPTER THIRTY-SEVEN

ADAM WALKED with his head down, hands in his pockets. All he could think about was Sylvia. He tried to focus on the case, sort through the few facts they had, the people involved, but all he saw in his mind was Sylvia. In bed. With another man.

His face grew hot despite the autumn breeze that whipped leaves across the grass of Washington Square.

He loved her. He thought she loved him. She'd always pushed him. Pushed him in his career. Pushed him in the choices he made. He'd thought she'd done that to help him. Not to push him away.

Had he done something wrong? Maybe he didn't pay her enough attention. Listen to her. Respect her needs, her wants.

"Detective."

Grace Evans' sharp voice caught him by surprise, tearing him out of his thoughts.

"Detective, you almost walked right into me. You should pay more attention when you walk. And why are you even walking around here, anyway? Don't you have somewhere else you should be?"

"Why did you want to marry Ryan-Mills?"

"What? I beg your pardon?" She looked around the deserted square as if looking for who else Adam might be talking to. A lone figure sat on a bench halfway round the square, reading, bundled against the breeze.

"Was it for the money?"

"How dare you? You insignificant little man. Who do you think you are, questioning me like that?" Her words were sharp, but she took a step back as she spoke, leaning a hand against the back of the wooden bench next to them for support.

"I'm the man who's going to find the truth, Ms. Evans. That's who I am. So tell me, what did you hope to gain from that marriage? Harry seems to think you were only interested in the money."

"Harry can go suck an egg."

"Oh?"

"Harry thinks everyone is only interested in money because that's all he cares about. It's all he ever wanted from his father. The money. We're not all like that."

"And what are you like? Really?"

She sat heavily on the bench and lowered her face into her scarf. Tears glistened in her pale eyes, though they could have been prompted by the cold breeze as much as the question. She blinked, shook her head, folded her hands on her lap.

"I am lonely. If you must know. I've buried two husbands. Two good men." She sniffed and pulled a handkerchief out of her coat pocket. "Not that it's any of your business."

"I'm sorry to have to do this. But it is my business. In a murder investigation, everything becomes my business." He gave her a moment as she sniffed, blinked again. "I'm sorry for your loss. Your husbands, I mean."

She nodded her acceptance of his condolences. "Two great men. They took care of me. They loved me. And they left me very well off." She looked up at Adam. "I don't need any more money. I need the company. That's all."

"Then why…?"

"Do I seem so cold?" She giggled. "An old woman, alone, rich? It's a dangerous world, Detective. Too many people preying on women like me. I need to be strong.

221

To take care of myself. As much as I don't want to. As much as I want someone to take care of me."

"I thought Marcus took care of you."

"Him? Ha." She shifted in her seat. "Oh, he tries well enough, I know, and he really is a genius in the kitchen. But he needs me to guide him more than he takes care of me. Constantly reminding him when the next bills are due, when it's time to switch my closets. He's not as efficient as he looks, Detective."

"Then why do you keep him on?"

"Oh, I don't know. He's a handsome man, anyway, nice to have around. And when I hired him he was the best applicant of the bunch. I guess I just don't have the heart to fire him."

Adam sat next to her, his hands still tucked into his pockets. "Even after all these years on the force, people never fail to surprise me."

She glanced at him. "Why do I get the feeling you're thinking about something very specific?"

Adam smiled. "How much did you know about Oliver Ryan-Mills?"

"What did I know? What a strange question. If you're asking if I know who killed him, or why, the answer is no, I do not."

"Did you know he gave financial support secretly to some group or person?"

Grave Evans sniffed. "Well... no, I suppose I didn't know. Exactly."

"What does that mean?"

"He had some... shall we say, peccadillos. Some opinions that didn't really fit with his public persona." She looked at Adam, then looked away across the square. "Let's just say I had some suspicions about his political and social views. I'm fairly certain his first wife did quite a lot to keep him in line. A role I was willing to play myself."

She looked down at her hands, and Adam thought about her comments. If Grace had some clue as to the

222

groups the judge was supporting, and his sons clearly knew, who else knew? And were those payments the motive for murder?

"I apologize if I was unpleasant toward you. I have a position in society, you understand. I really can't be seen mingling with police officers. You do understand, don't you?"

Adam smiled, shook his head. "I suppose I don't understand. Perhaps I have to learn."

The two sat together in silence. An unlikely couple. Looking out over the square as tourists came and went, residents walked and jogged by. As the wind blew the leaves in dances across the grass.

LIGHT BOUNCED off the bank manager's bald head. Matt shook himself and ran a hand over his own hair. Still there, thank God.

The floor to ceiling windows provided some shade from the street outside, a bluish hue covering the glass. But the reflection of the midday sun off the other steel and glass buildings along the street were too much for the weak tint. Sunlight passed through where curious stares from passersby on the sidewalk outside could not.

Matt leaned over to Pete, who seemed fixated on whatever conversation the bank manager was having with his staff. "Is he gonna do it?"

Pete nodded without moving his gaze. "He doesn't have a choice. He'll do it."

Matt let his eyes roam over the bank, restless in the comfortable chair. It was impressive how well Pete had worked the system, that was true. Only a few hours to get all the paperwork in place for access to Oliver Ryan-Mills' bank accounts and records. Matt didn't share Pete's enthusiasm for paperwork.

"What d'you think Kaminski's doing?" Pete didn't seem interested in talking, but Matt hated sitting there in silence. "He seemed pretty angry."

Pete dipped his head in acquiescence. "He'll manage.

He's checking out some art dealers, those who might have connections to Lubrano. At least it gives him something to do, gets his mind off it."

Matt sucked in his lips. That sounded a lot more interesting than sitting here waiting for a bunch of bankers. He glanced at Pete. "That'll be helpful; good he's doing it."

"Maybe." Pete still didn't look at him. "He's got too much on his mind right now. He's not focused. He needs to stay back, stay out of the way."

He settled back in his seat to wait, his foot bouncing against the wide wooden desk in front of them. How could Kaminski be focused? He just caught his girlfriend with another man. But at least he wasn't letting it stop him. Kaminski wasn't the one turning to paperwork to find the answers.

Matt's foot hit the desk hard, and he flinched, glancing at Pete. Pete didn't look over. Matt definitely had more in common with Kaminski than Pete. Then again, Kaminski was suspended. So there was that.

Five minutes later, after a thorough discussion with two other people present and at least one other on the phone, the bank manager returned, the warrant still in his hand.

"It seems everything is in order, officers. I'll be able to provide you with the records you need."

"Thank you, Mr. Walters, I appreciate that." Pete stood. "I just need to know who those payments were to." He handed Walters a copy of the bank statement, the questionable payments highlighted in yellow.

"Well…" Walters puffed out his cheeks. "For the cash withdrawals, there's no way to know, is there?" He looked at Pete and Matt. "You understand that, don't you?"

"Yes, sir." Pete nodded without giving away a clue as to what he was thinking. "And the checks?"

"Well, that's quite easy, really. I just need to pull up the cancelled checks." He sat down behind the heavy wooden desk. Pete glanced at Matt, then retook his seat.

"You have it all electronically?"

"Oh, yes. We scan the cancelled checks." He tapped a few keys on his keyboard. Matt watched as light from the computer screen hit his head. This man was far too shiny.

"Ah, here we are." He hit another key and a soft, purring sound let them know the sleek black printer standing against the wall was working.

Matt jumped up to grab the printout, flipping through the pages as he came back to the desk where Pete waited with his hand out.

"Let me see."

Matt handed half the sheets to Pete. "Here's one." He waved one of the pages.

"There's one here. Can you read yours?" Pete asked as he peered at the printed copy.

Matt stared at the scribble on the check. Oliver Ryan-Mills had had atrocious handwriting. Thin, wiry letters scrawled across the check, only the dollar amount truly legible. "Sons?" He said out loud.

"Well, that would be Harry and Thomas, I believe." Walters raised an eyebrow, leaning back on his desk chair.

"No, it's not made out to either of them. It's a name... Sons of something." Pete narrowed his eyes even more.

"Sons of Man," Matt announced. "That's what it says. Sons of Man."

"Oh, why that's..." Walters voice trailed off. "We have nothing do with that, of course. The bank, I mean."

"I know that, Mr. Walters." Pete stood. "Thank you for your service today, you've been very helpful." He grabbed all the records and headed out to Market Street. Matt jumped to keep up.

"That's the neo-Nazi group that's been gathering in the park." Matt spoke as soon as they were out on the street, dwarfed beneath the row of skyscrapers that lined the business district.

"I know." Pete nodded. "So it was a group he wouldn't want people to know about. This must be what Thomas was talking about, like Adam said."

"If he didn't want people to know, why'd he write a check?"

"Maybe he didn't always. Maybe the cash went to them, too." Pete shrugged. "I need to find out where that cash went."

"There's no way to do that."

Pete grinned. "Here's the thing about money. When one person spends it, it means someone else is getting it."

"Someone else?"

"Yep. Someone or something."

"But how can you find that? You can't go through the bank records of everyone involved in this case." Matt's opinion of Pete's investigative skills had risen with the discovery of Ryan-Mills' payments to the Sons of Man. But not that much. Paperwork might do it for Pete Lawler, but not for him.

"Can't I?" Pete smiled at Matt. "Even when I've got all this extra help?" He laughed when he saw Matt's expression. "This is what police work is, Matt. It's not all running around beating up bad guys, you know?"

Matt was about to object, but Pete's phone cut him off.

Pete kept his head low as he talked, his voice muffled by the collar of his coat, so Matt couldn't make out his words. His conversation didn't take long.

"Looks like we might not have to go through everybody's accounts after all."

"What'd you learn?"

"That was the medical examiner. In New Jersey."

"Ian Heyward's autopsy results?"

"Yep. And we just got a new direction for our investigation."

CHAPTER THIRTY-EIGHT

THE WIND PICKED up and Adam was hit with the smell of ginger. He took a breath, enjoying it, until the scents from a seafood market on the corner took over. Not so fresh fish, by the smell of it. He tucked his hands into his pockets and turned away from the fish vendor, looking south down 10th Street to Chinatown's Friendship Gate, just visible from this distance.

The tall, brightly colored arch didn't simply mark the entrance to Philadelphia's Chinatown neighborhood. As Adam had learned through his work with the Philadelphia International Council last summer, the gate was made using tiles from Tianjin, Philadelphia's sister city in China. It held pride of place in this international and vibrant neighborhood and practically glowed from its recent renovation.

Adam loved walking through this neighborhood, sidestepping around residents dropping into the many small boutique shops, tourists gaping at the array of goods spread out on street stands, office workers looking for a quick, savory bite from one of the many excellent restaurants. The atmosphere always energized him, and he was glad Pete had agreed to meet here, a block away from the precinct headquarters, to share what he'd learned from the Heyward autopsy. Adam's stomach grumbled and he realized he hadn't eaten anything all day. It just hadn't been that kind of day.

"You look like you're thinking about lunch." Pete's words interrupted his thoughts.

"That's crazy how you do that, partner. Yeah, I'm hungry. I'll grab something to eat after you share what you know."

Pete nodded and turned to walk down 10th Street. Adam kept pace, letting the stream of pedestrians flow around and between them as they spoke.

"We found a connection."

"To one of our suspects?" Adam asked as he stepped back next to Pete.

"Yep. And no surprise there. It's Roc Lubrano."

Adam let out a low whistle. "That's a break." He turned sideways to pass through a group of teenagers. "This is from the medical examiner's report?"

Pete nodded. "DNA match."

"Hmm." Adam was honestly surprised it had been that easy. "I would've thought the water'd wash any DNA evidence away."

"It probably did. But they found a fragment of a fingernail. Stuck in his teeth." Pete grimaced as he said it. "Looks like Mr. Lubrano beat the poor man to death with his bare hands."

Adam took a deep breath and thought about the scene he'd walked into down in Atlantic City. "That sounds like Mr. Lubrano. But even if he killed Ian Heyward, that doesn't necessarily mean he killed Judge Ryan-Mills, too."

They stopped at the next corner and waited for the light, even as a steady stream of locals crossed without waiting, zigzagging through the cars that slowed as they passed through this neighborhood.

"Now you're reading my mind." Pete grinned. "You're right, it doesn't. While forensics were doing their bit on the body, I went back through Oliver Ryan-Mills' finances."

"I thought you and Matt already went through those? Some great idea Matt had?" Adam didn't hide his humor at the fact that Pete had never shared with him how Matt had come up with this idea.

"Right." Pete grinned and didn't take the bait. "So there's still those large sums of cash, withdrawn at random intervals."

"More support for our friendly neo-Nazis?" Adam asked.

"Could be. But once I saw the report on Roc Lubrano, I took another look at his accounts, too. And guess what."

Adam stopped walking and turned to Pete. "They matched."

"They matched." Pete nodded. "For at least half the withdrawals by the judge, there was a matching deposit by Lubrano a day or two later."

"And why the hell would Judge Ryan-Mills be paying Roc Lubrano?"

Pete shrugged. "That's what I want to know. Maybe to get him to stop the casino?"

Adam shook his head. "No way. Ryan-Mills wouldn't have enough money for that. No, if my sense of Lubrano is right, that's blood money."

"Blackmail?" Pete kept his voice low, but even so an old woman passing by stopped to glance at them before moving on.

"Sure, why not?" Adam stepped up closer to the side of a building and Pete followed. "We know Roc Lubrano isn't above that kind of thing. And we know Ryan-Mills had a secret he wouldn't want anyone else learning about."

"So somehow Lubrano found out about Ryan-Mills' extracurricular activities and blackmailed him to keep them secret."

"Sounds right to me."

Adam turned to keep walking, taking a minute to sort through the facts they had, fitting all the pieces together until they made sense, discarding the loose ends that didn't fit into this particular puzzle. Pushing thoughts of

Sylvia out of the way. That was part of a completely different puzzle. He looked up and saw the convention center poking up above the buildings ahead of them. The city's neighborhoods were distinct, even when right on top of each other, themselves like pieces of a puzzle that fit neatly together, but only in one way.

"Which means Lubrano was telling the truth when he said he wanted Ryan-Mills alive," Pete said, interrupting his thoughts.

"He said he was worth more to him alive," Adam agreed. "You going to pick up Lubrano?"

"On my way now. Just waiting for a call from dispatch, they're locating him. Listen, Adam." Pete gave him a look he didn't like to see. A look full of pity. "Once this is over, if you need to talk... you know I'm here for you, right?"

Adam leaned back against a grimy wall as a crowd swarmed the sidewalk coming out of a restaurant, ignoring Pete's offer. Trying not to let it make him mad again.

Pete's phone rang and he grabbed it. After only a few words, his voice became high and tight and he cast a worried glance in Adam's direction. "He's where? You're sure?"

Adam stood up straight. "What's going on, Pete? I don't like that look in your eye."

"They found Roc Lubrano." He tucked his phone back in his pocket. "He's at Legg University."

"Legg? That's where Sylvia works. What's he doing there?"

"Apparently he's in the admin offices, meeting with Jim Murdsen and Sylvia Stanko."

CHAPTER THIRTY-NINE

ADAM JUMPED OUT of the cruiser before Pete had come to a full stop.

"Hold up," Pete called out to him as he turned off the car. "There's another car on its way, maybe more."

"I'm not waiting. And in case anyone asks, I didn't come with you, just came to talk to my girlfriend, right?" Adam slammed the door and took off toward the administrative building that housed Sylvia's office.

This was his own damn fault, and he knew it. He never should have gotten Sylvia involved in this or had her contact Jim Murdsen. What a jackass he'd been. She was right to be mad at him.

An image of her shoe tossed up against another man's shoe scuttled across his vision, but he pushed it away. Right now, he had to focus on helping her, getting her out of this safely. He could worry about the state of their relationship later. Once she was safe.

He tried to stay calm, but his hand shook as he reached for the side door to the building, and he took the steps up two at a time. Glancing out the stairwell window when he reached her floor, he saw two more squad cars pulling up next to Pete, the uniformed officers getting out and checking in with him on the plan.

Adam knew Pete well enough to know exactly what that plan would be. But he had no intention of waiting around. He pushed through the fire door into the hallway.

Sylvia's office was around the corner. As he stepped out into the hallway he thought he recognized Jim Murdsen's voice floating toward him. Then a door slammed and the voice was cut off. Adam jogged in that direction, his hand reaching for his weapon.

He stopped short of the door, pushing himself against the wall. He took another breath, then leaned to his left to look through the door's narrow window. Letting his breath out again, he leaned back against the wall.

Sylvia was there. Still safe. But Roc Lubrano was in there with her, leaning forward across her desk. Aggressive. Tough. If Murdsen was in there as well, he must have been standing next to the door, outside of Adam's limited view. Even if he was in there, though, Adam didn't imagine he'd be much help if the situation got out of hand.

One more breath. Adam focused on the moment, thought about what he needed to do. Checking to make sure he wasn't shaking anymore, he nodded to himself, stepped forward, and pushed the door open.

Lubrano turned to face him, a snarl disfiguring his features. Adam was struck again by how different Lubrano could look if he stopped making those faces. Murdsen stood exactly where Adam expected, backed up against the wall next to the door.

Sylvia's expression when Adam entered flashed a moment of surprise, then settled into one of caution, her eyes narrowed. She gave a slight shake with her head, but kept it still when Lubrano turned back to her.

Lubrano stood and turned to face Adam. "Detective Kaminski. What are you doing here?"

"I should be asking you that question."

The two men stood and stared at each other, each waiting for the other to move. Or speak. Adam kept his hands loose, but he could feel the heft of his weapon against his chest, knew exactly where it was and how fast he could grab it if he needed it. He'd wait Lubrano out, see how he reacted, before escalating the situation any more.

It was Murdsen who finally broke the silence. "Detective Kaminski, good to see you again. I brought Mr. Lubrano here to meet Sylvia. Just following up on your earlier request, you know?"

Murdsen looked hopefully at Adam, and Adam nodded. "About the stolen statue."

"I don't know what you're talking about," Lubrano jumped in. "What stolen statue?"

"That was the piece of art I mentioned to you, Mr. Lubrano. The piece I was trying to track down. The reason Sa— I mean, our common acquaintance, thought you and I should speak."

Lubrano shifted his eyes from Adam to Murdsen. "And why would I know anything about a stolen statue?"

Murdsen coughed. "Well, of course, I'm sure you don't. Our acquaintance never meant to imply that."

"You got that right. I thought we were meeting to talk about a legitimate business deal. But I see I was wrong." Lubrano sneered at Adam. "What was this, some lame attempt at a sting?"

"Nothing like that, Mr. Lubrano. I just need to talk to you. Wanna step outside?"

Lubrano's eyes narrowed. He looked again at Murdsen, then at Sylvia, who still sat silently.

"As tempting as that offer is, Detective, I think I'll pass."

"It's not a request, Mr. Lubrano." Pete spoke from the hallway, where he stood flanked by two uniformed officers.

At the sight of them, Sylvia stood with a gasp. "Adam, what's going on?"

Murdsen's face turned a shade paler than before.

Lubrano took a step back toward Sylvia's desk. Adam matched him, taking two steps toward him.

Lubrano nodded, adjusted both his sleeves, and walked out of the office.

As the uniformed officers cuffed him, Pete read him his rights. "I'm arresting you on suspicion of murder, the murders of Ian Heyward and Oliver Ryan-Mills."

ADAM WATCHED as Pete and the two officers escorted Roc Lubrano down the hall toward the elevator, then turned back to Sylvia's office. Jim Murdsen still hovered inside, near the door, but Adam hardly noticed him. He focused only on Sylvia.

Murdsen cleared his throat. "Ah, I'll just leave you two alone, shall I?"

When no one responded, he let himself out, pulling the door shut behind him.

"Adam, I'm so glad you were here." Sylvia stood and walked around her desk to Adam.

He couldn't help himself. Relief surged through him at the sight of her, feelings of love and longing that he couldn't ignore no matter how angry he was. He grabbed her and pulled her close, his hand against the back of her head. He shut his eyes and inhaled her familiar scent.

For that moment, all thoughts of murder and theft, Roc Lubrano, Oliver Ryan-Mills, even Julia went out of his head. His mind cleared as he felt Sylvia's touch.

The moment didn't last. The thoughts came back. The worry. The anger. He pushed her away, his hands still on her shoulders. She looked up at him. Her pale blue eyes filled with tears, one lone drop spilling out and running down her cheek.

His heart cracked.

"Talk to me, Sylvia. What's going on?"

"Adam, I am so sorry. I am, you have to believe me."

"I know. But why?"

She shrugged and sat back against her desk, hugging her arms across her body. "Oh, I don't know. There is no reason. No good reason. No justification. I made a mistake. A stupid, stupid mistake. I can't explain it. I don't know what I was thinking."

He nodded. Put his hand out to take hers.

"What's going on between us? What are we doing together?"

"I love you. And you love me. So we are together."

"And where do we go from here? Do we trust each other?"

"What do you mean? What are you asking me?"

"I don't know. Just, what are we building? If we'd stayed together, what kind of life could we have offered to our children?"

"Our children?" Sylvia raised her eyes to him. "You are thinking about our future?"

He smiled at her. "Of course I am. I was." He shook his head. "I always think about our future."

"Oh, Adam, sometimes I think you don't care about the future. Whenever I talk about it, you say there is something else you need to do, that your priorities are different from mine."

"So I don't want to talk about it. That doesn't mean I don't think about it. It doesn't mean I don't care."

"That's all I ever wanted from you. To know that you think about our future together, too."

She stood and stepped close to him, her face buried in his shoulder. "I am so sorry I made this mistake. I promise, I will never, never do that again. I am so sorry."

He held her close, feeling her heart beating against his own. Once he felt her heartbeat slow, he pulled himself away. "At least you're safe now. I was so worried about you."

"Thank you. For coming to help." She gave him a sad smile. "After what I did to you, I wouldn't blame you if you'd left me on my own with that man." She shut her eyes and shuddered.

"Tell me about him. What did he say to you?"

Sylvia shrugged. Frowned. "Not much, really. They weren't here long. Jim said that the statue had been sold to a dealer named Sal—"

"Sal?" Adam put his hands back on Sylvia's shoulders and looked down into her face. "Are you sure he said Sal?"

"Yes, I am sure. Why does it matter? You've caught him now, haven't you?"

"No, it's great. Sal Rivieri — that name has come up before, in connection with Roc Lubrano. It's one more piece of evidence to hold against him. That's good." He looked down at her. "Thank you. I am so sorry this put you in danger, but it was helpful. Thank you."

"I was not in real danger. Was I?"

He raised a shoulder. "Honestly, I was worried. Roc Lubrano is a murderer. And they were here talking about his connection to the murder weapon. I hate to think what could've happened…"

"Oh, I don't know about that. They said Sal was a friend of Harry, someone he's close with. So it couldn't have been that bad, could it?"

"A friend of Harry's? What do you mean?"

Sylvia shrugged. "Jim Murdsen. He said this man Sal was a friend of Harry. That's why they were talking about him, that's all. Adam, is everything all right?"

"Maybe not. Damn!" Adam spun away from Sylvia, reaching for his phone.

"Adam? What's wrong? You're scaring me." Sylvia followed after him, out of her office toward the stairs.

"I should've seen it sooner. I'm an idiot. I'm not thinking clearly." He really had been an idiot. Getting into the other guy's head was his strength, what he'd always been good at. How could he have missed it this time? He spoke quickly, not caring if Sylvia followed his train of thought. "It's the payments to the Son of Man, it must be. He wanted to stop those payments, and this was the only way."

"Who, Adam? Who?" Sylvia reached out to pull on

Adam's arm, and he turned to face her, one foot on the step below.

"Harry. It was Harry Ryan-Mills."

"But why would Harry kill his own father? Could money really be that important to him?"

"I don't know. But I gotta tell Pete." He took the stairs down two at a time, trying again on his phone to reach Pete. "To tell the truth" — he spoke loudly so Sylvia, falling behind, could still hear — "we don't know he did, just that he must have had the murder weapon. That's too great a coincidence, though."

"But why?" Sylvia panted as she ran to keep up.

"Could be shame. His father has been giving money to a neo-Nazi group, the Son of Man."

"What?" Sylvia's footsteps behind him stopped. "That's horrible."

He paused long enough to look over his shoulder, make sure she was okay. "Your friend Roc Lubrano knew about the payments and was blackmailing him."

"He's not my friend, don't say that." Sylvia pulled her lips into a tight line and picked up her pace again, trying to catch up.

"Harry must have wanted those payments to stop. Both of them, the payments to the Nazis and the payments to Roc Lubrano."

"So Roc Lubrano didn't kill Oliver Ryan-Mills?"

Adam heard a voice at the other end of the line. Finally. It had taken three times to get Pete to answer. "Pete, we've got a problem."

"Adam, is that you?"

Julia's voice over the phone brought him up short. Sylvia collided into him from the back, but he kept his balance. "Jules? Where are you? Where's Pete?"

"I'm at Mom and Dad's. Pete stepped out of the room for a minute. He left his phone, and when I saw it was you I figured I'd better answer. You kept calling."

"Julia, I gotta talk to Pete. Tell him to call me. Now."

He hung up the phone and spun around to face

Sylvia. "I gotta go. I can't wait for him to call me back. I love you!" he called as he ran through the doors out into the street, speaking automatically, in a hurry, forgetting how angry he was at her. How hurt.

"I love you, too." Her words floated after him.

CHAPTER FORTY

ADAM'S PHONE STARTED to ring as his taxi pulled up behind Pete's car. He saw the name on the display, saw Pete standing on the front stoop, phone to his ear. He didn't answer, just stepped out of the cab.

"Hey, I was trying to call you."

"Yeah, I saw." It took only a few steps to bring Adam up to the front stoop of his parents' house, where Pete waited in the chill afternoon sun. "What're you doing here?"

"Lubrano's being booked. That takes time, you know that. They'll call me when he's ready, then I'll go talk to him." Pete dropped his phone back in his pocket.

Adam waited, thinking there must be some other explanation coming, but Pete seemed done.

"Right, but why here?"

"Oh... uh... I just wanted to let Julia know she was free and clear. No longer a suspect, you know? Just doing my job..." His voice trailed off.

Adam laughed out loud, then realized his laugh sounded a little hysterical and bit his tongue. "You can stop lying to me, buddy. I do know what's going on with you and Julia."

Pete looked more worried now than he had when they'd confronted Lubrano. "You do?"

"For Chrissake, I'm a detective. A good one. You know that. I spend my life getting inside people's heads.

Did you seriously think I wouldn't notice that my partner — my best friend — was sleeping with my sister?"

Pete had the decency to look ashamed, though of sleeping with his sister or of lying about it, Adam couldn't be sure. "And are you okay with it?"

"What the hell, of course I'm not okay with it. She's my baby sister." Adam felt his anger growing again, threatening his judgment, and knew he needed to control it. He pushed the image in his mind away. Far, far away. "We got bigger problems right now. I don't think Lubrano killed Judge Ryan-Mills."

Pete shook his head and glanced at his watch. "Calm down, partner. He'll be through booking in another ten minutes, we can talk to him then."

"Everything okay out here?" Julia stuck her head out through the doorway. "You coming in?"

Adam turned his gaze on her, using the expression he'd used so many times in the past when he'd protected her, defended her, covered up for her. "You and I will talk later, got it?"

She tightened her lips into a mock frown and stepped back into the house.

"Listen to me, Pete. Harry had the statue. Julia's statue." He tried to keep his emotions in check, to make his voice sound reasonable.

"Okay, I'm listening. How do you know that?" Pete adopted his patient voice, one Adam had heard him use too many times in the past. On other people. Never before on him.

"Through his dealer." Adam clipped his words, speaking through his anger. "The dealer didn't work with Lubrano, he worked for Harry Ryan-Mills. Murdsen told Sylvia about it while he was there."

"Adam, that you?" John Kaminski's voice rumbled from inside the house. "Come in here, don't stand out on the stoop. Are you fighting with Pete about Julia?"

Why was everyone treating him like an invalid? He

loved his family, he really did, but they needed to work on their timing. He raised his voice. "We're good, Dad, it's about work." He turned back to Pete, his voice an urgent whisper. "Pete, buddy. Harry had the statue. He got it from his dealer, Sal. Jim Murdsen tracked it and he told Sylvia. And she just told me."

Understanding finally dawned in Pete's eyes. "So while I'm standing here waiting for Lubrano to be booked, the real murderer of Oliver Ryan-Mills might be packing up and leaving town."

"Or settling into his apartment. We gotta find him. Talk to him."

"Crap." Pete leaned into the front hallway to grab his jacket, pulling out his phone in the same movement. "Whoa, where're you going?" He put an arm out to block him as Adam tried to follow him down the path to his vehicle.

"I'm coming with you." Adam put a hand out to open the passenger door, but Pete slammed it shut.

"Like hell you are. It was one thing when Sylvia was in danger. But you've got no reason to come along on this one, Kaminski. Sorry, but no way. You're only a liability at this point, trust me."

Pete jogged around to the driver's side and started the car.

"Not a chance." Adam reached for the door again, then felt his father's hand on his shoulder.

"Adam, we should talk."

"Not now. I gotta help Pete." He turned to move his father away. He felt like a teenager again, running out after curfew. He always felt like a kid when he came back here to this house. To Dad's domain. His anger rose again, his hand shaking where it rested on the door handle.

"No, you don't." His father's voice was firm, his eyes even firmer. "I heard what happened to you. At work. With Sylvia."

"So?"

"You got a lot going on right now, son. You need to talk about it. Make sure you're okay."

Pete pulled the car away from the curb and stepped on the gas, his sirens lighting up when he was less than a block away. Adam watched the car go, fuming. At his father. At Pete. At Sylvia. His anger was spiraling out of control.

"Let us take care of you." His father put his hand back on his shoulder and Adam let it stay there. "You're in no condition to be running around chasing criminals, waving a gun."

Adam took a breath. Felt his shoulders sag. John Kaminski kept pushing. "You said you were staying on the case to help Julia. Well, you did it, right? She's not a suspect any more. So you can let Pete have this arrest."

Adam felt himself go still. His dad was right. He'd done what he needed to do. It was time to let this go and focus on his own problems.

JULIA ROSE from the sofa as he entered with his dad. His mother stood in the doorway, watching. A cluster of dirty glasses sat on the coffee table, like they'd all just finished a friendly drink.

"Adam?" Peggy Kaminski took a step forward, a sound of caution in her voice.

They all looked worried. About Sylvia maybe. Or about Pete and Julia. Or about getting suspended. He could take his pick, really.

"I guess Pete told you, huh? About us?" Julia tried on a light smile and Adam couldn't help but laugh.

"Why did you all think I didn't know? And why were you trying to keep it from me?"

Julia shrugged. "You can be pretty protective sometimes, you know? That's all."

Adam lowered himself onto the sofa, his head in his hands. "Yeah, I guess. Or maybe because I know what a jerk he can be sometimes. And what a ditz you can be."

Julia slapped him, smiling, but he didn't return the smile, just kept staring down at his knees, his head still in his hands.

"Pete told us about Sylvia, son. We're really sorry to hear about it. You know we're here for you if you need to talk."

John walked over to Adam and tried to sit on the sofa next to him, but Adam didn't move over. He resorted to patting Adam awkwardly on the shoulder, then settled into another chair. He glanced over at his wife and daughter, who each grabbed an empty glass from the coffee table and hightailed it back into the kitchen.

Adam raised his head to look at his father and shrugged. He felt his knee start to bounce up and down and put his hand firmly down on his leg to stop it.

"I don't know what's going to happen there. I don't."

"Have you spoken to her? About that, I mean, not about this investigation."

Adam nodded. "We spoke."

"Did she have anything to say for herself?"

"She said she was sorry. Said she'd never do it again."

John snorted. "They'll always say that."

Adam caught the edge in his father's voice and looked up sharply. "You got some experience in this I should I know about?"

"No, no," John answered quickly. Perhaps too quickly. "No, not like this. It's just... well, I guess it's good she's sorry." He grabbed a napkin that had been left lying on the coffee table when the women removed the glasses. He toyed with it for a moment, then turned to look at his son. "Do you think this is something you'll get past?"

Adam shook his head. "I don't see how."

John nodded. Tore the napkin up into thin strips as he kept his eyes turned down, away from his son.

"She says she thought I didn't want a future with her," Adam added. "Said she thought I didn't care about our future together."

John frowned. "That's a pretty strong statement. If she was worried about your future together, I'd say she found an ass-backwards way to fix it."

Adam laughed and felt tears welling up in his eyes. He shook his head and took a deep breath. "Yeah, whatever. I don't know what's going to happen. I did think about our future together, you know?"

He looked over at his father, who nodded, his eyes sad. "I know you did. That was always clear to me." John shook his head again. "Look at how much time you spend thinking about our family, huh? You get a chance to read those articles I gave you?" John seemed to be making an effort to change the topic of conversation, moving away from Sylvia. Adam had no problem following his lead.

"I did, yeah." Adam tried to refocus his thoughts. "Weird about that picture, huh? Of Great-grandpa? I spoke to a librarian about it."

"Yeah? What'd you find?"

"More unanswered questions. About the picture, about who painted it, and how it got here, to Philadelphia."

John nodded again, scrunching the tiny shreds of paper napkin into a ball and depositing it back on the scarred and scrubbed coffee table. "So there's still more for you to learn, is that it?" He turned his eyes to Adam, and Adam saw the age there once again. His father was getting older every day. He couldn't stand the thought that one day, he'd be gone.

He put a hand out to touch his father's knee. "Sure, why not? But Dad, you know I'm proud of our legacy. Of our family — your family. You know that, right?"

John smiled and put his hand over Adam's. "I know. Sylvia's worried about the future. You, you're worried about the past. You always have been."

Adam gave a small laugh, pulled his hand away. "I hate to think about losing you. What that would do to me."

He thought about the funeral he'd attended, of the two sons at the grave of their father, Oliver Ryan-Mills. The secrets they were keeping even then. Secrets they'd tried to keep hidden. He couldn't imagine watching his father being buried and knowing... knowing that he hated him, that he'd wanted him dead.

He looked over at his father. "In fact..."

He stood and grabbed his coat.

"Where are you going now?"

"I have an idea where Harry Ryan-Mills might be. Just going to check it out."

His father stood, concern painted across his face. "You need to be careful. If you have an idea, you should call Pete."

"I will. If he's there, I'll call Pete. I promise."

CHAPTER FORTY-ONE

ADAM LET THE TAXI driver drop him a few lanes down from the Ryan-Mills plot. He crossed the distance over the neatly trimmed grass, keeping what sparse trees there were between himself and the grave. He didn't know if he'd find Harry here or not, but if he did, he wanted the advantage to be his.

The November sun burned as brightly as it had all week. Such a dry week it had been. Unusually warm. Even the thick grass in the cemetery looked like it could use some water, though Adam was sure the gardeners had long since turned their irrigation off for the winter.

He approached the last tree between himself and Oliver Ryan-Mills' grave. Two figures stood by the freshly turned dirt. No stone yet marked the site; only the raw earth showed where a human being lay.

Adam stepped around the tree, bending to keep his profile low, his steps quiet. He could just make out their words, missing a few here and there.

Harry Ryan-Mills spoke to his brother. "Why're we here? There's not even a stone marker yet." He threw his hands out. "I don't like this, I'm going home."

"Home?" Thomas' voice surprised Adam with its strength. He hadn't heard Thomas mad at his brother before. "Whose home, Harry? Yours? Or Father's?" He practically spit the last word out.

Harry spun back toward his brother. "What do you

care?" His tone matched Thomas'. Angry. Fast. "You left, didn't you? You couldn't handle it here."

"Maybe so." Thomas took a step closer to the grave, closer to Harry who stood across it. "I couldn't be here anymore. Even with Mother."

A branch caught under Adam's foot, the crack sounding like fireworks in the quiet of the cemetery. Both brothers spun around to look at him, Thomas reaching a hand into his jacket pocket.

"Harry. Thomas." Adam kept his voice calm. "Came to pay your respects? Like me?"

Harry made a face of disbelief, his handsome features corrupting into distortion. "Respects? No one respected my father." He turned back to glare at Thomas. "No one."

Adam looked back and forth between the brothers. Harry had had the statue, that much he was sure of. But Thomas could easily have gotten it from his brother. Borrowed it. Even stolen it. Maybe Thomas had come back sooner from Chicago than he'd claimed. Pete had checked the flight manifest, hadn't he?

Thomas pulled his hand out of his pocket, a small pistol in his hand.

Harry took a step back. "What the hell?"

Adam took a step forward, both hands out. "You don't need to do this, Thomas."

"Stay where you are!" Thomas' voice had risen at least an octave. "I know what I'm doing. Because you and your partner are so friggin' incompetent."

Adam stopped moving, trying to make sense of Thomas' words.

Harry, on the other hand, seemed to have relaxed. "Beautiful. Just beautiful. Do you see this? Do you see what my family is like?"

"Shut up," Thomas was practically shrieking now, his hand shaking so badly the gun seemed to be waving back and forth in front of him. "Stop it."

"What are you trying to do, Thomas? Talk to me."

Adam didn't step forward this time, but kept his hands out in front of him, as if warding off whatever evil Thomas was exuding.

"I'm fixing it. Fixing what you morons weren't able to fix." He took a deep breath, seemed to get his hand back under control. Adam liked that even less.

"Why? Why did you kill your father?"

"My father?" Now it was Thomas' turn to laugh. "I didn't kill my father. Is that what you think happened?" His laugh turned to a giggle, his emotions clearly out of control. "No. I had an evil, bigoted father, Detective. And an even more evil big brother."

Adam risked a glance at Harry, who stood gloating at Thomas.

"It's time for this to end. For this legacy of hatred..." Thomas took a step closer to Harry, and Adam moved as well, closer to Thomas. But not too close.

Harry slid his hands in his pockets, a smile breaking out on his face. "You think I'm evil? You think *I'm* evil?" Harry's voice grew tighter as he repeated his question. "He had to be stopped. You know that."

"You had no right to kill our father." Thomas leveled the gun at his brother's chest.

"Thomas, don't do this. If your brother killed your father, we'll arrest him. He'll be punished." Adam took another step closer to Thomas as he spoke, and Thomas turned the gun toward him. He stopped moving.

"You couldn't figure it out. None of you. You even arrested the wrong person. But I did. I even tried to tell you, but did you care? Did you listen?" Thomas' voice dropped to a whisper. "Nobody listened to me."

Harry's eyes narrowed, his face dark. "Nobody listens because you don't have anything worth saying. What were you doing out in Chicago? Hiding? From Father and his problems. Or trying to get that stupid Grace Evans involved. You thought she could help him, didn't you?"

Thomas sniffed, a high, wheezy sound. "I wanted to

help him. Not hurt him."

"Well, I wanted to stop him. Get it? And I did."

Adam kept his eyes focused on the gun, but directed his words to Harry. "Why'd you kill him, Harry? Because of his support for the neo-Nazi group? The Son of Man?"

"Who?" Harry's look was incredulous. Adam felt like he was missing something obvious. "It wasn't about the neo-whatever... the Nazis. I wouldn't care if he was giving the money to fucking Mother Theresa." Harry's words came out faster as his temper rose and he swiped a hand across his mouth. "I just didn't want him giving away any more money. My money."

He turned his anger toward Adam, ignoring his brother and the gun pointed at him. His eyes were wide, staring wildly around him. Spittle flew out of his mouth as he started to shout, white flecks gathering at the corners of his lips. "That was my money he was throwing around. *My* money. To the white supremacists. To the casino developer. To fuckin' Grace Evans. I mean, what the hell was I supposed to do? Let him spend it all?"

"You don't deserve to live." Thomas spoke the words quietly. Too quietly.

Adam jumped at him as he pulled the trigger, throwing himself at Thomas and knocking him sideways, his hand grabbing for the gun. He didn't make it in time. The gun fired.

Harry hit the ground and rolled. Adam kept his grip tight on Thomas, his fingers locked around the gun still in Thomas' hand, and bent around to see if Harry was all right.

Harry was fine. The shot had gone wide. At first tentatively, as if not sure if he'd been hit, Harry stood. Shook himself off. Seeing Adam still struggling with Thomas, he turned and ran off deeper into the cemetery. Back the way Adam had come.

Adam refocused his energy on the man on the ground

below him. It wasn't too hard for him to roll Thomas over, trap his hands behind his back and retrieve the gun. By that point, Thomas had wilted, cowering on the ground, crying into the grass.

Adam stood, brushed himself off. Harry was nowhere to be seen. He pulled out his phone and called Pete.

CHAPTER FORTY-TWO

"TO A SUCCESSFUL case." Matt grinned and raised his coffee mug.

"To teamwork." Pete winked at Adam as he raised his.

"To friends," Adam finished the toast. "It's a shame this isn't Irish coffee, though." He grimaced as he downed the rest of his coffee and flagged the waitress over for more.

"Thanks for meeting me here, guys. I just wanted a chance to say thank you, for everything." Matt leaned forward, looking over the table at the two cops in the booth with him.

Adam saw the enthusiasm in his eyes, the excitement that he always felt, too, after a successful arrest. One that they knew would stick, no matter what Harry's lawyers came up with.

The diner wasn't quite as crowded this morning. The local fan club apparently didn't do an early breakfast on weekdays. Theirs was one of only a handful of occupied tables, one lone waitress moving without haste between her customers. Out on the sidewalk, no residents occupied their stoops at this time of day, though Adam had no doubt they'd be out again later that day. Like every day.

Harry hadn't made it very far after taking off from the cemetery the day before. Pete put out the call for Harry as soon as Adam had called him, filling him in on the excitement at the graveyard. Adam laughed under his breath as he thought about it.

"Something entertaining you, partner?"

Adam looked over at Pete, his familiar grin plastered to his face. "Just that it was so easy to catch Harry, that's all. What the hell kind of criminal goes home to pack a bag when he's on the run from the cops?"

They all laughed at that. Again. Finally. It felt good to be able to look at this case with hindsight. In reverse. With the danger to Julia behind them.

"Nah, he was no criminal mastermind, I'll grant you that." Pete looked up at the waitress as she placed their orders of French toast, fried eggs, and pancakes in front of them, getting all the orders right this time. "They rarely are though, are they?"

"Really? Do you usually catch them because of their own mistakes?" Matt asked, his enthusiasm still brimming over.

Adam nodded. "I'd love to say it was always down to our own exceptional detective skills, but, yeah, usually it's because they screw up."

Matt took a deep breath and shook his head. "One more thing I learned from this case."

"So, you off to Denali, then?" Adam asked, wiping up the pool of syrup with his pancakes.

Matt shook his head. "Actually, I got a better offer. Right here."

"Yeah?"

"Yeah. The chief said that if I could commit to hanging around for a while, he'd let me backstop behind John Hamilton, serving as another liaison with other law enforcement agencies."

"Oh, great." Pete rolled his eyes. "We can't get rid of you, can we?"

"Sure, have fun at my expense." Matt smiled with them. "That's okay, I can take it. Turns out I'm not as eager to leave Philly as I thought."

Pete laughed and put his silverware down on his empty plate. "Well, that's classic code for 'I met a girl.'"

Matt shook his head and grinned. "Yeah, maybe. We'll see. But this is a good offer for me. A chance to learn a little bit more about the job before I try to push myself into a position I'm not ready for."

"Wow." Adam wiped his mouth and looked around for the waitress. "You're smarter than most guys I know your age. It seems like everyone is rushing to get to the next promotion. The next career advancement."

Pete shook his head. "Don't go there, friend, I can hear Sylvia in your voice."

Adam grabbed for the bill the waitress dropped on the table, but Matt put his hand on it first. "This one's on me. As a thank-you."

"You didn't have to do that, buddy." Pete patted Matt on the shoulder as they stood, bundling up for the cold outside.

"No, I did," Matt answered him. "It's the least I could do. After how I screwed up…"

"We all make mistakes. You either learn from them and move on, or—"

"Or you let them weigh you down, and then you sink." Adam completed Pete's thought.

Out on the sidewalk, they shook hands, promised to get together again soon. Matt turned and headed north, up toward the park. Pete turned back to Adam. "Can I give you lift somewhere?"

"Just heading home. No point in driving, they'll have the street closed off for the Son of Man march. I'll walk."

Pete nodded and walked with him the half block to his car. "It's good to have this behind us, Kaminski, but you're still gonna have to face the music. You know that, right?"

Adam stopped, leaned against Pete's car, hands deep in his pockets. "Yeah. I know. But trust me, it was worth it. If this had gone differently… if Julia'd been arrested…"

"I know, partner. I get it. And whatever discipline they come up with, it'll pass. We'll be back to normal before you know it."

Adam tried to smile, but felt the corners of his mouth turning down. "Whatever normal is."

ADAM STOOD by the living room window, the thin curtain pulled back and the sash opened wide. The marchers formed a double line on the street below him. Walking two by two. Perhaps for security. He wouldn't want to be in the middle of that crowd.

He'd half expected no one to show up for the march. It would serve the group right for them to be ignored, their opinions meaning nothing to the residents of this diverse town. But he'd misjudged the neighborhood. The whole city, in fact.

The number of people lining the sidewalks far outnumbered the residents in this part of town. They had come from all over the city. From the artsy neighborhoods to the north, from the working class neighborhoods even more north of that, from the student neighborhoods in the west and the rough-and-tumble neighborhoods of the south, even from the privileged neighborhoods of Center City.

And they'd brought fruit. Bad, smelly, rotten fruit.

Adam laughed out loud.

"What do you see?" Sylvia came up quietly behind him, placing a hand gently on his back.

He let it stay there, but didn't turn toward her. "Just Philadelphia, being itself. Gotta figure a city that can boo Santa Claus would have no problem letting their feelings be heard when it comes to neo-Nazis."

She peered out the window around him, then shook her head sharply and stepped back into the apartment.

Adam took one more look up and down the street, trying to reassure himself that though the crowd was loud — and willing to use projectile fruit as a weapon — the march wouldn't turn into something more violent. He finally gave up, realizing that anything could happen. He couldn't predict the future. He shut the window and turned to face Sylvia.

She stood by the futon, waiting for him. A small bag packed with a few things she'd need overnight waited on the floor next to her.

"Is this goodbye?" She caught her breath as she asked the question, visibly fighting against the tears that gathered in her eyes.

"I'm not the man you want. Clearly. This is for the best." He tried to keep his voice calm, but could hear it breaking. Along with his heart.

"I'm so sorry. If I could take it back, I would. If I could change what I did…"

"But you can't." He turned away from her, seeking something that would catch his attention. Anything. A pile of magazines on the kitchen counter. A corkscrew left on the dining room table. The French press waiting in the drying rack next to the kitchen sink. It didn't work. All he could see was Sylvia pouring him coffee, sharing a glass of wine after work, relaxing on the futon, flipping through magazines.

"Just… why? Why?" He turned back to her and realized that he'd started to cry first. He'd lost control before she did.

The sight of his tears broke the dam for her, tears flowing freely down her cheeks.

"No reason, darling. Simply no reason at all. I was a fool. A stupid, stupid fool." She let herself drop onto the futon.

He stood for a moment more, then dropped down onto the far end.

"I'm not the man you want," he repeated.

"Yes" — she turned to him, moved a hand close to him but didn't touch him — "yes, you are."

"Don't you get it? I'm still suspended. There'll be a

hearing, there'll be discipline. I don't even know what."

"I know." Her voice was quiet, like a little girl. His strong, accomplished, demanding woman brought to tears and a quiet voice. He couldn't stand it.

He shoved himself off the sofa and paced around the room. "I thought my career was important to you. This will set me back years probably. No promotions in my future now."

She nodded, her lips quivering. "I know."

"Then why?" He tried to stand still but his legs shook beneath him and he kept moving, back and forth between the kitchen and the living room. A short walk.

"Because I love you. I have always loved you." She spoke into her lap, her face hanging down.

He thought about the time he'd spent with Sylvia. Her faith in him even when he'd been accused of murder. Her trust that he would always keep her safe, always succeed. But was she the woman he thought she was? The woman he needed her to be?

She had gone with him to see the face of his great-grandfather, a man who had struggled against evil, pure evil, fighting to save his family. His children. Adam thought about his own father, and what John Kaminski wanted for him. He felt the weight of generations heavy on his shoulders, the need to keep the family name, the family traditions.

"We all make mistakes," he said as much to himself as to her. "We either let them sink us, or we learn from them and move on."

"I made a mistake. I know that. I will not make another."

He didn't think about what he was about to do. Who was he to try to predict the future? He could only act on what he felt right now. On what he knew right now.

He knelt down in front of her. Took her hand in his. She turned her tearstained face up to look at him, a question plain across her brow.

"Sylvia Stanko, will you marry me?"

"Oh, yes." She leaned forward and sobbed. She put both her hands in his, the tears coming even faster now, even stronger. "Yes, I will."

Author's Note

Thank you for reading *All That Glitters*. I hope you enjoyed reading it as much as I enjoyed creating it. Of course, writing a book is never a solo effort. I am grateful for all the support I received from my early readers, mentors and friends who took the time to read, comment and critique, particularly Lois Steinberg for her review and comments and the fabulous professionals at TanMar Editorial and Bookfly Design. I also want to thank the Sisters in Crime and all the Guppies for sharing their wisdom, their experience and, when necessary, their commiserations. Most of all, I want to thank Chuck, for his unwavering belief in my writing.

In each of my books, I share some of my experiences in cities around the world – places I've lived, worked, considered home or just wished were my home. Philadelphia has been my home for many years, and while in some ways that made it easier to write about, in others it made it much harder. I must also include here my thanks to all my friends in Philadelphia who helped me experience the city and all it has to offer. Black market art in Philadelphia is something I have not had the opportunity to experience, so for that I relied on an exceptional book, which I highly recommend if you're interested in the subject. *Priceless: How I Went Undercover to Rescue the World's Stolen Treasures* by Robert K. Wittman and John Shiffman (Broadway Books, 2011) is both entertaining and informative, as Robert Wittman shares his experiences working undercover on the FBI Art Crime Team.

Adam Kaminski lives on, in my mind and in the other books in this series. If you liked this book and want to read more, please visit my website to see the other books featuring Adam Kaminski as he steps up to the challenge of catching the killer, no matter where in the world he is.

To keep up on news about the Adam Kaminski books, including the fourth book in the series (coming Spring 2016), sign up for my newsletter at my website, where you can also follow me on Twitter or Facebook.

www.janegorman.com